# The Book Lovers

## Victoria Connelly

Cover design by J D Smith.

Published by Cuthland Press
in association with Notting Hill Press.

ISBN: 978-1-910522-10-3

To June Martin with love.

# ACKNOWLEDGEMENTS

My thanks to Roy, Caroline Fardell, Kate Harris of the fabulous Harris & Harris Books in Clare, and Dave Charleston of The Open Road Bookshop in Stoke by Nayland.

To Anne Holden, Ellie Mead and Judy Bourner for inviting me to visit their book clubs with my note pad and pen. Thank you all for making me so welcome and for answering all my questions.

To Susan O'Shea for the wonderful name for Castle Clare's bakery – 'Well Bread'.

And, as ever, to my lovely readers who constantly make me smile with their kind messages. I really hope you love this new series.

# CHAPTER 1

'You've moved *where?*' Callie Logan's mother bellowed down the phone.

'Suffolk,' Callie said brightly.

'And what on *earth* is in Suffolk?'

'Owl Cottage.'

'Owl Cottage?'

'My new home,' Callie said.

'You've bought a house?'

'Well, I have to live *some*where.'

'Yes, but buying a house is so final, isn't it?' her mother said. 'I know things haven't been perfect between you and Piers over the last few months, but isn't moving to Suffolk a bit drastic? I mean, can't you give things another go?'

Callie twisted the simple gold wedding ring around her finger. She'd been trying desperately to get it off, but it seemed to be stuck.

'No, Mum, I can't give things another go. It's too late for that. Way too late,' she said and she heard her mother sighing.

'But I still don't understand what went wrong!'

Callie bit her lip. She'd never had a close relationship with either of her parents: they'd had Callie late in life and she'd always been made to feel that she was a rather awkward surprise. So she didn't feel that she could easily confide in her mother now. She'd only ever been vague with her mother about the failure of her marriage to Piers because she knew that she'd never be able to explain it in a way that her mother would understand. If she was perfectly honest, she wasn't sure how to explain it to herself.

'It just didn't work out, okay?' she said in a voice that had suddenly lost all of its colour.

'*All* that money on the wedding,' her mother said with a volley of angry tuts, 'and it only lasted four years. I don't know *what* your father's going to say.'

Callie closed her eyes, willing herself not to say anything she'd

1

regret. 'I've got to go,' she said instead.

'Well, don't expect me and your father to visit you in Norfolk.'

'Suffolk, Mum. I'm in Suffolk.'

'Same difference, isn't it? It's still miles from anywhere.'

Good, Callie thought as she hung up because, more than anything else, she needed to be miles from anywhere.

Callie Logan should never have married her publisher. That's where it had all begun to go wrong for her. She'd been perfectly content to be single, happily writing her books in her rented flat on the outskirts of London and going out with friends each weekend, but then Piers Blackmore had appeared on the scene, praising her children's book to high heaven and simultaneously sweeping her off her feet.

Perhaps it had been gratitude that had made her marry him because it had been Piers who'd offered her that all-important first book deal. She'd been so desperately hungry to be published as well as just desperately hungry after living on tinned soup and cereal bars for so many years whilst fighting off all the rejections from publishers and juggling several temping jobs that barely paid the rent.

'I'm going to make you a star,' he'd promised the twenty-five-year-old, his bright eyes shining and his mouth curved into that movie star grin of his which had knocked the very breath from her body. How charming he had been. She'd never met anyone like him before and she'd fallen for him hard. But the cracks had appeared very quickly.

Callie took a deep breath. She didn't want to think about all that now. Instead, she looked around the little Suffolk home she'd only just moved in to. The cottage was a perfect jumble of her possessions which mainly consisted of a great number of books. In fact, her cottage seemed to be entirely furnished completely with books. That was all Owl Cottage was really, she thought: books and beams. There were even books *on* the beams where they were nice and low and not too undulating.

She smiled in satisfaction and it was then that her eye caught a little plastic doll peeping from behind a cushion. It was the heroine from her series of books for girls which had been a runaway success, spawning a TV series and rather a lot of tacky plastic merchandise. Piers had kept his promise about making her famous, she thought. If only he'd kept his promise about making her happy.

She shook her head to dispel her negative thoughts because they had no place in her beautiful new home.

'I'm going to be happy here,' she told herself as she walked through the cosy book-lined rooms. 'Happy and single.'

It hadn't been as much of a wrench leaving London and her friends as she'd thought it would be. Other then the disaster that was her marriage, she'd enjoyed her time in the capital but, after starting proceedings for a divorce, she'd felt she needed a dramatic change and had fallen in love with Suffolk on a visit in the spring. It had just felt so right.

Callie took a little tour of her cottage now, gazing with affection at the bookshelves that the previous owner had squeezed into every available space. She remembered noticing that most of Mrs Morrison's collection had been gardening and cookery books with just a little line of fiction here and there. Callie had been lucky that old Mrs Morrison had been a fellow book lover and had agreed to leave a number of the bookcases as part of the sale.

'My daughter's told me that I can't have more than two boxes of books,' she'd told Callie, causing her to gasp. Just two boxes? It was unthinkable and yet Mrs Morrison seemed resigned.

'Some of these have been my constant companions for decades now. Some even predate my husband. But life moves on and old friends are often forced to leave us.'

Callie couldn't bear to think about parting with any of her books because they were very much her old friends too, and she looked at them now with affection. There were the rows of tattered Enid Blyton paperbacks and the much-loved pony books by the Pullein-Thompson sisters. Callie smiled as she remembered how her school friends had been divided into those who read romance and those who read pony stories and, thinking about her disastrous marriage, Callie now realised that she should have kept on reading the pony books into adulthood and not graduated to romance novels at all.

Twenty-nine was, perhaps, a little young to swear off love, she realised, but her bruised heart wasn't up to coping with another relationship and she'd promised herself that this move was going to be a whole new her. She was Callie Logan, writer, and she was going to dedicate herself to her books and readers – they deserved only the best from her after all their support over the years.

The only trouble was that Callie seemed to have dried up as far as inspiration was concerned. In fact, she hadn't been able to write a single decent thing since she'd left London.

Strange misgivings plagued her. What if she *couldn't* write in the countryside? She might have been brought up in a little village in Oxfordshire but, ever since she'd left home for university, she'd been in London, and that's where she'd begun her writing career. Despite the constant noise from traffic, road works and neighbours, Callie's words had poured onto the page in an effortless stream idea after idea filling notebooks and her fingers flying over the keyboard as she endeavoured to get everything down. There had been a brief period of adjustment when she'd moved into Piers' flat. He'd given her the third bedroom, clearing out the mass of gym equipment that he'd spent a small fortune on, but which he never had time to use, and buying her a corner desk and a brand-new computer.

'It's my wedding present to you,' he'd told her when he'd first shown it to her and Callie had loved it. It hadn't been the most romantic of gifts, she thought. Rather like the four-day honeymoon in Capri, squeezed between two important meetings he'd had in London. But that was Piers – ever practical and only romantic if he had the time.

Now, her desk was an old pine table in the second bedroom, overlooking her tiny front garden and the green at Newton St Clare. It was a beautiful village with no more than thirty houses, most of which were pre-nineteenth-century. Callie would never forget the first time she'd driven down the bluebell-lined lane that had led from the estate agents in Castle Clare, the nearest town. They say that there are pockets of the English countryside where you could easily think you'd travelled back in time at least fifty years and Newton St Clare was one of those places with its tiny flint and brick church, its graveyard wild with cow parsley and campion, its thatched cottages and old Tudor manor house sitting behind neat yew hedges.

Callie had panicked and had looked at the details of Owl Cottage which the estate agent had given her. Could she *really* afford to live in such a place? The answer had been a surprising yes. In fact, the place seemed incredibly cheap compared to the overinflated prices of property in London. Yes, the thatched cottage was small. You would have been able to fit at least two Owl Cottages inside Piers's deluxe London flat, but Callie loved it all the more because of that. She loved its simple cosiness and the fact that, even at her modest five feet and three inches, she could touch all of the ceilings.

She had parked her car, opened the little wooden gate into a perfect cottage garden filled with roses, lavender and honeysuckle, and had just stood there, drinking in the scent, the sight and the silence.

She stood there so long that the owner had stepped outside.

'Are you here to view the cottage?' she'd asked.

Callie had nodded. 'Yes please!' she'd said and old Mrs Morrison had laughed.

'I'm so glad you really like the place,' she'd said after Callie's viewing.

'Like it? I *love* it!' Callie had said, hearing the reprimanding voice of Piers in her head.

*'Don't tell her you love it! You should be finding fault with it so you can knock the price down.'* That's what he would have said, but Callie wasn't like that. If she loved something, she said so.

'And you plan on actually living here?' Mrs Morrison had said.

'Of course. Why wouldn't I?'

'Well, you get so many people buying these little places as holiday homes or investments and they don't really live in them at all.'

'But a place like this *has* to be lived in,' she'd said. 'I don't think I could bear to leave for a single minute.'

Callie had seen bright tears swimming in Mrs Morrison's eyes when she'd said that.

'And I could only bear to part with it for somebody who truly loves it,' she had told her.

So, the deal had been done and Callie was now the very proud owner of a seventeenth-century thatched cottage with sloping floors, an inglenook fireplace and more beams than she had ever seen in her life.

Owl Cottage. How she loved its name as well as everything about it. As she'd slowly got to know Suffolk, she'd become a little obsessed with the names of country cottages, noting how so many were named after popular animals and plants like Badger Cottage and Nightingale, Rose Cottage, Apple Tree and Jasmine. Her writer's mind pondered the fact that you never saw a Rat Cottage or a Nettle Cottage, and how lovely would Rose Bay Willow Herb Cottage sound even though the plant was considered a weed?

Yes, she was blissfully happy in her new home – happier than she had been in years. So why did she have writer's block? Did complacency breed stagnation? Surely she hadn't been there long enough to be stagnating? She certainly wasn't bored. In fact, she had plenty to do even if she couldn't write, she thought, picking up the old satchel-style handbag she'd bought at a car boot sale almost a decade ago and which had wound up Piers something terrible.

'Really, Callie!' he'd complained. 'Let me buy you a nice designer bag.'

But Callie loved her practical satchel and got a perverse thrill from taking it with her whenever they went out together, seeing the despairing little looks that Piers would give it. If she hadn't hidden it at the back of her wardrobe each night, she felt sure he would have chucked it into the Thames long ago. He could be such a snob sometimes, she thought as she got ready to go out.

Owl Cottage didn't have a driveway, but the quiet country lane it was on allowed for ample parking and, stepping out into the golden September sunshine, Callie got into her car and sat for a moment, drinking in the scene. It was still so strange to be there and not in the centre of London.

'But what if I can't write here?' she asked the empty car.

She'd written nine books during her time in London. There'd been several standalone novels as well as the *Perdita* series which had been the runaway success with the TV show and everything. The bookshops of London had displayed her titles in their windows and Callie had given talks, taught workshops, signed books and generally pretended to be a celebrity. She hadn't liked it, though. It had been a strange experience for her to be stared at and talked about when all she'd wanted to do was to lock herself away in the little study overlooking the river and write the next book.

But then, as her marriage had fallen apart, her inspiration for the *Perdita* stories had dried up and, although she'd managed to buy Owl Cottage from the proceeds of her books to date, she dreaded to think of what would happen in the future if she didn't write any more books.

Callie sighed. If she didn't find inspiration soon, she was going to run out of funds and her country idyll would be well and truly over.

# CHAPTER 2

Callie tried to put thoughts of impending penury out of her mind as she drunk in the landscape on the short drive to Castle Clare. She felt sure the Suffolk artists Gainsborough and Constable would still recognise it with its high hedgerows, gently rolling hills and the enormous expanse of sky.

As she entered Castle Clare, she was struck by the fact that it had more of the feeling of a village than a town as its few streets were wonderfully compact and there were floral displays everywhere despite the lateness of the season. Castle Clare, it seemed, was the kind of town that didn't need an excuse to bring out the hanging baskets.

The ruins of a castle dominated the little town, gazing down over the winding streets like a benevolent guardian. There were pubs, hairdressers, banks, a newsagents, a bakery and a cafe, a library, a hardware store that looked as if it stocked absolutely everything a home could possibly need and a little bit more, a gift shop, two antique shops as well as a three-storey antiques centre, and the estate agents which had sold her Owl Cottage. But, what Castle Clare was really famous for was its bookshops and it was one of the secondhand bookshops that Callie was heading to. She often found that a good browse around a few shelves usually got the cogs whirring and sincerely hoped that that would be the case now.

She knew that there were several bookshops in Castle Clare, most of them run by the Nightingale family, and she soon found the street she was after, just off Market Square. There was the shop which sold new books, its window full of the latest bestselling fiction, a handful of gardening books and a few titles promoting the local area. On the other side of the road was the smaller children's bookshop and Callie knew that she was going to lose herself for many an hour in there, but it was the secondhand bookshop which caught her attention with its old-fashioned shopfront painted in a deep green and its large bay window stuffed full of colourful books. The name "Nightingale's" was written in gold above the door. It was the same with the other two bookshops – just a simple "Nightingale's" because it was obvious what they were selling and everybody for miles around knew about the family and the trio of perfect shops.

What a treat it would be to have these three bookshops on her very doorstep, she thought. Not that she hadn't had plenty of bookshops to choose from when she'd lived in London, but those stores had promoted few titles outside the latest celebrity biography or the choice of the newest popular book club. No, in Callie's eyes, nothing could beat a proper independent bookshop where the owner had hand-picked the books through love rather than having to stock a limited list of bestsellers pushed by the publishers.

She opened the green painted door of the secondhand bookshop and smiled as an old-fashioned bell tinkled merrily. She couldn't remember the last time she'd heard such a joyous sound. For a moment, she just stood on the wooden floorboards, drinking in the silence and the wonderful aroma of secondhand books. There was nothing, absolutely nothing that could compete with the all-enveloping feeling of warmth and comfort that came from the scent of an old bookshop. It was a kind of mental sanctuary and Callie felt as if she had found her true home.

Looking around, she saw that there were neat quotes in black cursive letters on the brief spaces of wall which weren't covered by books. Callie read a few of them to herself.

"A room without books is like a body without a soul."

"A reader lives a thousand lives before he dies."

"Books are for people who wish they were somewhere else."

Callie smiled and then her eyes sought out the books again and there were shelves and shelves of them from the floors to the ceilings. The first room was a lovely big square one looking out onto the street. A till was tucked away on a corner table and that, too, was covered in books. There was also a pair of ornate library steps on either side of the room so that it was possible to reach the perilously high top shelves, and a long table stood in the middle of the room with a range of brightly-coloured fiction packed upon it for the idle browser who just happened to walk in off the street and who didn't want to crane their necks or crook their heads to examine book titles.

There was a narrow passageway leading off the front room and it called to Callie to walk down it and explore. It led to a smaller room which was completely book-lined and wonderfully silent now that the low-level bustle of shoppers and traffic had been left behind. She stood looking at the shelves, taking in the travel journals, and the literary memoirs which the narrow passage housed. She then walked on into the back room in which two small squashy sofas sat. There was an elderly gentleman with a shock of white hair sitting on one and he looked up as Callie came in, nodding absent-mindedly before returning to his book.

A staircase led up from the back of the room and each stair was loaded with books. Callie peered up it and saw a "Private" sign at the top. She then noticed that there was an open door to the right of the room and curiosity got the better of her and, to her delight, she discovered a tiny kitchen area with a sink and a draining board and a little worktop on which sat a few cheerful Penguin mugs in orange and white, a blue kettle and a sea-green Fortnum and Mason tin of biscuits. Everything was so bright and colourful. There was something to delight the eye wherever it rested, she thought with a smile as she recognised the delicious aroma of Earl Grey tea and ginger biscuits.

It was then that she heard footsteps on the stairs.

'Hello there,' a voice said and Callie watched as a dark-haired gentleman wearing glasses descended. He was wearing a sky-blue shirt which was open at the neck, a Tweed jacket, a pair of dark jeans and he had a slightly quizzical expression on his face as if he was surprised to see a customer in his shop. 'Can I help you with anything?' he asked as he approached her.

'Oh, no thank you,' Callie said.

'Were you after a cup of tea, perhaps?' he asked, motioning towards the kettle.

Callie's face flushed as she realised she was practically inside the kitchen. 'Sorry,' she said. 'I'm very nosy, I'm afraid.'

'It's no trouble,' he said.

'No, really, I'm just browsing.'

He nodded, the quizzical expression still in residence on his face. 'Grandpa, didn't you see the nice lady in the shop?'

'I did,' he said.

'And did you not think to offer her a cup of tea?'

'She seemed to be getting on with things herself,' he said, not looking up from his book.

The younger man turned back to Callie. 'You'll have to excuse Grandpa Joe,' he said. 'Once he's got his nose in a book, well, you couldn't shift him if his feet were on fire.'

Callie smiled and she couldn't help noticing the intense look in the brown eyes behind the grandson's glasses. They held not quite a sadness exactly, but a kind of weariness, perhaps, as if he'd seen more of the world than he would have liked to.

'Well,' he said at last, clapping his hands together and making her jump out of her thoughts. 'I'll leave you to it.'

She watched as he left the room, walking into the book-lined passageway that led to the front of the shop and she suddenly felt awkward about being left alone there with Grandpa Joe. She cleared her throat.

'This is a wonderful place,' she said.

'Oh, yes,' he said quietly, his eyes stuck to the pages in front of him.

Callie walked around the room, admiring the colourful spines of the books and the beautiful displays the owner had created. There was an old-fashioned music stand which held open a large hardback book about mythological creatures, its open pages revealing two finely illustrated dragons. Then there was a long shelf on which had been placed, facing out, several old books about flowers, each one's cover so enticingly beautiful that Callie felt her fingers itch to touch them and turn over every single page, but she resisted. Instead, she turned her attention to the ornate fireplace on whose mantelpiece stood a row of art books. She cocked her head to one side to take in the titles.

'The Raphael isn't for sale,' Grandpa Joe's voice came from behind his book.

'Pardon?'

'The book on Raphael. It's mine.'

'Oh,' Callie said. 'Why's it here then?'

'It fits,' he said without further explanation.

'Aren't you scared somebody will buy it?'

The old man shook his head. 'They wouldn't dare,' he said. 'Besides, it's alarmed.'

Callie blinked in surprise and turned back to look at the precious title. Was it really alarmed? Her fingers once again started to itch to touch it, but she didn't dare. Leaving the beautiful room and

Grandpa Joe, Callie walked through to the book-lined passageway, stopping to check out the titles and hoping that none were alarmed. Taking a chance, her arm stretched up and her fingers reached out to pull down a volume. She cursed her shortness of stature for which she was always penalised in such places, but she just managed to reach the book she'd spotted and brought it down for her inspection.

It was a rather handsome hardback with a blue and gold spine featuring a huge ship, its sails full and ready for adventure.

'On the Banks of the Amazon,' she read,

Whenever Callie was in a secondhand bookshop, there was a strict order of things which she did. She would have one quick look around, determining the overall size and layout of the shop and then she would slow things down a bit, going back to the places and the volumes which had caught her eye, taking her time examining them. This she did now with the blue and gold book, taking in the cover and the spine before opening it up and inhaling.

Ah, yes! That unmistakable, unmissable smell of an old book; how it hit her every time. It was a scent that she never tired of and yet it was always subtly different depending on the age of the book and its heritage. This one was very delicate, whispering its age across the decades, and Callie took a moment to embrace it, wondering about the life of this little tome and what stories it could tell in addition to the one between its covers.

She wasn't sure how long she had been standing there sniffing the book, but she slowly became aware that she was being watched by the man she'd seen coming down the stairs – the man she only knew as Grandpa Joe's grandson.

'Oh, I erm– ' she stopped. What did she think she was going to say? How on earth would she explain what she was doing? She could feel her face heating up and knew to her mortification that she was blushing.

'It's okay,' he said with a grin. 'I do it all the time. In fact, if you want a really good one, try this.'

She watched in bemusement as he reached up above her head and brought down a wonderfully old hardback in sage green. It was a 1925 edition of a collection of plays by George Bernard Shaw.

'Go on – sniff that!' he said, his dark eyes twinkling with mischief as he handed the book to her. She took it from him, wondering if he was just toying with her or if he was in earnest but, when she opened up the ragged fawn-coloured pages, she knew that he was serious.

'Wow!' she said. 'That's good.'

'Isn't it?' he said. 'I'm actually hoping nobody buys it because it's long been a favourite of mine.'

'It's like an ancient building where the fire has only just gone out.'

His smile widened and he nodded.

There then followed a strange few minutes in which the two of them went along the shelves, pulling out volume after volume and sniffing them.

'This one's good,' she said, holding it open for him to inhale.

'What about this one?' he asked.

She nodded in appreciation. 'I don't know what book it is, but I'd buy it for the scent alone.'

'You don't get that experience with an e-reader,' he said.

'No!' she said. 'I was trying to explain that to a friend of mine, but she just didn't understand.'

'Maybe they'll invent a scented e-reader one day – one for us old book fans,' he said as he handed her another title for her delectation.

'Have you tried placing an e-reader in between a couple of old books?'

'I can't say that I have,' he said. 'In fact, I've resisted buying one so far. I just love real books too much.'

'Oh, well I do too,' Callie said, fearful that he might think she was a traitor to the printed word, 'but there's room in my life for both.'

'I'm Sam, by the way,' he said, probably feeling that it was only proper to introduce himself after having shared so intimate a pastime as sniffing books. 'Sam Nightingale.'

'Hello,' she said. 'I'm Callie.'

'Good to meet you. Welcome to Nightingale's. I've not seen you in here before, have I?'

'No,' she said. 'I've only recently moved to Suffolk.'

'Oh?'

'From London,' she said and then silently cursed herself in case he thought she was one of those rich people who was coming into the county buying up all the pretty properties but not actually living there. 'I live here – all the time!' she added.

'Well, good,' he said with a nod.

'I mean, this is my home now,' she said, telling herself to calm down and act like a grown-up. Why did she even want this man's approval anyway?

Sam was still holding a book but returned it to its proper place now.

'I often think that the smell of books is like a good wine,' he said and Callie was glad he'd turned the conversation back to books. 'They have a vintage and just get better with age. Take this 1953 Penguin paperback. A very modest little novella, but get a whiff of that,' he said.

Callie took a sniff. 'Oh, yes!' she said. 'That's very good.'

'Indeed it is. So, what do you make of Kingston's *On the Banks of the Amazon*, then?'

'Subtle but delicious,' she said. 'Very slightly smoky.'

'I thought that too.'

'I wonder what its story is?' she said. 'Do you remember how it came to be here?'

'It came from a man who was clearing out his father's house. If I remember rightly, he turned up at the shop with three enormous boxes of books. There wasn't really much of value in them. A couple of nice volumes. This was one of the nicer books,' he said.

'That must be exciting,' Callie said. 'Never knowing what you're going to find in a collection.'

He nodded. 'Oh, yes,' he said. 'You never know if you're going to get lucky and discover a first folio Shakespeare amongst the *Reader's Digest* anthologies and the *Encyclopaedia Britannica*.'

Callie laughed.

'Actually,' Sam said, 'this book shouldn't be here at all. It's fiction.'

'Really? It's not autobiography?' Callie asked.

'It's written in the manner of an autobiography, but Kingston wrote a whole series of adventures for boys. See here?' He showed her the list of other books just before the title page.

Callie nodded. 'Ah, yes,' she said. 'It's a lovely book. I adore the mottled pages.'

'Foxing,' he said. 'That's what we call it.'

'Yes, I know,' Callie said, 'but I prefer 'mottled'. It's more poetic, I think. It doesn't sound so much like some affliction.'

He smiled. 'Have you seen the little book plate in the front?'

'Yes!' Callie said, turning to look at it again. It was a very pretty little plate decorated with ivy berries and an illuminated 'P' for the word 'Presented'. It had been presented to one 'R Webb', and had

13

been the second prize 'for regular attendance at Bible class'.

'I wonder what the first prize was,' Callie said.

'Probably a bible,' he said.

Callie laughed. 'I think I'd prefer the adventure story.'

'Me too,' he said. 'You know, it's books like this that make my job a daily joy. It's not particularly old or rare and it's not the sort of book that's going to fund my retirement or even a decent meal out, but it's still a privilege to handle it – to take in the beauty of its production and to think about its previous owners – its little history.'

Callie nodded, understanding completely. 'And look at the colour plates,' she said. 'Aren't they wonderful?' She flipped through the pages again, taking in the exquisite scenes of jungle life and one of a storm at sea in which you could almost feel the coldness of the waves.

'Have a look at the titles inside the back cover,' he said.

Callie opened the book from the back and saw a neat page of titles and authors.

'Recognise any?' he asked.

Callie's eyes scanned the names. J Macdonald Oxley. E Everett-Green. Angela Brazil. Lilian Timpson.

'Oh! Louisa M Alcott!' she said at last. 'Look – *Little Women.*'

He nodded. 'Just one name remembered out of all those books published,' he said with a little shake of his head. 'I often wonder what happened to the other authors. Were they just one-book wonders? Why didn't their titles span the decades to still be alive today?'

'Luck?' Callie suggested. 'Who's to say what makes a title resonate with its readers? You've only to look at any bestseller list to find a title which you truly believe has no place there.'

Sam nodded. 'Indeed. Or the dreaded celebrity book club recommendations,' he said. 'Always good for the bookselling business, but not always good for the soul. I do think people should find their own books and learn to develop their own reading habits.' He held out his hand for the book she was still holding.

'Oh, no!' she said quickly. 'I'm going to have to buy it now,' she said. 'I couldn't possibly leave without it.'

He smiled and she decided that he had a very nice smile which went a long way to softening that little edge which his eyes held.

'You're going to read it?' he asked.

Callie looked thoughtful. 'You know, I'm not sure, but I've got lots of books that I love which I haven't actually read.'

'Me too,' he said.

'And just look at the enjoyment we've already got from this book without even reading a single word of the story.'

He laughed. 'Indeed,' he said, making Callie smile. He liked that word, didn't he?

'You know that book very well,' she added as she followed him through to the front of the shop. 'Do you know every single book in your shop so well?'

He smiled. 'Pretty much,' he said.

'I'm impressed.'

'I shouldn't be if I were you. It's just my job.'

'But there are *thousands* of books here and your stock must change all the time.'

He shrugged. 'What can I say? Books are my thing.'

'Mine too,' she said. 'In fact, I was wondering if you might have a first edition of a title I've been after for a while.'

'Try me,' he said.

'It's a children's book called *Perdita's Key* by Callie Logan.'

'That's quite a new title, isn't it?'

'Yes,' she said. 'It first came out three years ago, but the first print run was very small.'

'Well, I don't believe we've got one in stock. Would you like me to try and get a copy for you?'

'It would have to be a first edition,' she said.

He nodded. 'Let me take the details down.' He walked over to a table where the till was and Callie watched as he opened a book and grabbed a pen. It was a beautiful black fountain pen with a gold nib.

'No computer?' she asked, half-amused, half-bewitched.

'Upstairs,' he said. 'I don't like it in the shop and writing things down helps fix them in my mind.'

Callie smiled. As a writer, she had always preferred the keyboard to pen and paper, only using notebooks for ideas she needed to jot down quickly. But, looking at the slow movement of black ink on the creamy white paper of his notebook, she fell in love with the idea of going back to basics. Maybe actually holding a pen in her hands would kick start her inspiration, she thought. It had to be worth a try at least.

'*Perdita's Key* by Callie Logan,' he read once he'd written it. 'First edition.'

'Please.'

'So it's just the one title you're after?' he asked.

'Yes. I have the others.'

'You collect children's books?'

'Kind of,' she said, biting her lip and not wishing to confess her little secret just yet.

'So, how do I get in touch with you?'

'I've got a card,' she said, reaching into her bag.

'Nice bag,' he said.

Callie looked up in surprise. Was he teasing her? He didn't appear to be. 'Oh, thank you,' she said, remembering all the churlish remarks she'd had from Piers about it. 'I can fit everything inside it. It's been known to hold up to six paperbacks.'

'What more could you ask from a handbag?' he said, his dark eyes sparkling with humour.

'The only problem is, I can never find anything in it,' she said as she rummaged around in its depths, her hand encountering sunglasses, purse, lip gloss, hairbrush, notebook and umbrella before finally finding the little wallet in which she kept her business cards. 'Here!' she said in triumph. 'I've just had them made.'

Sam took it from her and looked at the name. 'Caroline Logan,' he read. 'You're the author, aren't you?' he said with a wry grin.

Callie nodded. 'I'm afraid I gave my last copy of the book away by accident and it's quite hard to find now.'

He shook his head. 'I've *never* had an author buy their own book from me before,' he said. 'It's like that old commercial, isn't it?'

'The fly fishing book?'

'That's the one!'

'And do you have a copy of *that* in the shop?'

'Er, no,' he said, 'but the book really exists although it was written by Michael Russell who just uses the name J R Hartley to cash in on its popularity after the commercial. Perhaps I could order one for you?' He was grinning again.

'I think I'll just wait for my *Perdita*,' Callie said.

'Well, take a bookmark. It's got our number and website on it so you can keep in touch.'

Callie took it from him. 'Thank you,' she said, reading the words written across it.

Nightingale's – for books which make your heart sing.

'Very clever,' she said.

'My sister, Polly, came up with that.'

'I like it,' she said, handing over the money for the hardback she was buying and watching as Sam placed it in a brown paper bag with the shop's logo neatly stamped upon it.

'Enjoy your purchase,' he said, 'even if you don't actually read it.'

She smiled. 'Well,' she said, suddenly aware that she'd been in the shop for much longer than she'd intended and that she had enjoyed every single second, 'I'd better be going.'

'It was great to meet you,' he said, extending his hand across the books to shake hers.

'You too,' she said, turning to go.

'Oh,' he said suddenly, halting her before she reached the door. 'I'm thinking of setting up a book club. Perhaps you'd be interested in joining?'

'Perhaps,' she said and he nodded, his dark eyes holding her blue ones for a moment.

After a spot of shopping in the town, Callie drove through the country lanes back to Newton St Clare. The hedges were thick with dark, jewel-like elderberries and she rolled her window down to inhale the sweet air.

She'd really enjoyed her trip to Castle Clare and knew she would be returning to the bookshop. Sam Nightingale had definitely been intriguing and she'd so enjoyed their conversation about books. Being married to a publisher, one would have thought that Callie would have had her fill of conversations about books, but that hadn't been the case. Piers had had great enthusiasm for books, of course, but he usually talked about them in terms of making the bestseller lists or winning prizes. She couldn't actually remember him handling a book with the love and attention she had seen Sam Nightingale display.

She thought about Sam and the way his hands had cradled the book that was now sitting on the passenger seat in the brown paper bag. She thought of the little bookmark he had given her and she thought about the intense brown eyes which had held both humour and sadness too. She also thought about Grandpa Joe, the library steps, the funny little kitchen with the Penguin mugs, and she knew that she had found a very special place indeed.

Entering the village and passing the church with its black and white flint walls glinting in the sunlight and the spire leaning very slightly to the west, she felt like the luckiest girl alive. And there, overlooking the village green, was Owl Cottage, her little home. Pride and joy swelled her heart at how perfect it was, but then she felt a stab of pain as she remembered that the journey which had brought her there had resulted from a failed marriage. She could barely believe that the last few years had happened to her and that her youthful dreams of love and romance had withered.

Well, she thought as she got out of the car with her shopping bags, she couldn't change the past, but she could jolly well make sure that it wouldn't be repeated in the future and Callie had made a promise that, under no circumstances, would she ever fall in love again.

She opened the little wooden gate and saw something on the doorstep of Owl Cottage. At first glance she thought it was a skinny cat, but then she realised that it wasn't moving.

Dropping her shopping bags, she anxiously walked forward and swallowed hard when she saw what it was.

It was a dead rabbit.

# CHAPTER 3

Sam Nightingale had been struck from the first second he'd seen Callie Logan in the bookshop, despite swearing to himself that he was never going to be struck again by any woman – not after his divorce from Emma.

He raked a hand through his dark hair as he thought about his ex-wife and their last miserable months together. He still couldn't fathom what had gone wrong. Well, apart from what she'd done. But what on earth had made her do it? Had she been so unhappy with him, and had he simply misread the signs?

He should never have married Emma, he realised, but he'd been bowled over by her beauty and her charisma. She had been so unlike the other women he'd dated with her witty conversation and her charm, and he'd fallen for her big time. His parents had adored her too although his mother had warned him that Emma had a slightly flighty look about her – as though she wasn't the kind to settle down and be happy with life as the wife of a bookshop owner and, sure enough, she hadn't been.

Sam often wondered what had attracted Emma to him in the first place. She'd only ever briefly talked about her past relationships and Sam had got the impression that the men in her life had been hotshot city types who might have dazzled her with their money and possessions, but had been somewhat lacking when it had come to just being able to talk to a woman. But had Sam been really good at that? He remembered many wonderful nights sitting up with Emma, rambling from subject to subject, so what had gone wrong between them?

'Perhaps I'll never know,' he said to himself as he admired the colourful paperbacks on the table in the main room of the shop. Perhaps she'd just grown bored, her seven-year itch arriving a year early.

He tried to put Emma out of his mind. It was over, done, finished. It was as much a part of the past as his precious collection of nineteenth-century novels. Instead, he thought about Callie.

She had reminded him of a butterfly with her slender frame, her fair hair which had fallen so softly down to her shoulders, and the misty blue eyes which had been full of wonder as she'd surveyed his shop.

There was something about a woman who loved books, he thought. Something intrinsically attractive. There was always an instant bond between readers, he thought, and he'd felt it with Callie as soon as they'd started talking. She was as crazy about the written word and the whole universe of books as he was.

He smiled as he remembered the sight of her sniffing the Kingston hardback and how her face had flushed when she realised he'd been watching her. How could you not like a woman who took joy in such a simple thing as the scent of a book? That was something Emma had never understood.

'I don't know how you can stick your nose in those horrible old things,' she'd once said. 'You don't know where they've been or who else has had their noses in them.'

She had a point, he supposed, and yet the instinct in a natural born reader to do just that was very strong indeed.

He'd done his best to ignite a love of books in Emma, but it just never happened. He'd make gifts of some of the loveliest volumes he'd come across on his travels but, although she'd always thanked him, she'd always looked slightly disappointed to be given a book as a gift.

He straightened the rogue copy of *Oliver Twist* which nobody seemed to want. It had been in the bookshop for at least two years now. He thought about the number of customers who came to his shop every week, every month, every year. Some of them were good friends now and regular customers but, for the most part, they were tourists or idle passers-by who would drift in and out – sometimes without so much as a hello or goodbye – and he would never see them again. Which was Callie to be, he wondered? Would she be a regular customer? And would she really be interested in his little book club? She was probably much too busy with her writing. She didn't need a provincial book club. She probably had no end of friends in London to talk to about books.

He shook his head. Somehow, he couldn't imagine Callie feeling at home somewhere like The Ivy. Maybe that was why she had swapped

London for Suffolk. Perhaps their small town would suit her after all.

It was funny. The most important people in his life were all connected to books. It had been his Grandpa Joe and his wife, Nell, who had first opened the bookshop, raising their sons, Frank and Ralph, in the rooms above the shop in which Sam was now living. Uncle Ralph had gone on to become a university lecturer, teaching English Literature and Theatre Studies. He was particularly passionate about medieval poetry and mythology and he'd hoped to name the three children he'd had with his wife, Bonnie, after characters from Arthurian legend. But Bonnie had put her foot down after agreeing to Tristan, and so Sam's other cousins had been given the more traditional names of Luke and Megan.

Sam thought about his own siblings. He was the eldest child of Frank and Eleanor Nightingale. Then there was Polly, Josh, Bryony and Lara. The entire Nightingale family still lived in and around Castle Clare. A few of them had experimented with moving away in the past with Josh taking off to London for a couple of years and Polly teaching abroad, but they'd found their way back again. Castle Clare was one of those places that it was hard to stay away from for long.

Now, Bryony ran the children's bookshop opposite Sam's secondhand one, Josh ran the independent selling new books, and Polly, who was mother to six-year-old Archie, worked part-time in all three of the shops, taking over if there was a family crisis. His cousin, Tristan, was a freelance editor and, for the last few years, had been organising Castle Clare's very own literary festival. It wasn't quite of the stature of Hay-on-Wye, but it was definitely gaining a good reputation and the crowds were getting bigger and bigger each year. Megan worked in the tiny local library and Luke was a reporter with aspirations to either write a novel or to act. He was just waiting for the right story to fall into his lap or for the right director to cast him, he said.

Of course, the bookshop was how he'd met Emma too. She'd run inside during a downpour. That's how he got a lot of his customers, he thought with a grin – many of them discovered him whilst seeking shelter from the temperamental English weather. Emma had slipped on the pavement outside and had landed badly on her left hand which had been bleeding when she'd entered the shop. He'd taken her upstairs where her clothes had made a big puddle on his Persian rug. She'd then sat on his sofa, soaking that through too, but he hadn't cared. He'd bathed her injured hand, popped a plaster on it, given her a cup of tea and fallen in love. It had been as simple and as quick as that. The end hadn't been as simple or as quick unfortunately.

Straightening a lovely old edition of *A Midsummer Night's Dream*, Sam went into the back room.

'Tea, Grandpa?'

'Has she gone?' Grandpa Joe asked, looking up from his book.

'Who?' Sam asked.

Grandpa Joe tutted. 'The *girl*! Don't pretend she wasn't a looker and you didn't notice!'

'She's gone,' Sam said with a resigned sigh at his grandfather's summation, 'and don't think I didn't notice you checking her out.'

Grandpa Joe's bushy white eyebrows hovered over his dark eyes. 'Well, of course I checked her out. I'm not dead yet!'

Sam chuckled. 'Tea?'

'Yep.'

Sam moved on through the room, returning a copy of *Roses for an Empress* to its rightful home before making two cups of Earl Grey tea.

'Ginger biscuit?' he called through.

'Since when have I said no to a ginger biscuit?'

Sam reached for the tin and took out four ginger biscuits. Grandpa Joe liked to dunk.

'So,' Grandpa Joe said, putting his book down as Sam joined him on the sofa. He watched as the old man dunked his biscuit in the mug of tea, taking his time until the whole thing had almost dissolved. 'Did you get her number?'

'I did,' Sam said, 'in a professional capacity.'

'Same thing as personal,' Grandpa Joe said.

'It is not,' Sam said, 'and, before you say anything else, it would be totally unethical of me to call her if it wasn't book-related.'

'Everything's book-related if you put your mind to it,' Grandpa Joe said.

'It would be taking advantage–'

'So take advantage!' he said. 'What's wrong with that?'

'She might come back anyway, especially if I can get hold of the first edition she's after.'

'That's not guaranteed though, is it?' Grandpa Joe said. 'Ring her,

Sammy!'

He shook his head. 'No.'

Grandpa Joe sighed and Sam knew what was coming.

'What your Emma did was inexcusable,' he said, 'but you can't lock that heart of yours away forever. You've got to get yourself out there.'

'Out where?'

'Into the arena of love!'

'Oh, Grandpa!'

'What?' he said, dunking his second biscuit.

'You're being so melodramatic about it all. I just want a quiet life.'

'What? Shutting yourself away with these dusty old books? That's no life. That's a secondhand life – living through other people's experiences. It's not healthy.'

'I guess not, but it might be happier.'

'Really? You *truly* believe that?'

'No, not really,' Sam said, 'but it suited you, didn't it? And Dad too.'

'Yes but we'd already found our soulmates before we took on this place.'

Sam nodded, thinking of his Grandma Nell who had run the bookshop alongside his grandpa for so many years. When Nightingale's had first opened, it had sold everything under one roof: the new books, the secondhand ones and the children's but, slowly, as the business had expanded, they'd opened the other two shops which had been run by Sam's dad and Uncle Ralph before he'd become a university lecturer. Then Sam, Polly, Josh and Bryony had taken over. Their dad was still involved with the running of the bookshop, but preferred to do things from his computer at home these days, sourcing rare copies from the internet so that he could spend as much time as possible in his beloved garden.

Sam adored his family home, Campion House. It was a marvellous Georgian manor whose facade was covered with wisteria in late spring and roses in summer. Just one mile from the centre of Castle Clare, outside the village of Wintermarsh the house had been a renovation project which was the only reason his parents had been able to afford it, and Sam remembered some very cold childhood winters there when they'd been forced to wear coats, hats and gloves inside because there hadn't been any central heating.

Slowly but surely, as profits from the book business grew, the Nightingales breathed new life back into the house, restoring each room and turning it into the perfect family home which, his mother insisted, everyone returned to each Sunday for a family lunch – no excuses. Even though her children were all grown-up, Eleanor Nightingale liked to be sure that they each got at least one proper hot meal into them each week, especially young Lara who was studying Literature at university in Norwich. Lara couldn't always make the weekly lunches but, whenever she did, Eleanor always made sure that her youngest child got double helpings.

'I don't want you all running around surviving on microwaved rubbish,' she frequently told them. Anyway, it was a good chance to catch up with everybody's news and to swap stories from their three shops.

'That Mr Bray came in again today,' Josh would say.

'Did he take anything?' Polly would ask.

Josh would nod. 'The new Dan Brown.'

'Good heavens!' their father would exclaim. 'How the hell did he shoplift that? It's enormous! You'd think he'd choose a nice slim Penguin classic or something.'

'I saw him pinch a copy of *The Very Hungry Caterpillar*,' Bryony said. 'I didn't say anything because it was shop-soiled after Mrs Carter's boy wiped his nose on it.'

Sam would watch and listen to his family, marvelling at the good fortune that they all still got on. How lucky they were, he realised, knowing several of the friends he'd grown up with came from broken homes with parents who were distant either emotionally or geographically and siblings that had little to do with each other.

Sam's grandparents had moved into Campion House a few years ago when Frank and Eleanor had insisted that there was plenty of room and that their own house was far too much work for them in retirement. There had been little protest and Joe and Nell now had their own little wing on the ground floor, which had been extended to accommodate them.

'You over for Sunday lunch?' Grandpa Joe asked now as if reading Sam's mind.

'Of course,' Sam said. He didn't know why his grandpa asked him each week because it was always the same answer. In fact, in all the years of the great Sunday lunch tradition, Sam had only missed it once and that had been the week he'd had his honeymoon. He and Emma had gone to Venice and he'd done his best not to venture into too many of the amazing book binding shops there.

'You bringing anyone?' Grandpa Joe asked.

'No,' Sam said, taking a sip of his tea. 'When do I ever bring anyone?'

'Exactly,' Grandpa Joe said. 'It's time that you did.'

'Got anyone in mind, have you?' he asked with a wry smile.

'Just the one,' his grandpa said.

Sam's eyes narrowed. 'What exactly is it about this woman that's got you all worked up?'

He shrugged. 'I like the way she moved around the shop,' he said.

Sam smiled. He'd liked it too.

'And she opens a book nicely,' Grandpa Joe added.

'She sniffs them too,' Sam said.

'I thought she might. So, she's pretty damned perfect, then, I'd say.'

'We don't know her,' Sam said.

'That can be remedied.'

Sam got up from the sofa and took their mugs into the kitchen. 'I'm not going to get involved with anyone again, okay?' he called through. 'I'm done with all that.'

'You can't say that,' Grandpa Joe said.

'Why not?' Sam asked.

'Because you're not dead yet.'

Sam didn't reply, but he couldn't help acknowledging the fact that, since he'd broken up with Emma, a little bit of him had died inside.

Callie still hadn't fully recovered from the whole rabbit on the doorstep incident. The poor little helpless thing, she thought, as she took it round to her back garden and placed it on an old wooden bench. She didn't have the heart to put it in the bin. That just wouldn't be right. She'd have to give it a proper burial. But how had it got there in the first place? Had it been left by a neighbourhood cat? Or maybe it was something more sinister. Perhaps it was the locals' way of telling her that Londoners weren't welcome in the village. She'd heard about such things before – how some communities only welcomed you if you were fifth generation. Had she made an awful mistake in moving to the countryside?

'I'll stick it out,' she told herself, imagining putting up a pair of net curtains in the downstairs rooms so she could keep an eye on the outside world without being seen herself, and having the local police station on speed dial if there were any more unwanted gifts left on her doorstep.

There was an old shed in the little cottage garden and Callie opened it, finding a few basic tools that had seen better days. Choosing a spot under an ancient apple tree, she dug a little grave for the rabbit.

'Dear little thing,' she said after a few minutes' digging through the tough clay soil. 'Rest in peace.'

Returning inside, she realised that she was shaking. Oh, dear, she thought. She was much too sentimental for life in the country.

'Don't be silly,' she told herself. 'You just have to grow a backbone. A real strong country girl backbone.'

It was then that the tiniest glimmer of inspiration hit her, lighting up her eyes and sending her scurrying to her study to grab a notebook and pen. Sitting down at the old pine table, she began to write, her pen flying over the page. She wasn't sure how long she sat there for, but when she'd finished she had five pages of notes and two pages of what she felt was going to be a pretty exciting Chapter One.

The next couple of days continued in very much the same vein with Callie furiously scribbling and typing at her desk, briefly stopping for cups of tea and a bite to eat and then continuing with her story. How wonderful it felt to actually be writing again, she thought, to be putting the words down one at a time, creating sentences, paragraphs, chapters – a story. Writing was her drug and, when she wasn't able to write, the withdrawal symptoms were horrendous but, when she was flying high as she was right now, there was no better feeling in the world.

It was in the middle of one afternoon when Callie was gazing out of the window, daydreaming about a scene, her eyes only half-seeing the village green on the other side of the road. She was aware of a tall man with long brown hair walking across the green. Her eyes focused properly and she watched his easy strides as he crossed the lane. It looked as if he was heading straight towards Owl Cottage, but that couldn't be right, could it? What business would he have with her, she wondered? It was then that she saw he was carrying a strange package out of which a long feather was poking.

She watched, her heart racing as he opened her garden gate. He was going to leave a dead animal on her doorstep, wasn't he? She ran down the stairs, listening to the heavy footsteps walking up the path to the front door before moving into the living room and peering out of the window. The man was wearing a rather tatty wax jacket and a pair of green wellies. Callie watched him and, as he walked back down her path empty-handed, she opened her front door. Sure enough, there on the doorstep was a dead pheasant. She gasped.

'Excuse me!' she called after the departing man who was now on the other side of the road. '*Hey!*' Her cry was loud and sounded a lot more confident than she felt.

He turned and Callie found herself staring at a rather handsome face. 'You after me?' he asked.

'Yes!' Callie said. 'I mean, I think so. Did you leave this dead bird?'

She watched as he crossed the road towards her, his stride long and slow. A country stride, Callie decided, where nothing was rushed.

'Hello,' he said once he'd reached the gate. 'How can I help?'

'Is this yours?' Callie asked, nudging the dead bird with the toe of her boot.

'Not anymore,' he said. 'It's for Mrs Morrison,' he said.

'Oh, I see,' she said. 'Was that dead rabbit for Mrs Morrison too?'

'Yes,' he said. 'She likes a bit of rabbit. Makes a wonderful pie.'

Callie breathed a sigh of relief at the realisation that she hadn't been the victim of some townie ousting campaign.

'I think there's been some sort of misunderstanding,' she told him.

'Misunderstanding?'

'Mrs Morrison – she's no longer here,' Callie said.

'Oh, my God!' the man said, his handsome face creasing in anxiety. 'She's dead?'

'Oh, no!' Callie said, shaking her head. 'She's moved in with her daughter.'

'For good?'

'Yes,' Callie said.

'And you live here now?'

Callie nodded.

'What a shame,' he said, causing Callie to frown. 'I mean – not that *you're* here. That's not a shame at all.' He grinned and she couldn't help acknowledging how attractive his smile was. 'I mean it's a shame that I didn't get a chance to say goodbye.' He stroked his chin and Callie noticed how dark his skin was as if he'd spent the whole summer out of doors.

'I've been away, you see – travelling,' he continued and Callie saw that he had that traveller's look about him; that sort of worldly-wise confidence that comes from hiking through mountains, eating street food and hitching rides on anything that moved. 'Where's she now?' he asked.

'Hampshire,' Callie said.

'Oh,' he said and then he raked a hand through his dark, wild-looking hair.

'I have her address if you'd like to write,' Callie said.

He shook his head. 'I'm not much of a one for letters,' he said and he sighed. 'I'm going to miss her.'

Callie wasn't sure what to say so said nothing.

'Hey,' he said, 'I'm taking up your time. Sorry.' He turned to leave. 'You can keep the pheasant.'

'Oh, no,' Callie said quickly. 'I wouldn't know what to do with it.'

He turned back to face her. 'You're not from round here, are you?'

'No,' she said. 'Is it obvious?'

'Pretty much,' he said, but he was smiling and so she didn't take it as a reprimand.

She suddenly became aware that she was wearing her 'writing look' as she termed it and that meant that her long hair had been haphazardly tied up and she was wearing jogging bottoms with a hole in the left knee and a baggy cardigan in a rather astonishing shade of lime. She cleared her throat, feeling awkward and self-conscious.

'So, where are you from? London?'

She didn't like the way he said that with such assumption, but he was still smiling at her and a strange assortment of emotions whirled through her as he stared at her so intently. She didn't feel comfortable with those inquisitive eyes of his upon her and yet there was something innately attractive about him that made her realise that she didn't want him to leave just yet.

'Yes,' she said at last. 'I'm from London.'

He nodded. 'Can't stand the place myself. I went there once.'

'Just the once?' she said, a teasing tone to her voice.

'Once was enough,' he said. 'Couldn't breathe there. Couldn't walk properly.'

'You like to stride,' she said and then bit her tongue.

'What?' he said, sounding surprised.

'I – erm – I'm guessing – with the wellies and everything.'

'Oh, I see,' he said and his eyes twinkled merrily. 'Well, I guess I do like to stride. That's very observant of you.'

Callie gave a little smile. It was the first she'd offered him, but she had the feeling that it wouldn't be the last. 'I'm a writer,' she volunteered. 'It's my job to be observant.'

'I've never met a writer,' he said. 'What kind of things do you write?'

'Children's stories,' she said.

'Oh, you have kids?'

'No,' she said.

'You write for other people's kids?'

'I guess,' she said. 'I've never really thought about it like that.'

'Or perhaps you write for the kid inside you,' he said.

She blinked. 'Well, I'm not sure about that.' She could feel her face was heating up with the directness of his gaze and the pertness of his comments.

'Right,' he said, suddenly looking ill at ease standing in the middle of her path. 'I guess I'd better be going.'

Callie nodded, not knowing what else to do. 'I'm sorry you missed saying goodbye to Mrs Morrison,' she said.

'Me too,' he said, turning to leave and then he stopped. 'What did you do with it, by the way?'

'With what?'

'The rabbit?'

Callie bit her lip. 'I buried it.'

The man laughed. 'You didn't!'

'I most certainly did,' she said.

He shook his head. 'Well, I'll come back and cook you one sometime. I'm a pretty good cook,' he said.

She watched as he took the pheasant and opened the little gate, closing it behind him and striding across the road and the village green before disappearing into the trees beyond.

'Extraordinary man,' she said as she closed her front door, but what was even more extraordinary was the fact that he'd invited himself back and that she hadn't objected even though she didn't even know his name.

# CHAPTER 4

Sam Nightingale crossed the road from his bookshop in Castle Clare and opened the bright yellow door into his sister's shop.

'Bryony?' he called as he entered, her shop bell tinkling very much like his own did. Grandma Nell had bought each shop a bell, insisting that a shop wasn't a proper shop without one and nobody had dared to argue with her.

'I'm in the back!' Bryony called through. 'Come and see these new books!'

He recognised the excitement in her voice; it was always the same when a new delivery arrived. That experience never got old and it was one that Sam sometimes envied his sister but, then again, he couldn't imagine he'd be quite as comfortable selling new books. His home was with the secondhand, the pre-loved, the old.

'Just look at these!' Bryony said, not bothering to turn around as he entered the stock room. He wasn't offended; he knew he couldn't hope to compete with a box of new books.

He knelt down on the floor beside her as she handed him a glossy paperback. 'It's a new children's series by that imprint I was telling you about.' Her glossy dark hair swung over her shoulder, obscuring her face, but he didn't need to see it to know that she was smiling.

He looked at the book she had handed him.

'Smell that!' she said, looking at him with the same brown eyes which he'd inherited from their parents. 'New paper and ink!'

Sam grinned, thinking once more of Callie Logan – his new book-sniffing customer.

'And feel the embossed title,' she said, laughing as she ran her fingers along it. 'These are going *straight* in the window,' she said, her cheeks pink with excitement as she got up from the floor and dusted down her skirt which was one of the patchwork creations that she made herself and which had defined her for years. She was also wearing a long multi-coloured chiffon scarf which floated around her as she moved and a pair of biker boots with enormous zips and buckles. It was a very Bryony sort of look which Sam often thought was part child, part bohemian.

Sam followed her through to the shop. It was just a one-room shop but it was divided into several areas which included a small space enclosed by bookcases. In the middle of this was a handsome striped rug on which sat a collection of brightly coloured cushions and baby beanbags. This was the 'Reading Room' where Bryony held twice-weekly story-telling sessions which were very popular with the neighbourhood children and even more popular with their parents who would drop them off and then go for coffee and cake in Castle Clare's cafe, The Golden Biscuit.

'I actually wanted to talk to you about a children's series,' he said, watching as his sister carefully placed three of the shiny new paperbacks in the window, taking out a rather tired copy of *Harry Potter* whose cover was starting to warp.

'Oh, yes?'

'The *Perdita* series,' he said. 'Have you heard of it?'

'Heard of it?' Bryony said, flinging her dark hair over her shoulders as she stood up straight again. 'Of *course* I've heard of it! It's been all over the place. Made into a TV series too and all the usual plastic merchandise that comes with those sorts of things which parents expect me to stock.' She rolled her eyes. Plastic toys did not have a place in Bryony's beloved shop. 'What about it? You after a set or something?'

'No, no,' he said. 'Just the first one.'

'Perdita's Key?'

'That's the one,' he said, impressed by her encyclopaedic knowledge when it came to children's literature. 'A first edition.'

She sucked her teeth. 'You won't find one of those in a hurry,' she said. 'Small print run if I remember rightly.'

'I know,' he said. 'It was just on the off-chance of you having one kicking around.'

She shook her head. 'It might be worth quite a bit of money now if I did.'

'Really?'

'Oh, yes,' Bryony said as she walked into the Reading Room and plumped up the cushions. 'It's quite a collector's item now. Worth far more than the recommended retail price. Why do you want it? You got a collector for it?'

'You could say that,' Sam said.

'Who is it?'

'A new customer.'

Bryony stopped plumping cushions and looked at her brother and smiled. 'Who?'

He grinned back at her. 'Somebody called Callie Logan.'

Bryony's eyes doubled in size. 'Callie Logan? The author? The *actual* author?'

Sam nodded at her.

'What was she doing in your bookshop?'

'She lives here now.'

'Callie Logan lives in Castle Clare?'

'A little village just outside,' Sam said.

'Oh, my God! You have *got* to get her to come in here! I'll order some of her books. No! I'll order *all* of her books! We can set up a signing. No – wait! An event! A real author event with queues of people going down the street!'

'Bry!' Sam cried. 'I don't think she's into all that.'

'How do you know?' she asked, her hands on her hips as she squared up to him in defiance.

'It's just an impression I get,' he said. 'She's left London for Suffolk and I think she just wants a quiet life now.'

'Is she running away from something?'

'I don't know for sure,' he said, 'but I think she probably is.'

Bryony examined her brother. 'You like her, don't you?'

'Don't you start as well,' he said, suddenly pulling out a new edition of *Black Beauty* and finding it intensely interesting.

'Who else has started then?'

'Grandpa,' Sam said.

'The astute Grandpa Joe,' Bryony said nodding. 'Well, he should know.'

'Know what?'

'What's going on in that head of yours,' she said. 'He usually does. If you're ever trying to hide a secret, everybody knows to go to Grandpa and ask him what's going on.'

'Good grief!' Sam said. 'Is there *no* privacy in this family?'

'None whatsoever,' Bryony said. 'You should know that by now.'

He replaced the copy of *Black Beauty*.

'Aren't you going to buy that?' Bryony teased.

'Ha ha,' he said, turning to go.

'Sam?' she said as he reached the door.

'What?'

'Do you really like her?'

'I don't even know her,' he said. 'I wish everybody would stop making such a big fuss about her.'

Bryony frowned. 'Sorry,' she said. 'It's just that we're all so desperate to see you happy. You know, after Emma.'

He sighed. 'And I wish everybody would stop going on about her too,' he said, the bell jingling above his head as he marched out of the shop.

Sunday lunch at the Nightingales' was always something a bit special. The large dining room table at Campion House, which comfortably seated all ten members of the family as well as various guests, was set with a fine white linen tablecloth which had belonged to Grandma Nell's mother, the very best crockery, silver cutlery and beautiful crystal glasses.

The room itself was a splendid typical Georgian one with a high ceiling and enormous sash windows that let in plenty of Suffolk light, and boasted the added bonus of French windows which led out into the garden. In the summer months, the doors would be flung open so that the scent of flowers and cut grass would mingle with the food.

A huge walnut sideboard also graced the room and it was on this as well as on the table itself that Frank Nightingale would display flowers cut from his well-tended garden. He still hadn't decided if books or gardening was his paramount passion these days, but his wife Eleanor knew that he was at his happiest when in the midst of some huge herbaceous border, tackling an overgrown honeysuckle or staking delphiniums.

'I'm just going outside,' he'd call to Eleanor and she knew that, if he was taking a book with him, he would be gone for at least two or three hours. If there was no book in his hand, he would be much longer.

As Eleanor bustled around the table now, she stopped briefly to admire her husband's display of multi-coloured dahlias which sat shaggily on the sideboard as well as at the centre of the table. They were such joyful flowers, she thought, and so lovely to have in the house, even if it meant the occasional earwig crawling across the woodwork. She remembered the first time Frank had brought one into the house. It had been a brilliant sulphur-yellow flower and he'd tucked it behind her ear where it had looked so bright against her dark hair. Of course, her dark hair came out of a bottle these days, but it was still naturally thick and wavy and she wore it loose over her shoulders just as Frank liked it. Not long ago, she'd announced that she was going to get it cut.

'A nice short bob,' she'd told him. He'd nearly exploded.

She walked across the room and gazed out of the French windows towards the emerald lawn which sloped down to the herbaceous borders. How lucky they were to have this place, she thought, not for the first time, and how lucky they were to still use it as a family.

It had been difficult maintaining the Sunday lunch tradition over the years as her children had left for university at different times and then gone on to work, get married and make families of their own. Well, Sam and Polly were the only ones to have married and that hadn't ended well for either of them – if Polly's had, indeed, ended, which nobody was at all sure about since Sean Prior had gone missing three years ago. Polly was also the only one to have provided her and Frank with a grandchild: dear Archie. He was six now, and a little livewire.

Then there was Josh, Bryony and Lara. Bryony was currently working her way through a succession of very bad dates and putting on a brave face about it all, saying that it didn't matter and that she was dedicated to her work, but Eleanor could see the pain in her eyes and knew that her daughter was desperate to fall in love.

Josh, on the other hand, seemed to have no interest in falling in love at all. He had thrown himself into running his bookshop. Eleanor and Frank were so proud of the ideas he'd brought to the store, but a life couldn't be made up of books alone and Eleanor was worried that he was never going to settle down and make a family of his own. He just didn't seem interested. Mind you, Eleanor thought, Frank Nightingale hadn't been a bit interested in marriage until the day she had walked into his shop. She smiled at the memory, and hoped that all her children would be lucky in love one day soon.

The sound of a car pulling up on the gravel driveway brought Eleanor back to the present and, making sure the two family dogs, Hardy and Brontë, were out of the way in the boot room, she went to open the front door. She knew who the first arrival would be: Sam. He was always the first, arriving with a nice bottle of wine and then spending the minutes before lunch prowling the family bookshelves, seeing if there had been any new arrivals or if he was in the mood to borrow any old favourites.

'Hi, Mum,' he said as he joined her in the hallway a moment later, leaning forward to kiss her cheek.

'You look tired, Sam,' she said. 'What's the matter?'

'Nothing's the matter,' he said.

'No? Are you sure? Grandpa said–'

'What? What's Grandpa been saying?'

'That you should get out more.'

Sam shook his head and gave the sort of smile that had no joy in it at all. 'I get out plenty.'

'Like when? When was the last time you went out?' she asked him. 'What is this?'

'Tell me,' his mother said.

'This is ridiculous,' he said. 'Why is everyone picking on me?'

A screech of tyres outside marked the timely arrival of Josh, and Sam made the most of the opportunity by fleeing the scene.

'I'm not done with you yet, Sam!' Eleanor said before she was greeted by her youngest son, Josh.

'Hi, Mum,' he said, kissing her on the cheek and thrusting a bunch of flowers into her arms.

'Thanks, darling,' she said. 'Have you cut your hair again?'

'Yep.'

'I liked it longer.'

'I like it shorter,' he said with a grin and Eleanor realised, not for the first time, that she could no longer dictate her wishes to her children anymore. She could only voice an opinion which she hoped might be heard.

'Mum?' a voice called through from the hallway a moment later.

'We're in the kitchen, Bryony,' Eleanor called back through.

'Look who I found in the lane,' Bryony said as she appeared.

'Lara!' Eleanor cried, rushing towards her youngest daughter and embracing her. 'I thought you couldn't make it.'

'I nearly didn't,' Lara said, pushing her long hair out of her face. It was the colour of dark honey and was wavy like Eleanor and Bryony's. 'My car broke down again.'

'Oh, not again!' Eleanor said. 'I *do* worry about you in that old thing.'

'That old thing is all I can afford,' Lara said.

'Well, your dad's offered to buy you a new one.'

'Oh, Mum! You know I–'

'I know!' Eleanor interrupted. 'You want to do things for yourself.'

Lara nodded. 'I've got a new Saturday job at a garden centre. It doesn't pay much, but it helps a bit.'

'You should just catch the train and get one of us to pick you up at the station. Anyway, it's good to have you home.'

'I brought some washing,' Lara said.

'I would expect no less,' Eleanor said with a wry grin.

'The washing machines in our halls of residence are disgusting,' Lara said with a grimace. 'You don't want to know what I found in one last week.'

'I do,' Josh called through from the hall.

'Not before we've eaten,' Eleanor said in a warning tone.

The conversation continued as the Nightingale family prepared to serve lunch, making their way into the dining room. The seating arrangements were the same that they'd always been, with Frank at the head of the table and Eleanor to his left. Next to Eleanor was Sam, Polly and Archie. Grandpa Joe sat at the far table end with Nell to his left and then there was Josh, Bryony and Lara. It was always the same. If there were guests, they would be squeezed in as comfortably as possible next to the person they'd arrived with.

Now, Eleanor, Bryony and Lara brought in the food: a traditional roast with all the trimmings.

'Where's Polly?' Frank asked.

'Oh, she rang before. She's running late,' Eleanor told her husband.

'Not again. She's never on time, that girl.'

'Well, there's a lot to sort out when you're a single mum.'

'She should be used to it by now,' Josh said and received a glare from his mother in response.

'How can you say that? Her situation is *not* something you get used to,' Eleanor said.

'Don't forget it's the anniversary today,' Sam said. 'You know – since Sean–'

'How could we forget that?' Bryony said.

'I'm just reminding you. Don't go saying anything inappropriate,' Sam said.

'Like what?'

'Not you, Bry. I meant Josh.'

'Why would *I* say something inappropriate?' Josh said with a wounded look on his face.

'Because you usually do,' Bryony said.

Josh shook his head. 'I don't know why I come here every week to be insulted.'

'Because you'd miss it if you didn't,' Bryony said, giving her brother a little smile.

It was then that the front door slammed.

'We're here!'

'Come on through, Polly, we're just serving up,' Eleanor called through.

Polly appeared in the doorway a moment later, her dark hair had been neatly pinned at the back of her neck with a tortoiseshell hair grip that she'd had since high school and her face was pale and make-up free. Beside her was Archie with a big grin on his face.

'We nearly got squished by a tractor!' he said with glee.

'We did not nearly get squished,' his mother told him.

'He said bad words to you,' Archie said.

'Yes, well, some people don't have very good manners,' Polly said. 'Now, go and wash your hands before you eat.'

'I washed them before we left home,' Archie said.

'Yes and we don't know where you've put them since,' Polly said, patting his bottom in the direction of the cloakroom before sitting down at the table. 'This looks nice,' she said.

'Your father's parsnips,' Eleanor said.

Josh laughed. 'That sounds really rude, Mum!'

'Everything sounds rude to you,' Bryony said.

'I'll tell you something really rude if you want,' Josh said.

'Must you at the dinner table?' Eleanor said with a weary sigh.

'No – not rude as in filthy,' Josh said. 'Rude as in bad manners.'

'Oh, well that's okay I guess,' Eleanor said as she handed round the blue and white dish of roast potatoes, golden and crisp in their skins.

'Who's been rude?' Archie asked as he entered the room with his hands newly scrubbed.

'Well, little nephew,' Josh said, 'let me tell you. That crazy woman was in again.'

'What crazy woman?' Grandma Nell asked from her end of the table.

'The one who keeps asking for that monstrous book,' Josh said.

'What monstrous book?' Grandma Nell asked.

'The one that's been in all the papers and on the news,' Frank told his mother.

'The sexy book?' Grandma Nell said. At eighty-three years old, she was still on the ball when it came to all the latest book gossip.

'Grandma!' Polly cried, nodding towards Archie.

'What's a sexy book?' Archie immediately asked.

'It's a filthy dirty book that I refuse to sell in my shop,' Josh said.

'Why don't they clean it if it's dirty?' Archie said.

'That's a very good question, Arch,' Josh said.

'I don't know why you don't just stock it,' Grandpa Joe said. 'You could sell hundreds of copies in a week, I'm sure of it.'

'That's not the point,' Josh said.

'But I thought that was the whole point of running a shop,' Grandpa Joe said, his dark eyes sparkling with glee.

'You know that's not true, Grandpa. If making money from a shop was the only objective, I doubt very much if one would choose a shop selling books.'

Grandpa guffawed and then stuffed a parsnip into his mouth, obviously enjoying the Sunday lunch show immensely.

'I don't know where you got your standards from,' Eleanor told Josh, 'because it certainly wasn't from your father. He stocked any old book that sold.'

'I did not!' Frank said with a little grin.

'Frank Nightingale, you know you did and I know where you kept them all as well for your special customers!'

'Is this true, Dad?' Josh said, his eyes wide in surprise.

'They were literary classics,' Frank said in his defence.

'Literary filth more like,' Eleanor said.

Everybody laughed.

'Well, I'm not having that book in Nightingale's,' Josh said.

'Good for you,' Bryony said. 'One has to have standards.'

'I don't know why that woman keeps coming in,' Josh said. 'It would have been quicker for her to have bought it somewhere else, but she's got a real bee in her bonnet about it now. I'm going to have to get a restraining order on her or something.'

'Why don't you just buy one copy for her? You don't have to have it on display. Just keep it under the till,' Frank said.

Josh shook his head. 'It is not going to happen. I'm not having that book sully my shop.'

Eleanor smiled at her youngest son's convictions.

'Sam had an interesting visitor to his shop this week too,' Grandpa Joe said.

'Oh?' Frank said.

'Grandpa!' Sam said, a warning tone in his voice.

'Yes!' Bryony interrupted. 'Callie Logan!'

'The writer?' Polly said.

'*Yes*,' Bryony said, 'but Sam won't ask her to do a signing at the shop, the meanie!'

'Why not?' Eleanor asked. 'Castle Clare could do with a bit of livening up in between the literary festivals.'

'She's not that kind of person,' Sam said. 'I don't think she'd be interested.'

'What's she like, then?' Polly asked. Sam didn't answer so Polly turned her question to her grandpa. 'What's she like, Grandpa?'

Grandpa Joe stroked his chin and took his time in answering, enjoying being the centre of attention. 'She's a wispy, dreamy sort,' he said. 'Like "a faery's child".'

'Keats,' Josh said without a pause.

'Well done, son,' Frank said. He'd done his best to cram as much good poetry into his children as they'd grown up.

'I really think you should let me ask her to do an author event,' Bryony said with a pout. 'It would be a great way for her to get to know everyone.'

'There's no way he's going to ask her,' Polly said, 'not when you remember what happened with that dreadful Miriam Morley.'

Bryony tutted. 'That was just one unfortunate incident!'

'Unfortunate incident?' Polly said. 'She made Tilly Brady cry!'

'How was I to know she didn't like kids?' Bryony protested. 'I didn't know children's authors were allowed to hate children.'

Sam sighed. 'For goodness' sake!' he said. 'Can't we have this meal in peace?'

Silence descended and everybody stared at him, and then the laughter began.

'No chance!' Josh said.

'It wouldn't be normal, would it?' Bryony said.

'No, I guess not,' Sam said, resigned to the fact that, as long as he was a Nightingale, he couldn't hope for a single moment's peace.

# CHAPTER 5

A week after her first visit to Nightingale's, Callie found herself back in Castle Clare. She parked her car near the castle and walked the short distance into town, browsing in the enormous antiques centre and wondering if she could justify the purchase of a chaise longue. Deciding that it was a little too pretentious for her humble cottage, as well as a little too expensive, she made her way to the little local supermarket in the town square. How nice it was to shop in a small space, she decided as she picked up a basket and wandered down the tiny aisles. She'd been used to years of shopping in ginormous supermarkets with shelves full of endless choice and things flown in from abroad whether it was the season to eat them or not. Now, as she browsed the shelves, she saw locally-sourced seasonal produce and that made her unexpectedly happy.

Two bags of groceries later, Callie left the shop and found herself in Church Street. She hadn't intended to go there but, she told herself, the smallness of the town meant that she had found the street easily enough as she'd been window shopping.

She walked by the independent bookshop and stopped outside the window of the secondhand one. If she went in, would Sam Nightingale think she was hassling him with her order? Would he think her pushy? She hesitated and, in that moment, Sam Nightingale walked into the main room of the shop and spotted her through the window. There was no escaping him now and she found that she actually didn't want to.

'Hello,' she said, entering the shop with her two bags now in one hand as the bell tinkled above her.

'Hi,' he said, his brown eyes warm in welcome behind his glasses.

'I haven't come in about my book,' she said quickly. 'I'm not hassling you or anything.'

He smiled. 'That's okay even if you were,' he said. 'I don't mind being hassled. I'm afraid there's no joy yet for *Perdita's Key* but my secret army of book spotters is on the case!'

'Thanks,' she said. 'Good to know.'

'How's Kingston?' he asked.

'Kingston?'

'The book you bought,' he said.

'Oh!' Callie said, the light dawning on her. 'Kingston is very well. He's sitting on the coffee table in the living room whilst I admire that lovely blue and gold cover.'

Sam nodded. 'I do that with new books all the time. Each one has a special place on a table somewhere before being safely shelved.'

'Do you have books out on your tables all the time?' Callie asked.

'A few,' he said. 'Nice big hardbacks which demand their time in the spotlight. I have a lovely hardback about Benton End. You know the Cedric Morris place here in Suffolk?'

Callie shook her head.

'He was a painter and set up something of an artists' drop-in. The gardens there were magnificent and artists from all over would come to paint there and swap gossip. That's the book I'm flipping through at the moment, looking at the pictures, reading the highlighted paragraphs before diving into the main text. I like that slow way of getting to know a book.'

'I do too,' Callie said. 'It's like taking a tiny bite out of a delicious meal just to see what the flavours are.'

He laughed. 'Indeed,' he said. 'So which book are you nibbling at the moment?'

Callie looked thoughtful. 'I've got a number of them around the house, actually. There's a book about herbs on my coffee table which I'm flipping through with the greatest of intentions of actually growing some myself now that I've got a garden. There's also a wonderful book about chocolate which a friend bought me for Christmas. She really should know better as I eat far too many sweet things. Then there's a romance novel in the bathroom for lazy soaks in the bath and a book in my study about woodlands which I'm reading for research for the new story I've just started.'

Sam nodded. 'Sounds like a good, varied diet with most of the book groups represented,' he said.

Callie laughed.

'Have you read any Roger Deakin?' he asked.

'No,' Callie said. 'What's he written?'

'He wrote three amazing books about the countryside and I think you'd really like *Wildwood*. My brother's shop next door always stocks them.'

'Shall I–' she motioned to the door.

'Go and take a look,' he said with a nod.

Callie left the shop and entered the one next door. It had the same Georgian shopfront with a large window stuffed with books and the same sort of bell tinkled above the door when she opened it.

A dark-haired man was reaching up to a shelf, but turned around as she entered and Callie smiled as she looked at yet another handsome Nightingale bookseller.

'Hello,' he said. His hair was short and neat and he had a nice slim face with the same large brown eyes as Sam.

'You're Sam's brother, right?' Callie asked.

'Yes,' he said. 'Did he send you round?'

'He sent me in search of Roger Deakin,' Callie explained.

'Come this way,' he said. 'I'm Josh.' He held out a hand for her to shake.

'Callie,' she said.

He blinked. 'Callie Logan?'

She looked at him perplexed. 'How did you know?'

Josh gave a smile that was like a ramped-up version of Sam's, making Callie think that Sam's smile was only on half-wattage.

'Sam mentioned you'd visited the shop,' he said.

'He did?'

'We love authors here, you see,' Josh said. 'You know we have a literary festival in the summer?'

'I've heard about it,' she said, wondering what on earth Sam had said about her.

'Well, we always get excited when a new author comes to town.'

'I've come here to live,' Callie said.

'I know,' he said, again his full-beam smile washing over her. 'Don't worry – you'll get used to everyone knowing your business. That's small towns for you.'

'So I'm learning,' she said.

'Right,' he said, clapping his hands together, 'which title were you after.'

'Sam mentioned a book about a wood.'

Josh nodded. '*Wildwood*.' He moved into the second room of the shop and, reaching up to a shelf, carefully extracted a white paperback which he handed to Callie. She looked at the blue and green trees on its cover. Simple but beautiful.

'*Wildwood – a journey through trees*,' she read on the cover. 'Why haven't I heard of this before?'

Josh grinned. 'It's a great day when you meet a new writer, isn't it? It's like an introduction to a best friend you didn't know existed just hours before.'

Callie smiled. Josh talked exactly like his brother.

'There's *Notes from Walnut Tree Farm* which is about his life out at Mellis here in Suffolk. It's in journal style. The writing is beautiful. And then there's *Waterlog* – his great swimming adventure across the UK. He started off in his moat at home and then swam in everything from ponds and rivers and lakes and tarns.'

'Really?'

'Truly,' Josh said.

The bell above the door rang as another customer entered the shop.

'Excuse me,' Josh said, leaving her in the company of three wonderful books which she berated herself at never having met before. She was still holding *Wildwood* and ran her fingers over the fine matte cover, enjoying the feel of the indented name and title and marvelling at the quality of the paper before flipping through the book. It was a good thick book of nearly four hundred pages and each chapter had a beautiful little illustration after its title. Callie knew she had to have it and a surge of excitement filled her as she thought about the hours of pleasure that this book would give her. She could come back for the other two books; it would be something to look forward to when she had finished the first – the delayed gratification that a compulsive reader never tires of.

She walked through to the till in the first room, pausing a moment as she saw Josh dealing with a customer.

'But I've told you, I'm not stocking that book.'

'It's disgraceful!' the woman told him. 'Call yourself a bookshop when you don't hold the latest bestseller?'

'You are welcome to place an order and I can keep it here for you to collect,' he said, doing his best to keep his patience.

'I want to see it on display,' the woman said.

'That's not going to happen,' Josh said.

Callie blinked at his firm tone of voice. What on earth was this book they were talking about?

Luckily for Josh, the customer's mobile rang and she hurriedly left the shop a moment later.

'What did she want?' Callie asked, coming out from her hiding place in Fiction L to M.

'She wanted that damned awful book by F M Keynes,' Josh said. 'Pardon my Anglo-Saxon.'

'You're pardoned,' Callie said with a grin.

'You know the book?'

'Oh, yes,' Callie said. 'I've seen it around. One of my London friends said she was in one of those massive supermarkets and a shop assistant was taking down all the other titles so she could put rows and rows of that book up.'

Josh shook his head in despair. 'What is the world coming too? I've seen people reading it in public with no shame! At the bus stop, in the queue at the post office – I even saw one of our school teachers reading a copy down at Castle Park!'

Callie bit her lip to stop herself from laughing. She hadn't met such a young man with such strong principles since her days as a student and it was wonderfully refreshing.

'She just can't accept that I'm not going to stock that book in this shop,' Josh said.

'Will she come back?'

'Probably,' he said. 'She's been in three times already this week and I've already backed down and said I'd order her a copy just to get her off my back, but she's got this perverse notion about seeing it physically on display in the shop.'

'How bizarre!' Callie said. 'Maybe she's got a bet with a friend or something.'

'Or maybe she's just a pervert.'

They looked at each other and laughed.

'Well, I don't want a copy of that book,' Callie told him. 'I've found *Wildwood*.'

He grinned. 'Good,' he said. 'A nice sane customer with exemplary taste!'

She watched as he rang the book through the till before placing it in one of the brown paper bags with the Nightingale stamp on which she was fast becoming addicted to.

'And a bookmark for you,' he said, popping one inside the bag.

'For books which make your heart sing,' she said from memory.

'Exactly,' Josh said, 'and that bloody Keynes book does *not* make my heart sing!' He rolled his eyes and sighed again, but then his smile returned. 'It was very nice to meet you. I hope you'll visit again.'

'I think it's probably on the cards,' she said. 'It's hard for a writer to stay away from books for too long.'

He gave her a funny little salute that made her laugh and she left the shop, returning to the one just next door.

'I loved your brother's shop,' she said as she entered to the sound of the tinkling bell.

'I thought you would,' Sam said, stepping down off one of the antique library steps. 'You'll have to meet my sister too – she runs the children's bookshop opposite, and my cousin, Megan, runs the library.'

Callie looked surprised. 'Your whole family works with books?'

'Books, writing, editing, the literary festival–'

'Wow,' Callie said.

'Did Josh tell you about *Beechcombings*?' Sam asked. 'The Richard Mabey book.'

'No,' Callie said.

'He really should have. Never mind, though, I have a copy kicking around somewhere.'

Before she could ask him anything more, Sam disappeared, resurfacing a minute later with a pretty paperback. 'Here,' he said. 'A little something for you from me.'

'Oh, you must let me pay,' she said.

He shook his head. 'It's been kicking around for a while and has a particularly nasty beer stain on page seventeen.'

Callie grinned. 'Well, I'll take it off your hands, then, and just hope that the pertinent passage that I'm looking for as a reader *isn't* on page seventeen!' She popped it into the brown bag which Josh had given her, a feeling of great satisfaction filling her at the thought of two new books to look forward to.

'Listen, I'll leave you to look around,' Sam said and she watched as he walked across the room towards a stack of hardbacks teetering on an old wooden stool.

Callie realised that there were several important features to which she'd not paid due attention during her first visit to the shop like the wonderful beams. The shopfront might have been Georgian but the interior was obviously much older and the thick wooden beams looked ancient. Since she'd come to Suffolk, she realised that its architecture was very rich indeed and there were more medieval timber-framed buildings than she'd ever seen in her life.

Her first trip to the bookshop had been about finding her way around the shelves and discovering which books were kept where, but now she looked at the shop itself – at the little pieces of old furniture that were dotted around the rooms and the ornaments too. There was an old chipped Staffordshire pottery figure of Shakespeare wearing a gleaming white outfit decorated in delicate gold stripes and buttons. He was leaning on a plinth of books and had the dreamy look of a true poet. He had been placed up against a row of fine hardback editions of his own plays.

'I keep him safely tucked away on the top shelf,' Sam said as he saw her looking at it. 'There's always the urge for people to touch him and he's a bit delicate these days.'

'He's keeping an eye on everyone from up there,' Callie said.

'Especially me,' Sam said. 'I have a tendency to lose myself in a good book when I should be thinking about the literary needs of my customers.'

'I have to say I wasn't a big fan of Shakespeare in school,' Callie said. 'Our teacher made us read *The Merchant of Venice* around the class. I was Shylock's daughter, Jessica. It was an awful part and I didn't know what on earth was going on.'

Sam smiled. 'I got to play Petruchio in our school's production of *The Taming of the Shrew*. I've never worked so hard in my life as I did learning all those lines.'

'Tough role,' Callie said. 'I'm impressed. Do you still remember it all?'

'Bits and pieces,' he said. '"Now, by the world, it is a lusty wench; I love her ten times more than e'er I did. O, how I long to have some chat with her!"'

Callie laughed and Sam cleared his throat.

'It's quite ridiculous what the brain stores away, isn't it?'

'Quite,' she said, noticing that his cheeks had coloured up rather attractively.

'That's what I love about bookshops,' he said. 'There are so many worlds in this very modest space. You can time travel back to virtually any era from Shakespeare's England to the 1960s. You can become a soldier and fight a world war, you can climb Everest or explore a South American tepui with Arthur Conan Doyle, or milk a cow in nineteenth-century Dorset with Thomas Hardy or drink a Rolls Royce cocktail on a farm in Kent with H E Bates. Where else could you do all of this but in a bookshop?'

Callie nodded, smiling at his enthusiastic words.

'So many lifetimes can be lead within the covers of books,' she said, watching as he picked up a yellow-spined paperback that had been wrongly shelved and returned it to its rightful home.

'This is the popular paperback section – always a hit with the holidaymaker.'

'Wow!' Callie said, gazing up at the books which reached from floor to ceiling, their bright spines enticing her to lean forward and touch them – to pull them out and gobble them up.

'Some people are surprised that we have so many. They shake their heads and tut, but there's room for everything at Nightingale's.'

Callie nodded. 'There is still this big divide between literary and popular fiction, isn't there?'

'I'm afraid so,' Sam said. 'I've seen customers come in here and buy the latest Booker Prize winning title and I know they're not going to read it in a million years. They might struggle through the first chapter on a dark winter's night when they can't get out into the garden, but that's as far as it'll go and it'll soon appear on one of the tables at the church fete where people will nod towards it and say, "Didn't that book win a prize?" and then they pick up the John Grisham or Nora Roberts next to it instead.'

Callie laughed. 'I don't know why there's such snobbery. It seems very silly to me. Books are meant to give pleasure, aren't they?'

'Exactly,' he said. 'I like to split books into two groups. Just two. Books I want to read and books I don't.'

'And are there many in the books you don't want to read category?' Callie asked him.

'Not many,' he said with a little smile. 'I think most books have some sort of appeal to me as a bookseller if not a reader – even if it's just the font used for the title or the quality of the paper the publisher has printed it on. If a book crosses my path, I have to pick it up and examine it even if I have no intentions of reading it.'

'Me too,' she said, 'and I have an awful habit of picking up fellow authors' books and reading the first chapter before either shuddering in horror because the writing is so bad or shuddering in horror because it's so much better than my own. But don't tell anyone I said that!'

They laughed and their eyes met and there was one of those wonderful moments of connection between two people that so rarely happens in life. It was as if both their lives had been leading up to this quiet little moment in a bookshop in Suffolk, somewhere between G and L in the fiction department.

It was Sam who broke the spell first, clearing his throat.

'Listen,' he said, 'I hope this isn't too forward of me, but – well – I was wondering if you'd like to go for a meal sometime.'

'No,' Callie said, the word shooting out of her mouth before she had a chance to check it.

'Oh, okay,' Sam said, holding his hands in the air as if in surrender. 'I didn't mean to–'

'I've got to go,' she said, leaving the shop in a dash of carrier bags and embarrassment.

When she got back to the sanctuary of Owl Cottage, she could feel her heart was racing wildly and tears filled her eyes. Why had she done that? She could still see the wounded look upon Sam's face. It was as if her 'no' had been fired directly into his heart. She closed her eyes as hot tears spilled down her face. *Stupid, stupid girl*, she chided herself. What had Sam Nightingale done to deserve that from her? Nothing! Absolutely nothing. He was sweet and kind and interesting and they'd been getting on so well together. She liked him – *really* liked him.

Perhaps that was it, she thought. Perhaps it was the fear of liking somebody too much again. She couldn't risk it. Not after what had happened with Piers. She was still feeling so wounded and raw from that that she could never see herself becoming involved with anyone ever again.

'What is wrong with me?' she asked.

*You've been hurt*, a little voice inside her said and she knew it was true. Piers might not have hurt her physically, he hadn't ever even raised his voice at her let alone a hand, but he had certainly hurt her emotionally. All those lonely nights she'd spent when he'd been at work had left her feeling isolated and unloved and she'd come to believe it was her fault until her best friend, Heidi, had told her that it wasn't her fault at all.

'Piers is a pig!' she'd told Callie.

'Isn't that being a bit mean?' Callie had said.

'He's the one who's mean!' Heidi had said, but Callie couldn't help harbouring the thought that something must be innately wrong with her for her husband not to have wanted to spend time with her.

She caught her reflection in the glass of a framed picture, her eyes large and frightened.

'What is wrong with me?' she asked herself again.

She closed her eyes. She really didn't know the answer to that question, but one thing was certain: she was never ever going to get close to another man.

# CHAPTER 6

What on *earth* had he been thinking about, asking her out for dinner? Of course she didn't want to go out with him. She was a beautiful, famous author and he was a fusty old antiquarian. She was never going to say yes.

Sam Nightingale shook his head ruefully. And they'd been getting on together so well too, he thought, remembering the easy way they'd talked and laughed. It had been so relaxed with Callie and he'd really thought there had been a connection there.

'But you had to go and blow it!' he said to himself, cursing as he dusted a hardback copy of *The English Vicarage Garden* before giving it its moment in the spotlight on the music stand. The cover was a little dated, but it was a pretty book that would find its owner, he felt sure of that.

'What did you go and blow?' Grandpa Joe said from behind him.

'Grandpa!' Sam said. 'I wish you wouldn't creep up on me like that.'

'I don't creep,' he said with a little grunt.

'You do,' Sam said. 'You should wear proper shoes instead of those slippers so I can hear you coming.'

'I like these slippers,' Grandpa Joe said. 'They keep my feet warm.'

Sam shook his head at his grandfather's eccentric ways. He sometimes had a feeling that customers came into the shop to see Grandpa Joe as much as they came to see the books.

'Anyway,' his grandpa continued, 'what did you go and blow?'

Sam sighed. Grandpa Joe's ears were far too keen for his liking. Why couldn't he be nice and deaf like most eighty-three-year-olds?

'What did I blow?' Sam asked. 'The dust off this book.'

'Huh!' Grandpa Joe said. 'She was here again, wasn't she?'

'Who?'

'That nice young girl,' he said. 'The author girl.'

'Were you eavesdropping?'

'Me?'

'Yes, you!'

'Nah! I was out the back having a nap, but I heard the bell tinkle and the sound of voices. It was her, wasn't it?'

'Yes, it was her,' Sam admitted.

'And?'

'And nothing.'

'What did you talk about?'

Sam went behind the counter and started shuffling papers around that didn't need shuffling.

'Hey?' Grandpa Joe cried.

'What?' Sam cried back.

'What happened? Something happened here, didn't it? I can feel it in my bones.'

'That's arthritis,' Sam said.

His grandfather tutted but held Sam's gaze with his own steely one and he finally relented.

'She said no,' he told him.

'No to what?'

'To me,' Sam said. 'I asked her out to dinner and she said no.'

'Oh.'

'Indeed.'

'How did you ask her?'

'Too quickly?' Sam suggested.

'No, I mean the wording – what did you actually *say*?'

Sam frowned. 'I'm not sure. I kind of bumbled my way through it, I guess, but her no was–' he paused.

'What?'

'Final.'

'Are you sure?'

'Pretty much,' he said. 'She said "no" and then bolted out of the shop. We'd been getting on pretty well till then.' He cursed again.

'Language!'

'*Why* did I have to go and mess it up?' he said, slamming his hand down on a book resting by the till.

'Don't take it out on a book. No woman is worth that,' Grandpa Joe said.

'Sorry,' Sam said, picking the book up gently and rubbing it as if he might have bruised it.

'Make us a cup of tea,' Grandpa Joe said and Sam nodded, having the feeling that his grandpa didn't really want a cup of tea at all, but that it was just an excuse to get them both sitting down.

Sure enough, a few minutes later, they were on the sofa together in the backroom of the shop with their tea. It was a quiet day and Sam didn't feel too guilty about sitting down for a moment. It was one of the many perks of working there – just sitting perfectly still in the same room as a thousand books.

'Did I ever tell you the story of how I met your Grandma Nell?' Grandpa Joe asked at last.

'Yes,' Sam said, knowing that Grandpa Joe knew very well that he'd told him the story many times over the years and also knowing that he was going to hear it again now.

'Well, that didn't go too smoothly to begin with,' Grandpa Joe began undeterred. 'She was browsing in the library and I was watching her for an age, trying to pluck up the courage to go and speak to her. She was wearing this cute little hat and her hair was all in curls. Oh, how I wanted to twist those curls around my fingers.' He gave a little chuckle and Sam couldn't help but be charmed by his reminiscence. 'But she didn't look up at me once so I decided to take action. I went right up to her and said–'

'Excuse me – that's my book you're reading,' Sam interrupted.

'That's right,' Grandpa Joe said, 'and she said–'

'What do you mean *your* book? This is a public library. Books don't belong to any one person,' Sam said.

Grandpa Joe nodded. 'So I told her that I took that book out every other week. It was some encyclopaedia or other – I don't remember which now.'

'And she said, "Well, I'm going to take it out this week," and you said, "Perhaps we can share it."'

Grandpa Joe chuckled again. 'You know this story better than I do.'

'I should do by now,' Sam said.

'Anyway, we went for a cup of tea and looked through the book together. It was the start of a beautiful relationship, but she often told me that my cheeky manner with her that day in the library nearly had her running for the hills.'

'Did she?' Sam said, never having heard him confess that part before.

'Oh, yes,' he said, 'but it was my smile that saved the day. She said

I had an honest smile and we all know that you've got my smile.'

'I do?'

'Yep,' Grandpa Joe said. 'The quickest way to disarm a woman is to smile at her. She may not admit it but a woman likes to know that she can make a man smile. It's a kind of power, you see.'

Sam gave a little laugh.

'What?' Grandpa Joe said.

'I think it takes more than a little smile.'

'Oh, really?' he said, eyeing his grandson incredulously. 'Well, I dare say a spot of charm doesn't go amiss.'

'I shouldn't have rushed this,' he interrupted. 'I don't know what I was thinking.'

'That's it, though, isn't it – with matters of the heart?' Grandpa Joe said. 'You tend *not* to think.'

'I guess,' Sam said with a sigh, 'but perhaps it's a sign that it's not right for me.'

'What do you mean?'

'I mean, this whole relationship business. After what happened with Emma, I just can't see things working out for me.'

'But you *can* see yourself living a miserable solitary life for the rest of your days, is that it?'

Sam shook his head. 'I don't know,' he said. 'I don't want to think about it.' He got up from the sofa. 'I want to think about work, that's all. It's what I'm good at.'

'Oh, yes. Books never broke a man's heart, did they?' Grandpa Joe said, his tone ironic.

'That's right,' Sam said in all seriousness, 'although the latest Clive Mandrake thriller very nearly broke mine. Did you read it? It was *terrible.*'

'Don't be flip with me,' Grandpa Joe said. 'This place – this shop – is heaven, but don't let it become your tomb. Don't bury yourself here because that would be very easy to do.'

Sam walked through to the kitchen to wash up the day's tea mugs. As much as he loved his grandfather's company, he couldn't help wishing that the old man would keep his opinions on his love life to himself.

'And remember: books don't keep you warm at night!' Grandpa Joe called through to him.

'Haven't you got something to do somewhere, Grandpa?'

'No, no,' came his reply. 'I'm good here.'

Sam rolled his eyes.

Heidi Wray looked thoroughly out of place in the middle of the Suffolk countryside. Her tall, willowy figure encased in the very latest designer labels, her four inch heels and her immaculate chin-length raven-black hair were thrown into relief in the topsy-turvy overgrown front garden of Owl Cottage.

'How charming!' she said, looking at the green chaos she found herself in. 'It wouldn't suit my nails,' she said, flexing her magenta talons, 'but yours are perfectly suited to country life!'

'It's so good to see you, Heidi!' Callie said, giving her friend a warm hug. She was used to Heidi's compliments which bordered on insults and took them in her stride because she knew her friend meant well. 'You look amazing!'

'And you look–' Heidi paused, her heavily made-up eyes squinting at Callie, 'countryfied.'

'Countryfied?' Callie said in horror. 'What do you mean?'

'Well, I know you were always being *far* too creative and what not to bother about hairdressers and the like and – well – now you've fully embraced that *au naturel* look!'

'Oh, have I?'

'And how well it suits you!' Heidi said.

Callie smiled to herself as she pushed her *au naturel* hair out of her face and bent down to pick up Heidi's overnight bag. For all her painful honestly, Heidi was one of the few things Callie missed about her old life in London and she was glad her friend was staying with her although she had to admit to being surprised when Heidi had agreed to sleep on the sofa because she was the sort of woman who liked a little bit of luxury.

Heidi had lived in the same apartment block as Callie and Piers and the two of them had become instant friends after Heidi's Jack Russell Terrier, Horatio, had laddered Callie's stockings in a bid to say hello the day she'd moved in. Heidi had been mortified and had immediately replaced them with a stunning designer pair which must have cost a small fortune. Callie had been too afraid to wear them and they remained in their packet in a bedroom drawer.

'Come in and see the place,' Callie said, leading the way straight from the garden into the sitting room.

'No hallway! How quaint,' Heidi said.

'Everything is absolutely tiny,' Callie said unnecessarily.

'So I see,' Heidi said. 'However do you manage, sweetie?'

'Oh, there's plenty of room for me,' Callie said. 'I love it! And it's so peaceful.'

Heidi walked across to the window, ducking to avoid the low beams, and peered out at the view across the lane towards the common. 'Yes,' she said with one of her measured looks. 'It looks a bit too peaceful. Don't you get bored?'

'Not at all,' Callie said.

'But what on earth do you do all day?'

'I write, of course.'

'And at night?'

'I write some more and I read.'

Heidi grimaced. 'But what do you do for *entertainment?*'

'I don't need to be entertained,' Callie said.

'You are a queer creature!' she said.

Callie laughed. 'Believe it or not, this place suits me down to the ground. I don't think I've ever been so happy anywhere.'

'Really?' Heidi said.

Callie smiled. Heidi was a city girl born and bred and the thought of living anywhere without twenty-four-hour facilities right on her doorstep was completely alien to her.

'Well, it wouldn't suit me living in the back of beyond without a coffee bar.'

'Talking of which,' Callie said, moving through to the kitchen at the back of the house. Heidi followed her.

'Good God – are those pumpkins?' Heidi asked as she saw the back garden.

'Yes. The previous owner grew all sorts in the garden. I'm afraid I won't be able to keep it up, but I'm going to give it a go. I thought I'd start off with some radishes and beans and potatoes in the spring. They're meant to be easy.'

'Easy to buy,' Heidi said.

'Yes, but where's the fun in that?'

'I suppose,' she said, examining a nail. 'It wouldn't suit me though.'

'So you keep saying.'

Her friend looked up at her. 'I'm sorry!' she said, a big smile suddenly emerging. 'I'm not debunking this whole country life.'

'Aren't you?' Callie said with a little grin.

'Not at all! I'm really proud of you for making this move. It's *just* what you needed.'

'It is,' Callie said as she put the kettle on.

'So I'm really happy for you. Although I wouldn't want to visit here in the winter,' she said with a theatrical shiver. 'Have you thought about that? All those long, cold winter months?'

'I have,' Callie said, 'and I'm looking forward to getting really cosy with the wood burner.'

Heidi looked aghast again. 'Well, you have to be admired, but you wouldn't catch me handling logs.'

'Not with those nails!' Callie said.

'Exactly!' Heidi said. 'Do you like them? I've got a new girl and she's a miracle worker.'

Callie sincerely hoped that Heidi wouldn't examine her own poor stubby nails too closely because they probably still had dirt underneath them from speed weeding the garden path before her friend's arrival.

With the coffee made, they went through and sat in the living room and Heidi cleared her throat.

'What is it?' Callie said, knowing that this was a sign that she had something to say.

Heidi took a deep breath. 'It's Piers,' she said with a pout. 'He's seeing somebody.'

'What?' Callie said with a little laugh. 'Are you *sure*? He hasn't got time to see anyone.'

'Well, the woman I've seen has been in and out of his flat at least three times this week.'

'Well, perhaps that's his cleaner,' Callie suggested.

'A cleaner in high heels?' Heidi said. 'Cheap ones, mind.'

Callie shook her head, marvelling at Heidi's acute observations. Nothing passed her by especially in the shoe department.

'They went out together the other night too,' she continued. 'Arm in arm.'

'He's at the arm in arm stage already?' Callie said and she couldn't help but feel a little hurt.

'It was quite late when they got back. After midnight, anyway.'

'What night was this?'

'Last Wednesday,' Heidi said.

'A weekday?' Callie said. 'I don't believe it. He rarely went out during the week.'

'Well, he does now.'

Callie swallowed hard, thinking of the husband who had been permanently chained to his desk – the husband who never wanted to spend any time with her. This same husband was now gallivanting across the town with another woman on a *weekday*.

'So?' Heidi said.

'So what?' Callie asked, wondering what she was getting at.

'What I'm trying to say is, it's okay to move on,' Heidi said. 'Piers clearly has so why shouldn't you?'

'But I'm happy being on my own,' Callie said.

'Are you? Are you *really*? Stuck out here in the middle of a field–'

'It's the village common,' Callie corrected her, 'and I can't *bear* the thought of becoming involved again. I'm just learning to appreciate how much I like my own company again.'

'So there's nobody on the horizon? You've not got any lords of the manor anywhere? Or some nice hunky farmer type?'

Callie looked out of the window.

'Callie? *Have* you?'

'No, of course not,' she said, returning her gaze to her friend. 'There's nobody.'

'You hesitated for a moment there,' Heidi told her.

'Did I?'

'You certainly did,' Heidi said. 'Come on – there *is* somebody, isn't there?'

'Really there isn't,' Callie said, but she knew Heidi wasn't going to let it go until she'd had a full confession.

'Oh, come on, Callie! I came *all* this way to see you. You're not going to deny me all the juicy details, are you?'

'There's nothing juicy,' Callie said.

'But? I can *definitely* hear a "but" approaching!'

'But,' Callie said, giving in at last, 'there is someone I've made friends with. Or at least, I *thought* I'd made friends with.'

'Just friends?'

'Well,' Callie said, 'I think I might have even screwed that up.'

'How do you mean?'

'He asked me out to dinner and I said no.'

'Why did you do that?'

'Because I'm not interested in getting involved with anyone and, even if I was, it was all moving way too fast. We'd only just met.'

'Since when has that got anything to do with things? God, Callie – we're living in the twenty-first century. Things move quickly and you've got to be willing to move quickly too or else you'll miss out on a whole heap of life.'

'But I don't want a whole heap of life. I want a nice quiet simple life.'

'Well, you'll get that all right if you cocoon yourself up here, refusing dinner invitations from handsome young men!' Heidi said. 'He is handsome, isn't he?'

Callie smiled at her friend's incorrigible line of questioning. 'I think so,' she said.

'So, what's he like?'

Callie took a deep breath as she remembered Sam Nightingale. 'He's got dark hair and deep brown eyes. He wears glasses.'

'Sexy glasses?'

'Cute glasses.'

'Okay. I can approve of cute.'

'And he has this worldly wise look about him,' she said. 'It's the kind of face you could look at for hours and not be bored by. And we were getting on so well. I found it so easy to talk to him.' She paused.

'Then what?'

'I told you. He asked me out to dinner and I said no and then I ran out of his shop.'

'His shop?'

'A bookshop in Castle Clare. Nightingale's. There are three owned by his family and he runs the secondhand one.'

'And have you spoken to him since?'

'I haven't dared,' Callie said. 'I feel so embarrassed. I don't think I can ever go in there again now which is such a shame as it's a pretty amazing place. Just the sort of hideaway I love.'

Heidi sighed. 'You worry about things too much,' she said. 'I think you should get yourself along there as soon as you can and just act as if nothing happened.'

'I can't do that!'

'Don't you want to see him again?'

'I – well – *yes*! I guess so.'

'What about now?'

'Right now?'

'Sure – why not? I could come with you for some moral support,' Heidi said with a big grin.

Callie shook her head. She could think of nothing worse. 'I think I should just leave things for a while,' she said.

'Spoil sport!' her friend teased.

'I really don't want him to get the wrong idea.'

'And what would be the wrong idea?' Heidi asked.

'That I want a relationship.'

Heidi looked puzzled. 'Don't tell me that you just want him as a friend,' she said.

'How did you know I was going to say that?'

'Because I know you,' Heidi said. 'Besides, you've already confessed that he's handsome and cute.'

'I know, but that was just the observant writer in me.'

'Yeah, right!' Heidi said, obviously not convinced.

'Anyway, what's wrong with wanting a friend?'

'It's wrong because it's not right,' Heidi said. 'It's just not normal, is it?'

'Oh, don't give me that men and women can't be friends line,' Callie said.

'But it's true!' Heidi said.

'I don't believe that. That line was just made up for the movies.'

'Oh, really? Well, how many male friends can you name?' Heidi said, a look of defiance on her face.

Callie stared at her, determined to win this particular argument. 'You want to know how many?'

'I really do,' she said.

'Okay,' Callie began. 'There's Mr Parsons.'

'From the flat next door to Piers's?' Heidi said. 'But he's eighty.'

'So? We had many an interesting conversation in our time.'

Heidi shook her head. 'I bet he still secretly fancied you.'

'Don't be so disgusting,' Callie said. 'Then there was Phillip.'

'He's gay so it doesn't count,' Heidi said quickly.

Callie rolled her eyes. 'Okay – Bob Andersen down at the local deli.'

Heidi wrinkled her nose. 'Were you *really* friends with him?'

Callie nodded. 'We used to talk.'

'About what?'

'Cheese, mostly.'

Heidi shook her head. 'You know I'm right, don't you? You simply can't be friends with a man. It's just not anatomically possible.'

Callie folded her arms across her chest. 'Right,' she said.

'Right what?'

'I'm going to prove you wrong.'

'How?'

'I'm going to be friends with Sam Nightingale. *Friends!* Nothing more and nothing less.'

Heidi grinned. 'You'll be in bed with him before the month's out.'

Callie's mouth dropped open in horror. 'I will *not!*'

'And I'll be waiting to hear *all* the juicy details!'

# CHAPTER 7

It was the second day of Heidi's stay at Owl Cottage when the unexpected visitor arrived. Callie had persuaded Heidi to go on a walk in the surrounding fields that morning, lending her a pair of wellies and trying to convince her that it was quite safe to walk through a muddy puddle and that it wasn't going to swallow her whole.

They were just thinking about popping along to one of the local pubs for lunch when there was a knock at the door.

'Expecting someone?' Heidi said.

'No,' Callie said.

'Maybe it's your book guy coming to try his luck again.'

Callie's face reddened at the suggestion. He had her address, but he wouldn't just show up on her doorstep unannounced, would he? She didn't think he was that kind of person but maybe he would if he'd found her elusive first edition. Maybe she was going to have to face him again far sooner than she'd hoped and in front of the inquisitive eyes of Heidi too.

With her heart hammering in her chest, Callie walked to the front door and opened it.

'Hello,' the man said. It wasn't Sam Nightingale at all. It was – well – Callie didn't actually know his name. She just knew him as the man who'd left the dead rabbit on her doorstep.

'Oh, hello,' she said.

'It's Leo,' he said. 'Leo Wildman. You got my note?'

'What note?' Callie asked.

'You weren't expecting me?'

'No,' Callie said, looking confused.

'I didn't leave you a note?' he asked, looking crestfallen. 'I could have sworn I'd popped one through last night. Oh, I am hopeless. I have a terrible memory,' he said with a grin, raking a hand through his thick dark hair. 'I thought I'd come and cook that meal for you.'

'Meal?'

'Yeah,' he said. 'I've brought it all with me. You don't have to lift a finger.' He motioned to a neat wicker basket on the path behind him.

'Oh, that's kind of you, but I've got a—'

'Hello!' Heidi said, popping her head round the front door.

'— guest,' Callie said, finishing her sentence.

'I'm Heidi,' she said, extending her hand towards the dark-haired visitor and batting her eyelashes which were unnaturally curly and which had given Callie a fright when she'd found them on her bathroom window ledge the night before.

'I'm Leo,' he said brightly.

'Well, come in!' Heidi said, causing Callie to glare at her. 'You've brought food?'

'Certainly have,' he said, turning to pick up the basket. 'One rabbit and a few things foraged from the woods this morning.'

'Foraged?' Heidi said.

'Heidi's food all comes pre-wrapped from Waitrose,' Callie explained as she followed the two of them towards her kitchen, still baffled by the fact that this man was in her house.

'You bet it does,' Heidi said, 'but that doesn't mean I can't sample other ways of doing things, does it?' she said, giving Leo a wink.

'You sure this is okay?' he asked Callie. 'I mean, I can come back another time.'

Callie was quite sure he would too. 'No, no – go right ahead,' she said. 'What do you need?'

'Well, I've brought all the ingredients. Just tell me where the pans are and I'll get on with things.'

She watched in amazement as he pulled a chef's apron from the basket and got to work setting the ingredients out on her worktops. Who *was* this guy? And what on earth was he doing in her kitchen?

Heidi motioned to her behind his back.

'I'll – erm – leave you to it then,' Callie told Leo.

'Sure thing,' he said and the two women left the kitchen together.

'Oh, my God!' Heidi said as soon as they were back in the living room. 'Tell me everything – *quickly*!'

'I don't know what to tell you,' Callie said honestly.

'Who *is* he?'

'I'm not really sure. I only met him a few days ago and I didn't even know his name then. He left some dead animals on my doorstep.'

Heidi wrinkled her nose in obvious disgust.

'He didn't realise that I was living here, you see. He left them for the previous owner. This is only the second time I've met him.'

'Leo Wildman!' Heidi said, her eyes bright and wide as she spoke his name. 'I can't think of a more romantic name!'

'Shush! He'll hear you!'

'And I can't believe you didn't tell me about him!'

'But there was nothing to tell!' Callie said.

'The hell there wasn't!' Heidi said. 'A gorgeous wild man of the woods turns up on your doorstep and you *didn't think it was worth mentioning*? Have you turned into some sort of nun since moving to the country? You do realise how gorgeous he is, don't you? And he obviously likes you.'

'What do you mean?'

'Why else would he turn up on your doorstep with Thumper, offering to cook you lunch?'

'I think it was just his way of apologising for scaring me with those dead things on my doorstep – that's all.'

'Yeah, right!' Heidi said. 'He likes you, damn it! And I'm as jealous as hell. If I were you, I'd say yes.'

'To what?' Callie asked.

'To anything he asks you!'

Callie rolled her eyes. 'I don't know anything about him.'

'What's to know? He's gorgeous and he cooks. What more do you want?'

It was then that Leo's head popped round the living room door. 'Would you ladies like some wine? I took the liberty of bringing over a couple of bottles of pear wine, but there's some elderflower cordial too if you prefer.'

'Pear wine?' Heidi said with a laugh. 'This I've *got* to try!'

'Erm – how about you?' he asked nodding to Callie. 'I'm sorry, I don't know your name.'

'It's Callie,' she said, 'and I'll try the wine too.'

He nodded and smiled, leaving the room.

'He really didn't know your name?'

'I told you!' Callie said.

'The most gorgeous man in Suffolk turns up at your home – all fit and wild and smiley – and you don't even tell him your name?' Heidi said.

Callie shook her head, wishing her friend would rein herself in just a little bit.

Callie had to admit that the rabbit pie was pretty good even though she had to do her best to put all her favourite images of Benjamin Bunny and Peter Rabbit out of her head as she ate it. The pear wine was something else too.

'I've never tasted anything like this,' Heidi said, 'and I've had a lot of wine in my time!'

Leo grinned. 'You can't beat a bit of home-made,' he said. 'You should try my gooseberry sometime.'

Heidi roared with laughter. 'You should be selling these in London,' she told him. 'You'd make your fortune.'

'Really?'

'You bet! Londoners love all this rural stuff but can't be bothered to do it themselves. If you get yourself some nice-looking bottles and labels and then set up at a quality street market, you'll be quids in.'

He looked at her for a moment, but then shook his head. 'Nah!' he said at last. 'London's not for me. I could easily set up a stall in one of the market towns here in Suffolk if that's the way I wanted to go.'

'Yes, but you could charge *much* more if you went to London,' Heidi told him.

'But wouldn't it also cost me more to go there?' he said, raising a dark eyebrow.

'London isn't for everybody,' Callie told Heidi.

'Well, I know that,' Heidi said, 'but it wouldn't have to be forever. You could pop through on the train and do it all in a couple of days. You wouldn't even have to book a hotel – I've got a spare room you could use.'

Callie blushed on her friend's behalf, but Leo just laughed her suggestion off.

'I couldn't leave Truffle and Blewit,' he said.

'And they are what exactly?'

'My dogs!' he said with a laugh. 'Cocker spaniels – mother and son.'

'Well, couldn't a neighbour look after them?'

'I don't like leaving them,' he said. 'Blewit's just a youngster and needs training. But, I guess the truth is, I don't like leaving Suffolk much these days. I got all that wanderlust out of my system just recently and I really want to put down some roots now,' he said, catching Callie's eye again.

'Roots are good,' Callie said.

'Absolutely,' he said. 'Suffolk's a pretty special place too. You realise that once you've been away for a while.'

'Or if you're from London,' Callie said. 'I felt it as soon as I arrived here.'

He grinned. 'What made you choose it?'

Callie looked thoughtful. 'I wanted somewhere with no cities or motorways. Somewhere I could be sure of some peace and quiet.'

'You've got that all right,' Heidi said. 'It took me ages to get to sleep last night without the sound of traffic and my neighbours ringing in my ears.'

'I don't miss that at all,' Callie said with a little laugh.

'So I take it you live nearby,' Heidi said, turning her gaze to Leo again. Was it Callie's imagination or were her friend's false eyelashes working overtime?

'The next village,' Leo said. 'Monk's Green. It's within walking distance.'

'It's within walking distance,' Heidi said, turning to Callie who blushed instantly. 'Callie likes walking, don't you?'

'Well, you must pop over sometime,' he said. 'I'll introduce you to the spaniels.'

Heidi laughed. 'Now *that's* an invitation you don't get from men in London!'

'Did I say something funny?' Leo asked, a perplexed look on his face.

'Heidi just isn't used to the country,' Callie said, glaring at her friend in warning.

'Well, you're both welcome,' he said which made Heidi beam.

'Thank you,' Callie said.

'Listen,' Leo said, standing up a moment later, 'I'd better get going.'

'Oh, must you?' Heidi asked.

'I don't want to interrupt the whole of your day.'

'But you aren't,' Heidi assured him.

He gave a little lopsided smile. 'And I've got to get back to walk the dogs,' he said.

'Oh,' Heidi said.

'It's been really great to meet you both,' he said. 'I'll just tidy up in the kitchen and then get going.'

'Don't worry about that,' Callie said. 'I'll do that later.'

'Are you sure?'

'After the lovely meal you made us, it's the very least I can do.'

'You liked it?' he asked, genuinely looking surprised by her admission.

'Of course,' she said.

'Good,' he said. 'Well, maybe I can cook for you again sometime?'

Callie swallowed hard and tried to ignore the heated look that Heidi was giving her. 'That would be nice,' she said.

Leo nodded, his dark hair falling across his face as he reached for his tatty wax jacket and picked up his basket. Callie walked to the front door with him and opened it.

'Thanks for lunch,' she said and watched as he ducked to walk through the door.

'My pleasure,' he said, holding her gaze. 'Right – back to the dogs.'

Callie smiled. 'Bye,' she said, closing the door and leaping as she turned around and almost crashed into Heidi.

'Well,' her friend said, 'if that bookish bloke you've got your eye on doesn't work out, you could always give this wild man of the woods a go!'

Callie shook her head and began to clear the table, taking the dishes through to the kitchen.

'Don't tell me you're not at least intrigued by this guy?'

'Of course I'm *intrigued*,' Callie said. 'He's very interesting. From a writer's point of view, that is.'

'Writer's point of view!' Heidi scoffed. 'I'd say he's interesting from a *woman's* point of view! Did you see those arms? Please tell me you noticed those gorgeous strong arms. I bet he's cut his fair share of logs in his time. If I was you–'

'Heidi!' Callie said, knowing what her friend was going to say and hoping against hope that she could be stopped.

'If I was you,' Heidi went on undaunted, 'I'd fully embrace all that country life is offering you and have a wonderful mad fling with this foraging guy.'

'Heidi!' Callie said, chucking the dishcloth into the sink.

'*What?*' her friend asked looking baffled. 'What's wrong?'

Callie looked at her for a long drawn out moment.

'Callie?'

She took a deep breath. 'What if I'm not cut out for relationships? What if I just haven't got it in me and men can't love me?'

Heidi looked completely floored by this. 'You're joking, right?'

Callie shook her head. 'Why would I joke about something like that?'

'But you don't really feel that way, do you?'

Tears rose into Callie's eyes. 'I don't know what to feel,' she said in a very small voice.

'Oh, my God!' Heidi said, placing an arm around her shoulders and leading her through to the living room where they sat down on the sofa together. 'Piers did a real hatchet job on you, didn't he?'

Callie reached inside her pocket for a tissue and dabbed her eyes. She wasn't going to cry, she told herself. The time for tears was over and there had been plenty of them too. She'd promised herself that she'd left all her sadness behind her in London. But Heidi's presence had reminded her so much of the life she'd left behind and, with Heidi telling her to get involved with somebody new, it was just too much for Callie.

'What you went through with Piers,' Heidi began, 'well, I can't imagine what it was like.'

Callie closed her eyes. 'I thought the baby would help,' she said in a small voice. 'I really thought that having a child would make all the difference.'

'Don't torture yourself,' Heidi said, clasping her hands in hers.

'He couldn't ignore a child, could he? That's what I thought. But I'll never forget his words when I lost it. "It's for the best," he said. Can you believe he said that? He didn't want me and he certainly didn't want a family with me.'

'Piers was a selfish idiot who hadn't grown up, that's all,' Heidi told her. 'The way he treated you was inexcusable and the quicker you forget about it, the better.'

'I don't think I can ever forget about it,' Callie said.

They sat quietly for a little while, the song of a robin bright and clear from the garden.

'I'm so sorry I pushed you with Leo,' Heidi said at last.

'It's all right,' Callie said. 'I'm sorry I'm so tetchy.'

'I think you've a right to be a little tetchy after what you've been through.'

Callie blew her nose. 'I thought I was through all this. I thought I was beginning to feel... to feel like me again.'

Heidi smiled sympathetically. 'I think you're being a bit optimistic there. It might take a bit longer than a few months to get over something like a miscarriage and the breakdown of a marriage.'

Callie sighed. 'Nobody would want to be with me even if I *wasn't* a complete wreck at the moment and liable to dissolve in a pool of tears.'

'But that's rubbish! That bookshop guy asked you out didn't he?'

'Yes, but he doesn't know what a narrow escape he's had,' Callie said.

'And Mr Wildman of the Woods looked like he wanted to show you his foraging skills.'

Callie gave a tiny smile.

'You are a gorgeous, sexy woman that any man in his right mind would want to be with.'

'Any man except my husband,' Callie said.

Heidi shook her head. 'We won't have his name mentioned here now, will we? He was a buffoon of the highest order. He'll probably wake up screaming in the middle of the night and realise what he's lost one of these days.'

'I doubt it,' Callie said sadly.

'And, in the meantime, you'll be getting on with your wonderful new life here, won't you?'

Callie nodded. 'Yes,' she said. 'A life filled with reading and writing and absolutely *no* men!'

Heidi groaned. 'That sounds *awful!*' she said. 'I know it's probably the last thing you want to hear right now, but I really think that throwing yourself into another relationship is the very best thing. Now, hear me out,' Heidi said, raising her hand as Callie was about to interrupt her, 'I'm not saying a new relationship has to be serious with some kind of end game in mind. Quite the contrary. I think it should be fun and frivolous. You shouldn't think about it at all – just go for it!'

'But that sounds so shallow and–'

'Shallow can be very good from time to time,' Heidi interrupted, 'and I think your time for a bit of shallow is here and *now*. And Leo might just be the one to help.'

'But isn't that horribly unfair to him?' Callie asked.

'Are you *kidding* me? Didn't you see the way he was looking at you? He looked like he wanted to take you to the nearest farmyard and make hay with you whilst the sun shines!'

'I don't think I can do it,' she said. 'I'm not like that. I don't just have flings.'

'Well, at least think about it, won't you? Think about being kind to yourself and having a bit of fun. You really do deserve it.'

# CHAPTER 8

Polly Prior nee Nightingale, was in her brother Sam's shop. So far that morning, she'd made a packed lunch for Archie, hung out a wash load, done a quick repair to Archie's school blazer which he'd caught on a bramble, walked and fed their spaniel, Dickens, and then made another packed lunch after Dickens had eaten the first one. She'd then driven their Land Rover through the narrow lanes from their village towards Castle Clare, hoping that the tractor she'd immediately got stuck behind wasn't going to make Archie late for school.

By the time she reached the bookshop, she should have been shattered. Instead, she'd taken a deep breath, made sure that her long dark hair was still held neatly at the nape of her neck with her tortoiseshell hairgrip, made herself a cup of tea and begun work.

When her brother came down the stairs from his flat above the shop half an hour later, she'd served three customers, reorganised a shelf of paperback Penguins which had been annoying her, and had dusted the window display.

'Sorry I'm so late,' Sam said.

'It's a long commute, isn't it?' Polly teased.

'Very funny,' he said. 'I had to make a call and it took far longer than expected.'

'Good news?' she asked.

'Could be,' he said. 'There's a collector who's thinning out his shelves and wants my opinion. I'll pop over later today.'

'Well, I can stay until three,' Polly said.

'Grandpa's coming in after lunch,' Sam said. 'He can cover whilst I'm out.'

Polly nodded before walking across the room to return a little pile of books which a browser had left on the library steps, to their rightful home.

'Everything okay?' Sam asked.

'Of course,' she said, putting the last of the books away. 'Why

71

wouldn't it be?'

Sam shrugged. 'I was worried about you on Sunday,' he said.

'Oh?' she said, turning to look at him.

'You were very quiet.'

She quickly turned her attention to the latest blockbusting thriller to have found its way into the shop. Actually, eight copies had found their way into the shop in the last month. It was the kind of fiction which folks seemed to gobble up and then discard. She ran her fingers over the gold embossed title.

'I'm always quiet,' she told her brother.

'No you're not,' he said. 'At least you weren't until–'

'Don't,' she said. 'I don't want to talk about it.'

'We're all worried about you,' he said gently.

'I know,' she said. 'Mum took me to one side after lunch. I was hoping she wouldn't, but there was no getting away from it.'

'Because she cares about you.'

She nodded. 'But I'm fine so you can all stop worrying, okay?'

'Are you?' Sam's expression was so gentle and concerned that it made Polly's eyes vibrate with tears and she really didn't want to fall apart in the middle of the bookshop. 'I wish you'd talk to me, Poll. We used to talk about everything, remember?'

She nodded, thinking back to how close the two of them had been growing up. As the two eldest Nightingale children, they'd formed an unbreakable bond, creating imaginary worlds together, making dens in the grounds of Campion House and sharing all the heartbreaks and the joys of growing up. Polly adored her eldest brother, but she had to admit to having kept her feelings locked away over the last few years. Perhaps it was just a part of growing up, she thought – part of life's natural cycle. One couldn't expect to run back to one's family all the time, although she knew that her family was always there for her no matter how independent she thought herself and no matter how well she thought she was coping.

'Why don't we have a cup of tea, eh?' he said. 'I want an excuse to say "Polly put the kettle on".'

She groaned, but couldn't help laughing too. It was a favourite family joke which nobody seemed to have grown tired of.

A few minutes later, two mugs of Earl Grey had been made, scenting the back room of the bookshop.

'How are you coping?' Sam said without any preamble. 'I mean, how are you *really* coping?'

Polly took a long sip of tea, knowing that there was no hiding from her brother now. She felt his eyes upon her and, as much as she would have liked to have brushed him off with a flippant remark, she knew she wouldn't get away with it.

'I'm not really sure,' she said honestly.

'What do you mean?'

'I mean, I try not to think about it all. I fill my days with work, with Archie, the house, the garden. Did you know we grew patty pans and marrows this year? There are masses of them. You'll have to take some from us. We'll never eat them all ourselves.'

'Polly,' he said, 'I don't want to talk about marrows. I want to talk about you.'

'I know,' she said, taking another sip of tea.

'What's happening?'

'Nothing,' she said. 'What do you expect to be happening? He's been forgotten. Nobody's interested in what's happened to him now.'

'Did anybody get in touch with you?'

'Oh, yes,' she said. 'I got the usual anniversary phone call but nobody knows anything new.'

Sam shook his head. 'I can't believe nobody's doing anything.'

'They've done all they can,' Polly said. 'What more is there to do?'

He frowned at her. 'You sound as if you've given up.'

'What else *can* I do?' she said, her voice hollow and helpless. 'I feel like I'm in a strange sort of limbo where I can't move on. I sometimes wish that—' she stopped.

'What?'

'I can't say it. It's too awful.'

'Tell me,' Sam said. 'You can tell me anything.'

She looked at him, his eyes wide with concern and she knew that she could, indeed, tell him anything and so she did.

'I sometimes wish that they'd find his body,' she said in a hushed tone. 'Then, at least, I could move on.'

'Oh, Polly.' Sam reached out a hand and held hers. 'I wish there was something I could do.'

'But you do so much already.'

'Are you kidding?'

'This job. I don't know what I would have done without it.'

'But that's nothing.'

'It's *everything*,' she told him. 'I would've gone out of my mind without it. The thought of being in the house on my own all day when Archie's at school.' She shook her head. 'The evening's are bad enough when he's gone to bed.'

'You should call me,' Sam said.

'I can't call you every night,' she said.

'Yes you can,' he said. 'Of *course* you can. You know that.' There was a pause. 'How's Archie coping?'

'He's fine. He doesn't know about the anniversaries. He doesn't even know when his dad's birthday was. He was so young when it all happened,' she said. 'He occasionally asks me questions and I'll say something vague and then feel guilt-ridden the rest of the day because I can't bear to tell him the truth.'

'So he still thinks Sean is working away from home?'

Polly nodded. 'I feel terrible about lying to him, but what can I do? Tell him that his father's missing? That he walked out of the house one day and just never returned?'

They gazed at each other, not knowing what to say

'Listen,' Sam said at last, 'Antonia Jessop was in last week.'

'Oh, she's such a bossy boots,' Polly said. 'I hope she wasn't giving you any grief.'

'Well, just a bit, but she also said something that I've not been able to shake from my mind.'

'What?'

'She'd just got back from a holiday to her sister's and, whilst she was there, she took part in a book club and she wanted to know why Castle Clare doesn't have one what with all our bookshops and the festival and everything.'

'Didn't there used to be one?' Polly asked. 'I'm sure I've heard Aunt Bonnie talking about one.'

'That's what I said. Apparently, it all fell apart. Nobody took enough interest in it to keep it going.'

'That's a shame,' Polly said.

Sam nodded. 'It is, isn't it?'

Polly watched him carefully. 'You're not thinking of setting one up, are you?'

'Actually, I am.'

'Really?'

'Yes, why not? Just think about it. We're perfectly placed here to run one with all our bookshops and the library too. It would be a great way to bring the community together during the months when the festival isn't on.'

'You're really serious about this?'

Sam laughed. 'Don't you think it would be great?'

'I'm just thinking of the administrative nightmare and the organisation it will take.'

'Ah, yes,' Sam said. 'About that—'

'What?' Polly asked, immediately on her guard.

'What you said about your evenings at home,' Sam began hesitantly, 'well, I was kind of hoping you might want to help me out.'

'Sam Nightingale – that is so like you to think up a brilliant project and then hand all the work over to somebody else.'

'That is *not* so like me,' he protested, making her smile.

'So what did you have in mind?'

He shrugged. 'I just thought you could do a bit of research about book clubs, see what sort of ideas you can come up with, how often we should run them and the sort of things we could discuss at meetings.'

'Like whether or not Antonia Jessop is going to be in charge?' Polly said raising an eyebrow.

'She is most definitely not going to be in charge,' Sam said sternly.

'I'm very glad to hear it. She'd totally take over everything,' Polly said. 'So, are you going to hold meetings here?'

'Yes. To begin with at least. It's pretty central and we have the kitchen and plenty of seating available if I bring some chairs from upstairs. We can always borrow more chairs from the village hall if it's really popular.'

Polly grinned at his enthusiasm.

'It's good to see you smile,' he told her. 'There hasn't been enough of that lately.' He squeezed her hand. 'So, are you going to help me with this?'

Polly cast her eyes to the ceiling, delaying her response.

'Polleeee?'

'Of *course* I'll help you, you oaf!' she finally said.

'Good!' he said.

'As long as I get to choose a book.'

'That seems fair although I've already planned the first choice.'

'Oh, you have, have you?'

'Far from the Madding Crowd.'

'You and Thomas Hardy!' Polly said. 'I really can't understand what you and Dad see in him.'

'Then you'd better enrol in the book club and find out!' he said with a wink.

It was with mixed feelings that Callie saw Heidi leave. On the one hand, she was glad not to be living under her close scrutiny but, on the other, it was like saying goodbye to her past all over again. Heidi was heading back to the place Callie had once called home and she was left on her own in a rural village where she didn't really know anyone.

She shook her head. There was no need to get all maudlin. No need at all, she told herself. She was blissfully happy in her little cottage and she had chosen to leave London.

'And I know *several* people,' she said, thinking about the new neighbours she'd made friends with and Leo Wildman and Sam and Josh Nightingale.

She thought about the strange way that Leo had just turned up on her doorstep with his rabbit pie, taking over her kitchen and chatting away about gooseberry wine. She'd never met anyone like him before, with his slightly feral good looks and his affable manner. He'd certainly made an impression on Heidi because her friend had already texted her twice since she'd left, with teasing little messages about Callie's 'wild man of the woods'.

Callie couldn't deny that it would be fun to get to know Leo better but, as her eye caught sight of the hardback adventure book she'd bought in Castle Clare, her thoughts turned to another man, Sam Nightingale, and a wave of regret washed over her as she thought about how she'd run out of his shop. She still felt awful about that but hadn't had a chance to make things right with Heidi staying with her. But Heidi wasn't there now, was she?

She grabbed her satchel and car keys. It was always best to do these things right away, wasn't it? If she left it any longer, she might lose her nerve completely.

Getting into her car, she looked across the village green which was bathed in the kind of mellow autumn light that always made her stop whatever she was doing just to take it all in, but she didn't have time to dawdle today because she was on a mission.

She was just passing the church when she was forced to brake. The Ford in front of her had come to a stop just as it was passing a Jeep on the other side of the road. Callie watched as the woman in the Ford wound her window down and proceeded to hold a conversation with the driver in the Jeep.

'*Really?*' Callie said out loud to herself, thinking how rude it was that neither of the drivers seemed to be considering her and then something occurred to her – something she remembered Mrs Morrison saying to her.

'You're in the country now, dear.'

Callie had been late arriving for her second viewing of Owl Cottage because she'd got stuck behind a slow moving farm vehicle, but Mrs Morrison hadn't seemed to be worried by that.

'You might find everything's a little slower than what you're used to in London.'

Callie grinned as she remembered. 'And so it is,' she said, watching as the Ford and the Jeep finally moved on.

It was as she was driving through the beech wood on the way in to Castle Clare that she saw an old green mud-splattered Land Rover heading towards her. It was flashing its lights at her. Callie frowned and slowed down, wondering if there was an accident up ahead but, as the Land Rover came to a stop, she saw that it was Leo Wildman.

'Hello there!' he called through the open window as Callie pulled up alongside him and wound her own window down. 'I recognised your car,' he said.

'You did?'

He nodded and she realised that it wouldn't be too hard for somebody who could probably identify a mushroom at ten paces to recognise a car parked outside somebody's house.

'That friend of yours gone?' he asked her.

'Yes,' Callie said. 'Back to London. She was serious about you selling your produce there,' she told him. 'She mentioned it again before she left.'

Leo shook his head. 'London's not for me. Not enough puffballs for a start.'

'Puffballs?'

He nodded. 'It's a massive white fungus. I'm off to a little place I know where there's a few growing. Can't tell you where, mind,' he said, tapping the side of his nose.

Callie laughed. 'Well, I'd better not delay you.'

'Where're you heading, then?' he asked.

'Just into Castle Clare.'

'Are you around tomorrow evening?'

'Erm–'

'I'll pick you up at six, okay? For a spot of dinner.'

'Oh, all right,' Callie said.

It was then that a car horn honked from behind and Callie realised that an irate driver was intent on moving her on.

'Probably from London,' she said to Leo and he laughed, his handsome face lighting up.

'I'll see you tomorrow,' he said, driving off.

Five minutes later, Callie had parked her car in the square at Castle Clare and was sat staring ahead at the market cross in front of her. Was she doing the right thing, she wondered? Maybe it would be easier just to leave things as they were between her and Sam.

*And how was that?* A little voice inside Callie asked. Would it be right for Callie to let Sam go on thinking that she was a rude person who had no regard for his feelings? Did she want him to think that she didn't want anything to do with him? That was probably the impression she'd left him with and she knew she couldn't let him go on believing that because she wasn't a rude person and she cared desperately that she might have hurt his feelings.

Getting out of the car, she took a deep, confidence-enhancing breath. Even if she felt like turning and running in the opposite direction as soon as she walked through the door to Nightingale's, she had to go through with it. She was a grown-up and she owed this man an apology if nothing else.

However, as soon as she opened the shiny green door and heard the shop bell ringing above her head, Callie couldn't help but want to hide behind the biggest atlas she could find. It was a silly idea to have come. Sam had probably forgotten all about her by now and she was making a big deal about nothing. It would be better if she left and forgot about the whole thing.

She'd just turned to leave when she heard a voice behind her.

'Hello. Can I help you?'

It was a woman's voice and Callie turned to see an attractive woman in her mid-thirties. She had long dark hair tied back and her skin was porcelain-pale. Deep, expressive eyes looked directly at Callie and she couldn't help thinking that there was something other-worldly about the woman; she had an aura of vulnerability that was wholly compelling. But it was rude to stare and Callie switched off her writer's inquisitiveness and focused on her mission.

'I was hoping to see Sam,' Callie said, her voice sounding weird and croaky.

'He's just popped out,' the woman said. 'He shouldn't be long. Can I help with anything?'

'No, no,' Callie said. 'I'll wait for Sam.'

The woman smiled. 'I'm Polly,' she said, coming forward and shaking her hand.

'Oh! You must be Sam's sister,' Callie said, noticing the family resemblance.

'That's right.'

'You're the one who came up with the lovely phrase on the bookmarks.'

Polly smiled. 'I'm glad you like it.'

'I'm Callie,' she said, watching as Polly's eyebrows rose a fraction.

'Callie Logan?'

'Yes,' she said.

'We heard you'd been into the shop,' Polly said, making her wonder just how many people the word "we" referred to.

'Occupational hazard,' she said. 'It's physically impossible for a writer to walk by a bookshop without going inside.'

'That's good to know,' Polly said. 'So how is Suffolk suiting you?'

'Great. I like the peace and quiet,' Callie said.

'It's quiet all right,' Polly said. 'I live in a village just outside Castle Clare and there's nothing *but* quiet there.' They smiled at each other. 'I'm afraid we've not tracked down that first edition you were after yet.'

'Oh, please don't think I'm hassling you about that,' Callie said. 'I just wanted to speak to Sam. About something else.' She could feel her face heating up with embarrassment and she was mightily relieved to hear the sound of the bell above the door as Sam returned.

'Callie!' he said in surprise.

'Hello,' she said.

He looked at her and then at Polly. 'I see you've met my sister,' he said.

'Yes!' Callie said.

'Callie's slowly working her way around our entire family,' he told Polly. 'She's met Grandpa, Josh and now you.'

'She'll have to pop across the road and meet Bryony,' Polly said. 'She's dying to meet you!'

'Is she?' Callie asked.

'She said she's ordered a box of your books and she'll be hoping you'll sign them for her,' Sam said.

'I'd be happy to,' Callie said, and an awkward silence descended upon the three of them.

'I'll go and make some tea,' Polly said after a moment. 'Callie?'

'No, thank you,' she said, waiting until Polly had left the room.

'I'm afraid we haven't got your book yet,' Sam said.

'I know,' Callie said quickly. 'I didn't come about the book.'

'No?' Sam said, his dark eyes filling with surprise.

Callie anxiously twisted a ring on her right hand as she summoned up the courage to say what she had to say.

'I've been wanting to apologise to you,' she said at last.

He frowned. 'But it should be *me* apologising to *you*,' he said. 'I shouldn't have hounded you like that.'

'You didn't hound me,' she said. 'I *completely* overreacted and it's been bothering me ever since. I just–' she paused. 'I just wasn't expecting it.'

'I know,' he nodded. 'It was unfair of me to put you in that situation when we'd only just met.'

'It's not that,' she said, holding his gaze. 'I – well – I've just got out of a bad relationship. A marriage, actually.'

Sam gave a tiny smile. 'Me too,' he said.

'Really?' she said, her eyes widening.

'Really.'

'I'm sorry.'

'Don't be,' he said. 'It was all for the best.'

'Mine too,' she said in a quiet voice. 'Didn't make it any easier, though.'

'No,' Sam said.

'And I think I'm still getting my head around things which is probably why I was so rude when you–'

'You don't have to explain,' he told her.

'But I do,' she said. 'I want to. You've been nothing but kind to me and I've really enjoyed all our conversations about books.'

'Me too,' he said.

'And I'd like to be friends,' she said. 'I really would.'

Sam nodded. 'Me too,' he said again.

Callie breathed a sigh of relief. 'Great,' she said.

'So we're good?' he asked her, his smile stretching across his face. She liked his smile.

'We're good,' she said.

'Well, as my newest friend, I wonder if you'll take a look at this for me?'

Curious, she followed him to the counter where he picked up an A4 piece of paper and handed it to her. She read it and looked up at him.

'It's the book club you mentioned,' she said.

'Aha,' he said. 'You think it's a bad idea, do you?'

'Oh, no,' she said. 'It's just—'

'A lot of admin?' he said.

Callie laughed. 'I was going to say that it could be a lot of aggro. I joined one when I was in London and it was fine to begin with, but it became more and more competitive.'

'Do you mean in the choice of books?'

'Oh, no,' Callie said. 'We met in people's homes, you see, and it was agreed that the guest house would provide tea and coffee and maybe a bowl of crisps or some scones or something. Anyway, each month, things got more and more elaborate with gourmet food being laid on and expensive floral decorations everywhere. The focus didn't seem to be on the books anymore but rather on who could outdo all the rest with their decor and their catering. One woman even hired a butler to serve drinks.'

'No way!' Sam said incredulously.

'I'm not joking,' Callie said. 'It all got too much for me.'

'I'm not surprised,' he said. 'Well, if I promise not to hire any butlers and serve nothing more than a few ginger biscuits, will you come to ours?'

Callie smiled. 'I'd be happy to.'

It was then that Polly walked through with two cups of tea.

'Callie's going to join our book club,' Sam told her with a grin.

'Oh, good,' Polly said. 'I was beginning to worry that it was just going to be me and Sam sitting in a room on our own together.'

# CHAPTER 9

Six o'clock seemed terribly early to be going out to dinner, but Callie reminded herself that she wasn't in London anymore and that maybe things were done differently in the country. Maybe everybody went to bed much earlier and got up when the cock crowed or something, especially somebody like Leo, who seemed to be so in tune with the natural world.

Still, as she peered out of her bedroom window to see if his old Land Rover was in sight, she couldn't help wondering what the evening held in store for her. For one thing, she had absolutely no idea where they were going and that caused a problem in the wardrobe department. She was pretty sure that he wasn't the sort to try and wow her with a posh restaurant, but how much should she dress up? It was impossible to know. Should she go all out in the pretty lace-trimmed dress she'd bought from her favourite little boutique in London or should she play it safe with a pair of smart trousers and a jacket?

There were so few opportunities for a writer to get dressed up, she thought to herself as she opened her wardrobe. Usually, she would spend the day alone, wearing a practical pair of jeans or a tracksuit bottom and an extra large jumper or baggy cardigan. Sitting at a desk all day made one feel the cold and so Callie had learned to counter this with layer upon layer of unflattering clothes. Leo had already seen her in one of her infamous writer's ensembles, she thought, mortified by the memory. It was one of the reasons why she wanted to get dressed up tonight: she wanted to banish that appalling image from his mind.

Her hand hovered over the lace-trimmed dress as the thought sank in that she wanted to look attractive for this man. Why was that so important to her? Was this a date? Or was it just two new friends getting to know each other a little bit better? More importantly, was Leo thinking of it as a date?

She really couldn't remember the last time she'd been on a date. It must have been with Piers before they'd got married. The early days had been good; he'd made time for her then, impressing her with expensive restaurants and dress circle seats at West End theatres. They had been wonderfully exuberant, extravagant dates, but Leo was definitely no Piers and she liked him for that precise reason.

She was just putting on her lace-trimmed dress when her phone beeped. It was a text from Heidi.

Hi Gorgeous! Seen anymore of the wild man of the woods? x

Callie grinned. It was as if Heidi could sense what was going on even though she was a hundred miles away. Callie texted her back.

Going out to dinner this evening!

OMG! the reply came back. I am soooooo jealous! Send him my love! x

Callie shook her head at Heidi's response and knew that she would now be plagued with calls and texts from her friend until she'd found out what had happened.

And what was going to happen? Heidi had encouraged her to have a fling, but she knew she wasn't ready for that. Still, she couldn't deny the fact that Mr Leo Wildman was a very interesting man, and the fact that he was also easy on the eye was a wonderful bonus.

She had to admit to being a little nervous about the evening that lay ahead of her, but she comforted herself that she was only going out for a few short hours and that she would be back in the safety of Owl Cottage before she knew it.

The front door knocker sounded and Callie knew that it was time to put her misgivings firmly on the back burner and, instead, focus on enjoying the evening ahead.

When she opened the door, Leo was standing there wearing a striped shirt under a tweed jacket which was a definite step up from the tatty wax coat she was used to seeing him in, but it hinted more of dinner at a cosy local pub rather than at a restaurant. Callie suddenly felt ridiculously overdressed.

'Oh, dear,' she said. 'Should I change?'

'No, no,' he said lightly. 'You look great. Come on.'

He'd left his Land Rover running and opened the door for her and she climbed in. It was a long way up when you were wearing a dress and Callie was beginning to wish that she'd opted for a practical pair of trousers. Still, it was too late now.

'You okay?' Leo asked, flashing her a smile as she did up her seatbelt.

'Good, thank you.'

'I've been looking forward to this,' he said.

'Have you?' she asked in surprise.

He nodded. 'We always seem to be meeting in passing, don't we? Or when somebody else is around.'

'I suppose we do,' Callie said.

'And I'd like to get to know you without any of that other stuff going on.' There was a pause. 'Is that okay with you?'

Callie looked at him, taking in the dark hair that was a tad too long and the irrepressible smile.

'That's okay with me,' she said.

It wasn't until they turned off a country lane into a wood that Callie began to get nervous. They'd passed several pubs so far and, each time Callie had spotted one, she'd felt sure they were going to stop but they hadn't. Now, the Land Rover was bumping down a woodland track and they were soon completely surrounded by trees. Was there a grand hotel at the end of an unmade track or should she start to panic, Callie wondered?

'Leo?' she said.

'Nearly there,' he said as the Land Rover bounced in and out of several large potholes. There definitely wasn't a hotel at the end of this track, was there, Callie thought?

'Right,' Leo announced a moment later, bringing the Land Rover to a stop and cutting the engine, 'we're here.'

'Here?' Callie said in surprise.

'We walk from here,' he said, jumping out of his door and running around to Callie's.

Callie looked out at the rutted woodland track in front of them and at the leaves, puddles and fallen debris, and then she looked down at the high-heeled boots she'd chosen to wear.

'Why didn't you tell me to change?' she asked Leo.

'Because I've got an extra pair of wellies in the back,' he announced unperturbed, taking her left foot in his hands and unzipping her boot and removing it. Callie gasped as he repeated the manoeuvre with her right boot, the warmth of his hands on her near-bare skin.

'Don't move,' he told her, opening the tailgate and rummaging around. 'Here we go,' he said a moment later, proffering a pair of green wellies and some thick Fair Isle socks.

'We're really going into the woods?' she asked.

'Only a quarter of a mile,' he said.

Callie's mouth dropped open.

'It's all right,' he said. 'You won't have to carry anything.'

Callie watched in bemusement as he disappeared again, coming back with a large wicker hamper, a cooler bag and folded a couple of tartan blankets over his arm.

'Ready?' he said, a wide grin stretched across his face.

'You're mad,' she said. 'Totally mad!'

'It has been said,' he told her, and then he laughed and Callie could only join in. This, she thought, was the weirdest date of her life, but she couldn't help acknowledging the fact that she was enjoying it in a strange kind of way.

With her feet snug in her socks and oversized wellies, Callie followed Leo into the woods. It was wonderfully silent with the last rays of the sun strobing through the grey trunks of the beech trees.

'This place is a sea of bluebells in the spring,' he told her. 'I'll bring you back then.'

Callie smiled. She liked the idea of that.

They continued to walk, passing fallen trees, ditches full of debris from winters long ago and little cities of mushrooms.

'They're good on toast,' Leo said. 'But don't ever eat those ones,' he said, pointing to some fungi growing out of a rotting log. 'They'll have you in hospital within the hour.'

'Noted,' Callie said, following him as he marched further into the wood.

It was strange for Callie to be in a wood in the evening and the experience reminded her of her childhood growing up in rural Oxfordshire when she would venture far afield with a bold group of friends to explore the woods and fields. She smiled as she remembered those long lost days, thinking how sad it was that she'd morphed into the kind of adult who never went deeper into the countryside than the nearest post box. When had that wondrous need to explore died? When she'd moved to London? When she'd grown up? And where had it gone? Callie had the sneaking suspicion that it was just lying buried deep within her; that it had never gone away because the young heroes and heroines in her stories were always having such adventures as the one she was on tonight. Perhaps, she thought, she'd been living vicariously through them. Well, no more, she told herself. If her move to the countryside had told her one thing, it was that there was a glorious world of exploring if only she took the time to leave her desk, pull on a pair of boots and get out there to discover it all.

'Here,' Leo said at last as they reached a clearing in the wood. There were a couple of old tree stumps across which Leo placed the tartan rugs and she watched in awe as he gathered kindling and logs, making up a fire in the centre of the clearing.

'Do you have the landowner's permission to do that?' Callie asked as he lit it, suddenly anxious that they'd be set upon by an irate gamekeeper toting a rifle.

Leo looked up at her, amusement sparkling in his eyes. 'I *am* the landowner,' he said.

'Really?'

'Well, jointly with my brother, Rick. We bought this little bit of woodland when it came up for sale recently. We'd always wanted a wood. Our dad used to bring us out this way all the time,' he said. 'We lived for those days. Hiking, foraging, camping out – it was great.'

'Does your father live nearby?'

'No,' Leo said, 'he died three years ago.'

'Oh, I'm sorry.'

'We miss him. Every day.'

'And your mother?'

'She lives in Cavendish,' he said. 'You know it?'

'Yes, I've driven through. It's very pretty.'

'Well, she used to hate it when we'd all traipse back after one of our weekends in the wild. We'd be caked in mud and we'd fill her kitchen with all the produce we'd found.'

'And she didn't like that?'

'She liked neatly-wrapped food that came from the supermarket not stuff that had been dug out of a ditch or plucked from a hedge.'

'That's a shame,' Callie said.

'It was, wasn't it? But at least you appreciate a bit of wild cooking, don't you?'

'I think I'm about to find out,' she said.

'Oh, yeah,' Leo said, winking at her.

# CHAPTER 10

Callie watched as Leo emptied the hamper, laying out plates, glasses, a bottle of wine and all the pots and pans needed to make them dinner. The fire was now blazing, sending out its welcome warmth into the darkening wood. Still, despite its heat, Callie was glad that she'd grabbed a jacket as she'd left home and she put it on now.

'So, what about your parents?' Leo asked.

'They live in Oxfordshire,' Callie said.

'And you didn't want to move there when leaving London?'

'Oh, no!' she said. 'I couldn't go back.'

'And what do Mr and Mrs Logan think of your new home in Suffolk?'

'They've not seen it yet,' she said. 'I don't suppose they will.'

Leo frowned. 'What do you mean?'

Callie shrugged. 'They're not really interested, you know?'

'No,' Leo said, 'I don't.'

Callie gave a sad little smile. 'They've got their own lives and I've got mine. We really don't see a lot of each other.'

'You're not close?'

'Never were,' Callie said. 'I think I was a surprise baby. I don't think they really planned to have children at all and, when I came along, they didn't know what to do with me.'

Leo looked at her, a dumbfounded expression on his face. 'That's the saddest thing I've ever heard.'

'Don't let it make you sad!' Callie cried. 'It's not – really. It's just the way it is. I've never known any different and it's made me wonderfully independent which is just what I needed when my marriage was falling apart.'

'I'm sorry to hear that,' he said, 'about your marriage too.'

She nodded. 'At least I was able to make the right decision in leaving, knowing that I'm perfectly all right on my own and that I don't actually need to rely on anyone else like my parents.'

'But that's a crazy way to live,' Leo said. 'I can't imagine not being close to my parents. When Dad was alive, I felt like he was just as much of a good mate as a father.'

Callie gazed into the flames of the fire, watching them dancing and spiralling ever higher.

'You've been lucky to have that,' she said. 'You know, I didn't realise anything was unusual for ages. We moved house a lot when I was young and it was difficult to make friends and it wasn't until I went to university and saw my friends there ringing their parents or going back home at the weekends that I started to realise that my own set up was a bit odd. Then there's all the messages on social media sites – you know the ones that say something like "Repost this if your parents are your best friends". And I look at all the messages underneath and the photos friends would post of themselves with their parents, and I know there might actually be something wrong with the way mine behave. But what can you do? You can't choose your family, can you? And they care about me in their own way.'

'Are you *sure* about that?' Leo asked.

Callie laughed. 'No, not really. Mum's already said she's not traipsing all the way to Suffolk to see me. It's too far, really.'

Leo looked baffled by this. 'Callie – our Uncle Ed got on a plane from South Africa so he could be at my brother's graduation.'

'Really?' she said. 'Well, that's nice. Maybe he'll come and visit me when he's next in Suffolk.'

'I'm sure he'd be on the first flight to the UK if you invited him.'

They smiled at each other and she watched as Leo poured green soup from a plastic container into a little pan which he placed on a hook suspended over the fire which had died down a little now and was perfect for cooking over.

'What's this?' she asked when he decanted it into bowls a few minutes later and presented it to her.

'Try it first,' he said.

'It's good,' she said after taking her first spoonful. 'It tastes really fresh and–' she paused, trying to come up with the right words to describe the unique taste. '*Green!*' she said at last.

'It tastes *green*?' Leo said.

'It's the *greenest* thing I've ever tasted.'

They both laughed.

'Go on then – tell me what I've just eaten,' she said.

'Nettle soup.'

'Nettle!' she cried.

'You said you liked it,' Leo said. 'Now don't go changing your mind just because you know what it is.'

'I'm not going to change my mind,' Callie said. 'I'm just surprised. I didn't know you could eat nettles.'

'Well, it's bulked out with potato and onion and other goodies otherwise it would just be a thin green gruel.'

'And I'm thankful that you didn't present me with *that* version,' Callie said, her eyes sparkling in merriment.

'Nettles are very good for you – full of iron and vitamins and, of course, they're free,' he said. 'And it's a wonderful kind of gardener's revenge to be able to chop them down and eat them, don't you think? Only it's best to pick them when they're young, and always wear gloves.'

'Ah, yes,' Callie said.

'I always make gallons of it in the spring and then freeze it and couldn't resist sharing it with you tonight even though it's out of season and one should always strive to eat in harmony with the seasons.'

Callie nodded. 'I'll try and remember that.'

'So, that was your starter,' he said, taking her empty bowl away from her.

'You mean there's more?'

'Of course. I didn't bring you all this way for a measly bowl of soup,' he said, placing some oil in a frying pan. Callie watched as Leo began chopping mushrooms on a mini chopping board from out of the hamper before flinging them into the pan to sizzle. He then brought out a box containing three eggs which he cracked into a bowl, seasoning it, and adding a piece of hard cheese.

'Just how many ingredients did you bring tonight?' Callie asked, fascinated by the parade of food which was coming out of the hamper.

'Just enough,' he said, pouring the eggy mix into the pan. 'Wild mushroom omelette,' he said, 'with free-range eggs and garnished with wild marjoram.'

'Wow!' Callie said.

'I hope you like mushrooms,' he said. 'My last girlfriend didn't think much of all this foraging. I'd bring her home some of nature's very best and she'd look at it as if I was trying to poison her. Mind you, there was that incident with the dodgy mushrooms, but you're bound to make mistakes every now and then and she was only sick the once.'

— Callie gulped and looked down at the omelette he was serving up for her with some misgiving.

'And then there were all the flowers I picked for her,' he said as he passed Callie a knife and fork. "These are wild, aren't they? You didn't buy them," she'd say.'

'Oh, dear,' Callie said. 'I always think wild flowers are the most beautiful.'

'Me too!' he said. 'You see – *you* understand these things. Apart from the rabbit, that is.'

'I'm sorry about that,' she said, taking a bit of her omelette.

'Well, you are a city girl,' he said with a teasing smile.

'Not anymore,' she said, lifting one of her wellie-clad feet up.

'Yep – forget designer shoes from now on.'

'You know, I never really understood the whole women-and-shoes thing anyway,' she said.

'Then you should blend right in here.'

Callie was thrilled to hear that.

'How's your omelette?' he asked.

'Good,' she said. 'Very good.'

'Not too green?'

'Not at all. It's good and shroomy. I just hope they're the right kind of shrooms,' she said.

'Cheeky!' he said.

They ate in silence for a while, listening to the sound of the evening wind in the trees and the distant sound of crows cawing and pheasants crying.

'I thought they said that the countryside was quiet,' she said.

'Ah, that's a myth.'

'I was hanging some washing out on the line the other day and I heard the most unearthly sound imaginable. It was like somebody was being murdered.'

'What was it?' Leo asked.

'I think it was a pig squealing.'

Leo nodded. 'That'll be Bill Symonds. He keeps a few up at the farm near you. His bacon's the best in Suffolk.'

'Is everything about food with you?'

'Pretty much,' he said, stuffing the last of his omelette into his mouth. 'Yum!'

Callie laughed. He seemed to make her laugh with the greatest of ease, she noted.

He took her empty plate from her.

'What's next?' she asked.

'I thought we could have a glass of wine before pudding,' he said. 'Took the liberty of bringing a bottle of my best cowslip.'

'Cowslip wine?' Callie said. Now, she'd heard everything.

Leo reached for the bottle and opened it, pouring the pale yellow wine into two glasses.

'It's beautiful,' Callie said, looking at the way it glowed against the light from the fire. She took a sip. 'Oh!'

'Good?'

'It's marvellous. It's like drinking sunshine.'

'I thought you might like it,' he said. 'Women tend to like the light florals.'

Callie's right eyebrow rose. 'You've plied a lot of women with cowslip wine, have you?'

Leo laughed. 'I'm just making an observation,' he said.

Callie smiled. She could well believe that she wasn't the first woman to be brought into the woods by Leo Wildman with his bottles of cowslip wine.

'Well, it's very good,' she said, 'and it's really lovely to see this place.'

'It's my favourite place in the whole world,' he said.

'It does have a magical feel about it,' Callie admitted, peering up into the autumn foliage of the beeches which were fast losing their colour in the approaching darkness.

'I've hiked in the foothills of the Himalayas and walked through South American rainforests,' Leo said, 'but nothing compares to an English wood on an autumn evening when the air is just beginning to crisp at the edges and the scent of wood smoke lingers in the air.'

Callie looked at him, impressed. 'That's very poetic,' she said.

'Oh, I don't know about that,' he said, running a hand through his dark hair. 'I'm just saying it how it is.'

'Do you read poetry?' she asked him.

'God no!' he said. 'I don't read very much at all. Only a bit of non-fiction occasionally.'

Callie was surprisingly disappointed by this admission.

'Rick loves books, though,' Leo went on. 'He's writing one right now. A guide to English woodlands. I'm helping him a bit with the practical side of things, but not with the writing.'

'I can't imagine a world without writing,' Callie said, taking another sip of her cowslip wine.

'But doesn't sitting indoors all day drive you mad?'

'Not at all,' she said. 'I guess I'm an indoor kind of person, but I am going to make an effort to get out more now I'm living here.'

'And maybe I can help in that department,' he said, his dark eyes glittering in the light of the fire. He was, she thought, the most handsome man she'd ever seen. 'More wine?'

She nodded and he leaned across to refill her glass. 'Now,' he said, 'pudding.'

It was no surprise that, tucked away in a small cooler bag inside the hamper, were two terracotta pots.

'Blackberry fool,' he said, passing her a pot and a spoon.

Callie beamed. 'Lovely!'

'Home-made but not too sweet,' he said.

'I have never been so spoilt,' she said, tasting the delicious, creamy concoction. 'My husband – my soon to be *ex*-husband – never cooked.'

'What *never*?'

'Nope,' she said. 'He liked me to cook for him or to go out somewhere hideously expensive.'

'And you didn't like that?'

'I didn't ever mind cooking for him,' she said, 'but restaurants can be pretty tiresome after a while, particularly when you've got nothing to say to the person sitting opposite you.'

Leo shook his head. 'I'm sorry to hear that.'

Callie shrugged. 'It's all in the past now.'

'Good,' he said.

They finished their blackberry fools and sat quietly, watching the mesmeric flames of the fire. Callie was definitely having a moment, and the writer in her wanted to reach into the dainty handbag she'd brought with her for her notebook and pen and scribble some thoughts down: about how beautiful the fire was and how cosy it felt to be in the heart of an English wood after the sun had set and the crows had roosted for the night. She wanted to capture the sights, sounds and smells of it all. And the tastes too. The tastes which Leo Wildman had conjured up for her.

'You look thoughtful,' he said, bringing her out of herself.

'I was just thinking how magical this has all been,' she said.

'I'm glad you've enjoyed it.'

'I have. I really have.'

They sat for a while longer, watching the fire and listening to the distant hoots of an owl out hunting for the evening.

'I should get you home,' Leo said at last, tidying everything away and making sure the fire was out.

'I was getting anxious that you might be about to take me further into the woods to watch badgers or something,' Callie confessed.

'That could be arranged,' he said.

Callie laughed, instantly believing him.

The walk back to the Land Rover was an adventure for Callie who had never been outside without the aid of street lighting before. Leo held a torch in his right hand and the thin beam of light was all they had to guide them along the twisting woodland path.

'You okay?' he asked as they hopped over a fallen tree trunk.

'I'm fine,' Callie said, taking care not to tear her dress on the rough bark as she buttoned up her jacket to keep warm. There were very few men, Callie thought, who could get away with bringing a woman into the woods at night when she was wearing her best dress and had been expecting to be wined and dined in style. Mind you, she *had* been wined and dined, and in the loveliest, most unique of styles too.

Callie smiled in the darkness as she thought about the nettle soup and the cowslip wine, and the way Leo had looked at her, his eyes glittering in the firelight. It had been an evening that she would never forget.

When they arrived back at Newton St Clare, Leo killed the engine and made to get out of the car.

'It's okay – I think I can make it to my front door all right.'

'You sure, city girl? It's pretty dark.'

'I think I'm beginning to get used to the lack of street lighting now.'

'Yes, but you also had rather a lot of that cowslip wine,' he pointed out.

'Are you saying I'm tipsy?' she asked, her voice laced with mock annoyance. Actually, come to think of it, she was feeling wonderfully light and mellow.

'Certainly not,' he said, 'but it's my job as your host to make sure you make it home safely.'

'Well, okay then,' Callie said and Leo hopped out and ran round to her side of the car, opening the door.

'I've still got your wellies on!' she exclaimed.

'So you have,' he said. 'Let me help.'

Before she could stop him, Leo's hands had clasped her boots, easing them off, his dark hair tickling her knees below the hemline of her dress.

'Socks next,' he said, gently pulling each one off.

'Oooh, that's cold now!' Callie said as he took the second sock off.

'Ah!' Leo said, looking up into her face. 'That's because this came off with it.' He held up a translucent stocking and Callie could feel herself blushing as he placed it in her hand.

'I'd better put my own boots on myself,' she said, suddenly feeling very sober.

Leo stood back as Callie thrust one stockinged foot and one unstockinged foot into her high-heeled boots. He then proffered a hand towards her which she took because the ground suddenly looked a long way down from her seat in the Land Rover.

'Must be the cowslip wine,' she said.

'What's that?' Leo asked.

'Erm, I'm feeling a little sleepy.'

He opened the garden gate.

'Here we are,' he said and she could just make out his features in the dim glow from the light she'd left on in the living room. 'I've had a really great evening, Callie.'

'Me too,' she said. 'It wasn't what I was expecting but I loved it!'

Their faces hovered closely together in the semi-darkness.

'Can I see you again?' he asked, his voice almost a whisper.

Callie nodded. 'Yes,' she said. 'I'd like that.' As they stood there a moment longer, Callie realised that she was holding her breath, wondering, anticipating what would happen next.

'Goodnight, Callie,' Leo said at last, reaching a hand towards her and squeezing her delicate fingers in his great wood-roughened ones.

She laughed nervously at the unexpected touch.

'Goodnight,' she said, watching as he walked down her garden path, closing the gate behind him and driving off into the inky darkness of the Suffolk countryside.

# CHAPTER 11

There was something very special about a bookshop on a rainy afternoon, Sam always thought. It became a very special sort of a world: a safe and cosy place where you could hide away without feeling the least bit guilty.

Alas, rain wasn't always good for business because people seemed to be hurrying to get home and the majority of customers who did come into the shop when it was raining were usually just trying to find somewhere to shelter. Sam didn't mind this too much because it was the accidental browser who often became the regular customer. A serendipitous rainfall would often help people discover the magic of Nightingale's.

It was on just such a rainy afternoon at the beginning of October when there were several rather wet-around-the-edges customers that the shop phone rang. Grandpa Joe was in his favourite place in the back room chortling his way through a *Tintin* hardback and Polly had gone into Bryony's shop across the road to help her rearrange her window display.

'Nightingale's,' Sam said as he picked up the phone. As soon as he heard the silence on the other end of the line, instinct told him to hang up, but he didn't. He couldn't. Instead, he waited for the habitual sigh that followed the silence.

'Sam?'

'Emma,' he said, his natural ease seeming to drain away from him in an instant.

'I don't want to waste time so I'm just going to ask you straight,' she began. Sam was used to that with Emma. Whenever she had something on her mind, she wouldn't bother with any sort of preamble – she'd just come straight to the point. 'I can't find that book you gave me.'

'Which book?' Sam asked. He'd given her a lot of books during their marriage. None had really been appreciated, he feared.

'That expensive one. The one you said was a collector's piece.'

Sam sighed to himself. She couldn't even remember the name of it, could she? He thought of the beautiful gilt-embossed anthology of love poems he'd given her. It was a first edition from the 1850s and was a glory to behold. Indeed, he'd never seen a more handsome book in all his years as an antiquarian.

'The poetry anthology?'

'Yes,' she said. 'That's the one. Have you got it?'

'No, of course not,' Sam said. 'Why would I have it?'

'Don't lie to me,' Emma said. 'I know you have it.'

'Emma, why would I take that from you? It was a gift to you.'

'You're lying, Sam. I *know* you are. That was a valuable book.'

'Yes it was, but that doesn't mean I took it back from you,' he said, doing his best to remain calm which was never an easy thing around Emma. 'Look, I can't talk now. I'm in the shop.'

'Yes, and you've probably just sold that book, haven't you?'

'No, I haven't,' Sam said. 'How could you honestly think that? You've probably just mislaid it.'

'I don't just mislay things,' she shouted down the phone.

No, Sam thought, apart from your scruples about sleeping with other men whilst you're married. But he didn't say anything.

'I'm sorry I can't help you with this,' he said.

'Sam – don't make me send Aidan over,' Emma said, her voice a cold warning.

'What's Aidan got to do with this?' Sam asked, thinking of Emma's loose cannon of a brother, Aidan Jones. He was short and stocky with arms built more like legs after spending way too much time in the gym. Sam had never warmed to him particularly after he'd got into a fight on Sam's stag night and had been arrested. He was, to quote his brother, Josh, "A foul-mouthed philistine" and Sam didn't relish the idea of his ex-wife using Aidan as some sort of go-between.

'If you don't give me back that book, I'll send Aidan over to get it,' she said, hanging up before Sam could say anything else.

He replaced the receiver and took a deep breath, wondering what on earth had just happened.

'Grandpa?' he said, walking through to the back room.

Grandpa Joe looked up from his *Tintin* book. 'You okay?'

'That was Emma on the phone.'

'Thought it might be,' Grandpa Joe said. 'Your voice goes all tight and unnatural whenever you talk to her.'

'Does it?'

'Sure does.'

Sam ran a hand through his hair. 'She thinks I've stolen a book I gave her.'

'What book?'

'The nineteenth-century poetry anthology.'

'Ah, yes – nice book that,' Grandpa Joe said. 'Well, did you?'

'Grandpa!' Sam said in exasperation. 'Of course I didn't steal it!'

'Just making sure,' he said with a wink.

'I thought she was out of my life for good now,' he said, 'but she keeps popping up to unsettle me.'

'I never warmed to that woman,' Grandpa Joe said, his white eyebrows hovering menacingly low.

'Grandpa, you fell for her just as hard as I did.'

'How can you say that?'

'Because you were all over her when I first brought her home.'

'Ah,' Grandpa Joe said, 'I was as hoodwinked as you in those early days.'

Sam shook his head. 'Listen,' he said, 'would you mind manning the till for me for a bit? I'm going to pop across the road.'

Grandpa Joe put his copy of *Tintin* aside and stood up. 'Going to get some sisterly advice?'

'Something like that,' Sam said.

A minute later and Sam had left one Nightingale bookshop for another.

'Hey!' Bryony said as her brother walked through the door. She was wearing a flowing floral dress in lavender and lime and a pair of enormous silver hoop earrings.

'Polly! Sam's here,' she called through to the storeroom.

Polly, who was helping Bryony out until she had to go and collect Archie from school, emerged from the storeroom.

'You need me?' she asked.

'No, no,' he said.

'You okay?' Polly asked as she surveyed her brother.

'Emma just rang,' he said.

'What did *she* want?' Bryony said, her dark eyes narrowed.

'She thinks I've stolen a book I once gave her.'

'What?' Polly asked. 'Are you kidding?'

'I am not kidding,' Sam said.

'Well, did you?' Bryony said.

Sam glared at her. 'I hope you're joking.'

'I know you and books,' she said. 'You wouldn't want to see a good book go to waste, and weren't you always saying that she never appreciated books like us?'

'Nobody appreciates books like us,' Polly said.

'She's threatened to send Aidan round,' Sam confided.

'Oh, blimey,' Bryony said. 'That Neanderthal.'

'I thought I'd better warn you,' Sam said, remembering what had happened at his wedding. They'd hired a glorious marquee which had been set up in the garden at Campion House for his and Emma's wedding reception. Of course, Aidan had been there, tanking up on as much champagne as he could get his hands on and then grabbing Bryony's bottom on the dance floor which had resulted in a slapped face, much to the amusement of the guests.

'I don't want to see that brother-in-law of yours *ever* again,' Bryony told Sam now.

'*Ex* brother-in-law,' Sam said. 'I don't exactly relish the idea of seeing him either.'

'What are you going to do?' Polly asked, concern in her voice.

'I don't think there's much I can do,' Sam said. 'Anyway, she was probably bluffing.'

'I wouldn't be so sure,' Bryony said. 'Honestly, Sam, 'I don't know why you put up with her nonsense. She's just trying it on with you. She's probably hoping you'll write her out a cheque or something to keep the peace. Tell us what you saw in her again.'

'Don't be so heartless, Bry,' Polly said.

'But she's been nothing but trouble from day one.'

'That's not true,' Sam said. 'I remember you two gossiping in the kitchen together every Sunday.'

Bryony looked sheepish. 'Well, that was just in support of my dopey brother,' she said.

'So, how's your love life then?' he asked. 'Seeing as you're so quick to judge everybody else's.'

'Oh, no!' Polly said. 'Don't talk about Bryony's love life – *please!*'

'Why?' Sam asked. 'What have I missed?'

'Nothing,' Bryony said. 'Absolutely nothing and *that's* the point!'

'No,' Polly said. 'There has been *some* progress.'

Bryony stared at her older sister, obviously nonplussed.

'*Colin!*' Polly cried.

'Oh!' Bryony said. 'Well, that's not really news, is it?'

'What isn't news?' Sam asked.

'Colin asked me out again,' Bryony said.

'Colin from Well Bread next door?'

'Of course *that* Colin,' Polly said in exasperation.

'Well, he's a good guy,' he told her, thinking of the young man who'd opened up the bakery in Castle Clare five years ago and had really made a name for himself. People came from all over the county for his delicious cob loaves and pastries.

Bryony slumped down onto a yellow beanbag in the children's corner of the shop.

'I'm seriously thinking of dating him,' she said, her elbows resting on her knees and her head in her hands.

'Shouldn't you sound more excited by the prospect of dating someone?' Sam asked, looking at the funny sight of his sister so close to the floor. Her dark hair was cascading wildly over her shoulders and was in stark contrast to Polly's which was neatly pinned back in a bun. Sam smiled at the pair of them as he knelt down to Bryony's level. How very different they were, he thought, and how very much he loved them both.

'There are only so many cream cakes and flapjacks a girl can accept before agreeing to a date,' Bryony said.

'He's worn you down with an onslaught of sugar,' Polly said. 'That's plain cheating. No woman can survive wooing by sugar.'

'Honestly, it's going to do my waistline no good at all,' Bryony said.

'Maybe your first date should be a very long walk,' Sam suggested, receiving a play punch from Bryony which nearly toppled him over.

'Why is there such a shortage of decent men in Suffolk?' she asked.

Sam shrugged. 'Maybe you should become like me and dedicate your life to the printed word.'

'Maybe,' she said.

'Nah. Don't do that, Bry. You'll find your perfect match,' Sam said.

'How can you be so sure?' she asked. 'I mean, it didn't exactly work out for you, did it?'

'I know,' he said. 'But it's easier to remain optimistic for other people.'

'But you've not seriously given up on meeting someone, have you, Sam?' Polly asked.

'I seriously have,' he told her, standing back up to full height. 'I am through with all that. The only romance I want is the sort that is safely tucked between two covers and a spine.'

'But what about that Callie woman? She was lovely.'

'You've met her?' Bryony asked Polly.

'She came into the shop the other day,' Polly said.

'Am I the *only* Nightingale not to have met Callie Logan?'

Polly laughed. 'You'll get your chance, I'm sure.'

'So, are you seeing her?' Bryony asked, gazing up at Sam from her beanbag.

'Only in a professional manner,' he replied.

Bryony rolled her eyes. 'Well, that's boring!'

'She was very pretty,' Polly said.

'What's she like?' Bryony asked her sister.

Polly looked thoughtful. 'She looked cautious, I thought.'

'Of what?' Bryony asked.

'Of everything,' Polly said.

'What do we know about her?' Bryony said, turning her gaze towards her brother again.

'We know that she minds her own business unlike some people,' Sam said, a stern expression on his face.

Bryony stuck her tongue out at him. 'I'm going to Google her.'

'Please don't,' Sam said, making to leave the shop.

'I'm going to Google her as soon as you leave the shop and I shall print out and highlight anything interesting for you.'

'I'm not interested,' Sam said, the bell tinkling above his head as he opened the door.

'The antiquarian doth protest too much!' Bryony said, laughing.

Sam ignored her and returned to the sanctuary of his own bookshop.

It was just ten minutes before closing time when the trouble began. Sam recognised the white van immediately. It pulled up next to the kerb outside Sam's shop, blocking the light and causing a woman with a buggy to swerve in alarm.

'Oh, no,' Sam said, watching as the short stocky figure of Aidan

Jones got out, scratching his groin before reaching into the van and bringing out a large cardboard box.

Sam frowned as his ex-brother-in-law pushed the shop door open so hard that Sam genuinely thought that it would come off his hinges. Aidan had always reminded Sam of Popeye, only without any of the cartoon character's endearing qualities.

'Sammy!' Aidan bellowed across the shop, startling an elderly lady who'd been happily thumbing her way through a Jilly Cooper paperback.

'What do you want, Aidan?' Sam asked, watching as the elderly lady decided to leave the shop without the pre-loved copy of *Riders*.

'I think you know what I want,' Aidan said with a sniff.

'Look, I don't want any trouble,' Sam said.

'You'll not get any trouble outta me,' Aidan said, running his hand over his nail-brush short hair. 'That's not what I've come 'ere for. I've come for that book, only I don't know what I'm lookin' for, see, and Emma doesn't seem to know what it is neither so I'm takin' all the old books in your personal collection.'

'What do you mean, you're taking *all* of them?'

'I'm to take any *old* book, sis said.'

Before Sam could say anything, Aidan had walked into the back room and was legging it up the stairs. For someone so short, he couldn't half move fast, Sam thought.

'Now, just you wait a minute– ' Sam said, sprinting up the stairs behind him. 'You can't barge in to my home like this.'

'Gonna stop me, are you?'

'What's going on?' Grandpa Joe shouted from his home on the sofa in the back room of the bookshop.

'Just stay there, Grandpa,' Sam called down below before following Aidan into the tiny flat above the shop.

'Wow!' Aidan said as he eyed up the sparse furnishings. 'You got this nice an' cosy, ain't you?'

'Please leave now,' Sam said, ignoring his sarcasm and trying to remain calm.

'I ain't leaving until I've got what I came for.'

'You have no right to be here.'

'No?' he said, a sly grin on his face as he threw the cardboard box down beside a bookcase. 'Emma thinks I've got a right to be here.'

'Well, she's mistaken.'

'We'll see about that, won't we?' Aidan said as he began picking random hardbacks from the bookcase in front of him.

'Do *not* touch those books!' Sam shouted, striding forward and reaching out to touch Aidan's left shoulder.

'I wouldn't do that if I was you,' Aidan said and Sam couldn't help noticing a touch of mischievousness in his voice as if he was, perhaps, baiting him.

'What's going on in here?' an angry voice came from the landing and Sam turned to see Grandpa Joe entering the room.

'Just wait downstairs please, Grandpa.'

'What the hell is he doing?' Grandpa cried.

In the brief moment that Sam had turned away from Aidan, he'd managed to half fill the cardboard box with old hardback books.

'Put those back,' Sam said.

'What's going on?' Grandpa Joe said. 'Why's he got those books?'

'Grandpa – go downstairs.'

'I'm not going anywhere,' he said. 'You just put those books back right now.'

'Get out of my way, old man.'

'Grandpa!' Sam shouted but, as fast as he moved forward, Aidan was faster, pushing into the old man with the heavy box of books, causing him to topple and crash into the chair behind him, falling to the floor.

Sam's eyes widened in horror at the callous act and he felt a great rage building inside him, but he didn't have time to take action because Aidan had predicted what would happen next and had dropped the box of books before shooting his right fist into Sam's belly. The move completely winded him and he could only glare up in surprise at Aidan.

'What? You thought I'd be so low as to punch a guy in the face when he wears glasses?'

Aidan grabbed the box and raced down the stairs.

'Grandpa? Are you all right?' Sam was instantly beside his grandpa who was still on the floor.

'Did he get away?'

'Just sit still for a minute,' Sam said.

'Let me at him!'

'Grandpa – sit *still*!'

Grandpa Joe let out a weary sigh.

'Sam?' a voice cried from downstairs and Sam heard the sound of at least two pairs of feet on the uncarpeted staircase. It was Polly and Bryony.

'We're in here,' Sam called and the two sisters ran into the room.

'Are you okay?' Polly crouched down next to her grandfather. 'We saw the van outside the shop and guessed there'd be trouble.'

'That jerk, Aidan, knocked Grandpa over,' Sam said, 'and ran off with a load of my books.'

'He winded you!' Grandpa Joe said.

'I'm calling the police,' Bryony said.

'Don't!' Sam said.

'Sam!' she cried. 'You've just been assaulted and robbed!'

'And that's enough. We don't need the police here too and tongues wagging in town for the next three months.'

'Oh, my goodness – you're bleeding,' Polly said, noticing a thin line of blood on Grandpa Joe's lip.

'I think I bit my lip as I fell,' he said.

'Let me get that fixed up,' Polly said, heading for Sam's tiny bathroom.

'What the hell did Aidan think he was doing?' Bryony said.

'He doesn't think,' Grandpa Joe said. 'He isn't capable.'

'I should have belted him,' Sam said.

'If you'd have so much as laid a finger on him, he would have killed you,' Polly said as she emerged from the bathroom with some damp cotton wool and a bottle of TCP. Sam knew she was probably right. Aidan was always getting into fights and he enjoyed every single one of them.

'What did he take?' Bryony asked.

'I don't think that matters right now,' Polly said, as she dabbed Grandpa Joe's lip with TCP.

'Ouch!' he cried. 'It matters to me what he took because it's Nightingale property.'

'Yes, a Neanderthal like Aidan Jones shouldn't be allowed to handle any sort of books let alone Nightingale books,' Bryony said.

'Were they expensive books?' Polly asked.

'Very likely,' Sam said. 'He wiped out most of the hardbacks from this case.'

'And what was there?' Bryony asked.

'Some nineteenth-century editions, a couple of Hogarth Press books–'

'Jeepers!' Bryony exclaimed.

'Is he going to bring them back?' Polly asked, standing back up to full height and helping Grandpa up from the floor.

'How the hell should I know?' Sam said, raking a hand through his hair.

'What are you going to do?' Grandpa Joe asked, slumping onto the sofa in the middle of the living room.

'I'm not sure there's a lot I can do,' Sam said, 'but, when Emma realises I was telling her the truth about the book of poems, maybe she'll return the books her idiot brother took.'

Polly sat down next to her grandfather. 'You okay?'

He nodded. 'Nothing a brandy wouldn't fix.'

Polly nodded. 'Sam?'

'Top of the cabinet,' he said.

'Pour us all one,' Bryony said.

Four brandies were poured and Sam pulled out two wooden chairs from the table for himself and Bryony. Emma had taken custody of most of the marital furniture when they'd split up and Sam had had to start from scratch with cast offs from his family and pieces he'd picked up secondhand.

'Well,' Grandpa Joe began after a generous slurp of brandy, 'never say life as an antiquarian is dull!'

'It's not funny, Grandpa,' Polly said. 'You could have been seriously hurt.'

'I'm not worried about that,' he said with a harrumph, 'I'm worried about those books.'

'Forget the books,' Polly said. 'Are you quite sure you didn't bang your head?'

'Stop fussing, girl,' he said. 'You're worse than your grandmother.'

Polly tutted which made Sam smile. Polly was always being told how very much she took after Grandma Nell. She was forever fussing around, making sure everyone had eaten enough or that they were wearing enough warm clothes. It was an endearing trait, but it was obvious that Grandpa was in no mood to be mollycoddled.

'What are we going to do?' Grandpa Joe asked, his great gnarly hands clenching his knees.

'We are going to shut up shop, that's what we're going to do,' Sam said.

'Is that all?'

'That's all,' he said.

Grandpa muttered something into his thick white moustache.

'What?' Sam said as he made towards the door. 'What would you have me do. Grandpa? Run down the street shouting blue murder? Getting the police involved and making this into an even uglier mess than it already is?'

'Maybe you should buy a Rottweiler,' Bryony said.

'Or at least get CCTV,' Polly said.

'I can't afford that,' Sam said.

'Well, at least keep your private living quarters locked when you're down in the shop so that maniacs like Aidan Jones can't just barge in and take what they want,' Bryony said.

'Okay,' he said, 'I'll lock my door.'

Sam left the room, walking downstairs to close up the shop. He tidied the area around the till and then went around the place, realigning books and returning the copy of Jilly Cooper's *Riders* that had been placed in the crime section when the elderly browser had hurriedly left the shop as Aidan Jones had arrived.

Sam took his glasses off and pinched his nose, trying desperately to put the memory out of his head. He shuddered to think what he might have lost from his personal collection of beloved books that day. Could he rely on Emma to do the decent thing and return them to him? He wasn't at all sure about that. One thing he was sure about, though, was that he was never going to lose his heart to a woman again.

# CHAPTER 12

When Sam came downstairs to open the shop the next morning, he was baffled to see a number of people standing around outside the window, some bent double over the pavement.

He unlocked the door, turned the "open" sign around and went to see what was going on. The first person he recognised was Lily Ann Taylor. She was in her mid-fifties, was a regular customer at the Nightingale's bookshops and loved nothing more than a bargain.

'Good morning, Lily Ann,' he said with a smile. 'What's happening here, then?'

'Mr Nightingale!' Lily Ann exclaimed, clapping her hands together in excitement. 'Are you doing a giveaway here?'

'Pardon?' he said, looking at the group of people who were huddled around what looked like a cardboard box. He squeezed himself between two ladies and his mouth dropped open in horror as he saw what they were all so interested in.

'My books,' he said, instantly recognising the hardbacks which Aidan Jones had taken just the day before. So, he'd brought them back, Sam thought. But when had he dropped them off? Exactly *how* long had they been hanging around on the pavement for all and sundry to pick through?

'They *are* free to take, aren't they?' an elderly lady with a large tartan shopper asked, a look in her eyes which seemed to suggest she was ready to fill it to the brim with Sam's precious books if they were, indeed, free.

'No,' Sam said. 'NO!'

The woman dropped one of the books back into the box in shock.

'Sorry,' Sam said. 'I'm really sorry, everybody, but these books are part of my own collection.'

'Then what are they doing on the street?' she asked him.

'There's been a mistake,' Sam said. 'They shouldn't be out here at all, I'm afraid. I'm really sorry to confuse you all.'

'But Winston has already taken one,' the elderly woman said, nodding down the street.

'Oh, blimey!' Sam exclaimed, taking the heavy box up from the pavement and hurrying into the shop with it before coming back outside and locking the door behind him.

'Where did he go?' Sam asked. 'Where did Mr Kneller go?'

'Towards the church, I think,' Lily Ann said.

Sam began to run, weaving his way through the morning shoppers out in Castle Clare, but he couldn't see any sign of Winston Kneller. He was probably long gone, Sam thought. Long gone with one of his favourite books.

Turning right into Market Square, Sam was heartily relieved to spot the old man.

'Mr Kneller,' he cried, catching up with him outside the Co-op supermarket.

'Sam?' the old man said as he turned around on hearing his name. 'You all right there?' He was wearing a jaunty brown felt hat and a slim red and white scarf. He gave a cheeky little smile and Sam thought, not for the first time, that Winston Kneller had the kind of face that one would expect to find on a Toby jug.

'Mr Kneller,' he said, 'I'm sorry to chase after you like that, but I believe you have one of my books.'

Mr Kneller looked down into the canvas shopping bag he was holding in which was a can of tomato soup, a packet of cheese-topped rolls and a bag of dog treats. And a beautiful old hardback book.

'You mean this?' he said, taking the book out of the bag.

Sam nodded. 'It's not for sale, I'm afraid.'

'I know,' he said. 'It was free. That's what Lily Ann told me.'

'I'm afraid she's wrong,' Sam said. 'Somebody was returning my books and left them outside the shop. They should never have been there. I'm really sorry for the confusion.'

'Oh,' Mr Kneller said, reluctantly handing the book back to Sam. It was a very rare first edition printed by the Hogarth Press. 'That's a shame.'

'But do come into the shop sometime. We have many reasonably priced books actually for sale,' he said with a little smile.

Mr Kneller tipped his hat. 'I will,' he said.

'And perhaps you'd be interested in our new book club,' Sam

added.

'A book club?'

'We're setting one up to meet in the shop. You'd be most welcome. I'll send you the details.'

'Will there be refreshments?' the old man asked.

'Tea, coffee and biscuits,' Sam said, 'and if Antonia Jessop joins, which I'm sure she will, there'll be cakes too no doubt.'

Mr Kneller's old eyes lit up at the mention of cakes. 'Count me in,' he said, waving a gloved hand at Sam before he went on his way.

Sam watched him go and then returned to his shop, hoping that his Hogarth Press book didn't smell of dog biscuits.

He was just moving the box of books to a safe place behind the counter when Bryony came into the shop.

'What have you been up to?' she asked. 'It looked like the entire population of Castle Clare was outside your shop. You having a sale or something?'

'No, I'm not having a sale,' Sam said.

It was as Bryony approached the till that she saw the cardboard box. 'Are they your books?'

'Yes,' Sam said.

'Oh, thank goodness for that! Are they all there?'

'I'm just checking now.'

'Want a hand?' she asked.

'I'm going to get them upstairs before anyone else tries to run off with them,' he said.

'I'll lock the door here for a minute.'

The two of them then took the books up to Sam's flat, popping the box on the landing floor whilst he got his key out.

'Glad to see you're taking security more seriously now,' Bryony said.

'After seeing half of Suffolk trying to run off with my first editions and having Aidan breaking in, I am definitely taking security more seriously,' he said, shaking his head at the memory.

Ten minutes later and the books were all safely restored to Sam's shelves and the two of them had returned downstairs to reopen the shop.

'Do you think you'll hear from Emma again?' Bryony asked.

'I sincerely hope not,' he said.

'Dear Sam,' she said, taking her brother's hand and squeezing it.

'You deserve to find the loveliest, kindest girl in the world!'

'What I deserve,' Sam said, 'is to be left alone in peace.'

Bryony shook her head. 'As if we're *ever* going to let that happen to you!' she said with a grin.

The writing had been going well. As Callie reached what she hoped was the halfway point of her new story, she took a moment to enjoy the sensation. She had something, she thought. She really had something. She wasn't *quite* sure what it was yet, but her agent had looked at the first few chapters and had seemed enthusiastic about it so that was a good sign.

Rolling her shoulders back, she realised just how stiff she had become from the hours she'd been spending at the keyboard. She needed a good walk, she thought as she got up from her chair and walked to the little window which looked out over the front garden and on towards the common. She'd been walking a lot more over the last few weeks but, now that it was the end of October, the clocks would be going back and the nights would be drawing in, meaning less time in the great outdoors. What would she and Leo do then, she wondered?

A blush heated her face as she thought of the implications of that question. Since the bonfire supper in the woods, she had seen Leo several times each week. Most of their dates had been walks. She'd decided that she liked the sort of man who considered that a walk along a river in search of mushrooms was a very good date to take somebody on, and she couldn't help being charmed by the fact that he'd turned up for such a date in wellies and a cap. After the terrible mistake she'd made of dressing up for her first date with Leo, she'd soon learned that trousers and sturdy footwear was the way to go. In fact, he'd been teaching her how to dress properly and there'd been a very interesting shopping trip after that first walk, with Leo insisting that Callie had to start dressing as if she meant to stay in the country and not like she was just visiting it.

'What do you mean?' she'd protested.

Leo had looked down at the pink wellies with blue dots on them and had shaken his head.

'They will *not* do,' he said. 'Maybe they'll do for a walk down a dry lane to the post box, but they'll split and crack before the winter's out and they won't keep you warm if you're standing in the middle of a field, trust me.'

Callie didn't like to say that she had no plans for standing around in the middle of fields, but maybe that's what she was destined for if she continued to date Leo. So she ditched her gorgeously girly pink wellies and bought a pair of heavy duty black ones which felt very snug indeed, she had to admit.

She'd also bought herself a tweed coat once she'd received her royalty cheque for her books. It seemed to bury her and had more pockets than she could ever hope to fill.

'What are all these for?' she'd asked Leo.

'Oh, shotgun cartridges and dead partridges,' he'd told her without blinking. Her mouth had dropped open. 'Or, in your case, a notepad and pen.'

She'd smiled at him and watched as Leo had chosen a rather fetching woolly hat for her.

'I haven't worn a hat since I was seven,' she said.

'Well, you will now unless you want your ears to fall off with frostbite,' he'd told her. 'East Anglian winters can be brutal.'

So, she was wearing the proper clothes for the second walk they went on and that's when she'd been introduced to Truffle and Blewit who were utterly adorable and instantly gave Callie their approval as they'd walked across the fields together.

'I wanted to show you one of my favourite views of Suffolk,' Leo said. 'Well, it's one of my favourite views in the world.'

They walked up a gentle hill, keeping to a footpath which skirted a wood. The field to the right had recently been ploughed, leaving corduroy-like ridges across the land. Since moving to Suffolk, Callie had fallen in love with the fields, watching the ever-changing colours and the wildlife that called this special place home.

The air was cool and she was thankful for her new coat and hat, and her boots had already been baptised in Suffolk mud. She would look like a real country girl in no time, she thought. She was even beginning to recognise the plants around her. She'd spotted lipstick-pink spindle berries in a hedgerow as they'd parked the Land Rover, and had even noticed a couple of parasol mushrooms as they'd entered a field.

'I'll come back for those later,' Leo said as he strode ahead of her, her hand in his. How quickly they had taken to holding hands, Callie thought. The first time had been when she was climbing over a very high stile. Leo was waiting for her on the other side and held a strong hand out to her and, when she'd placed her hand in his, he hadn't let go of it once she was safely down on the ground.

As they reached the top of the hill, the valley below spread out before them, the river winding its way through lush green fields. There were little copses dotted around the landscape, and cottages, farmhouses and pretty churches which all looked as if they had been a part of the landscape forever.

What a joy it was going to be to live through each of the seasons in the English countryside, Callie thought as she took in the view. This is my home now, she said to herself and how wonderful it would be to glory in the changing light and colours, the sounds and the scents of each passing day.

'Do you like it?' Leo asked her after they'd been standing in silence together for a good long time.

'I love it,' she said, watching as the clouds broke and a shaft of sunlight lit the valley, bathing everything in a golden light.

'You'd have to go a long way to beat a view like this and I'm not sure there is one.'

'You really love this place, don't you?' she said, looking at him as his dark hair flew around his face in the breeze.

'It's a part of me,' he said. 'See that little bend in the river after the thatched cottage?'

Callie looked towards the spot he was pointing at. 'Yes?'

'I learnt to swim there.'

'Did you?'

He nodded. 'One hot summer evening.'

'Who taught you?'

'I did,' he said. 'Just after my brother pushed me in.'

'Oh, no!'

'It was okay,' he said. 'I was a pretty fast learner, luckily, and I got my own back as soon as I was out of the water because I then pushed him in.'

Callie laughed.

'And that field over there – the one which slopes down towards the churchyard – I ate my first foraged mushroom there which actually turned out to be a really bad idea because it was a toadstool and made me very sick.'

'It didn't put you off foraging, though.'

'No,' he said. 'It made me even more determined to find out more and get things right next time.'

'What else?' Callie asked, liking this potted history of Leo and seeing the landscape through his eyes.

'Let me see,' he said, surveying the scene before him. 'Ah, yes. See that big old oak tree?'

'It's magnificent,' Callie said. 'It must be hundreds of years old.'

'At least five hundred years,' he said, 'and it's got my initials carved into it.'

'You vandal!' she teased.

'Well, I had something very important to commemorate there,' he said.

'What was that?' she asked.

'My first kiss,' he said, his dark eyes watching for her response.

'Oh, I see,' Callie said. She wasn't at all sure that she wanted to hear about Leo Wildman's first kiss.

'It was a pretty memorable occasion,' he told her.

'Right,' she said.

'But I didn't really have anything to compare it with back then,' he said, 'and I don't think it's going to be as memorable as this kiss.'

Before Callie could process his words properly, he'd lowered his head and kissed her, his mouth firm and warm on hers.

Callie thought of that day now as she looked out of her study window. She thought of the coolness of the breeze and the warmth of Leo's hand and the fire in his kiss.

Their third date had been slightly more formal. Leo had introduced her to one of his favourite pubs and they'd had lunch by an open fire. Then, as was becoming a routine, they went for a walk. This time, through a pretty Suffolk village full of pink cottages and medieval houses. They had held hands and shared a kiss as they'd crossed over a bridge.

Heidi would be delighted, Callie thought, only she hadn't actually told her friend that she'd been seeing Leo. She'd been putting the moment off because it was a wonderful little secret and, up until now, it had all been fairly casual. Callie was happy with that, but telling her friend about Leo would make it all so real and she wasn't sure she was ready for that yet. Not so soon after leaving Piers.

At the moment, everything was nice and light. She looked forward to seeing Leo because there was no pressure. It was fun. But Heidi's advice about having a fling kept haunting Callie and she couldn't help wondering when the actual *fling* part of a fling was meant to happen, and did she really want it to happen?

She really liked Leo: he was handsome, easy to talk to, and he was certainly a lot of fun to be with. But something inside Callie was holding her back. It wasn't just the fact that she didn't want to get involved with another man – not seriously anyway – there was something about Leo that... what? She really couldn't work out what it was. Heidi would tell her she was crazy – that this wasn't the time to be picky, and perhaps that was right. And yet Callie couldn't help thinking that she might be making a huge mistake if she took things any further with Leo Wildman than a kiss on a windswept hilltop.

# CHAPTER 13

It was a dreary afternoon at the beginning of November when Callie's phone rang.

'Callie? It's Sam.'

'Hi, Sam,' she said, surprised at how thrilled she was to hear from him.

'I was just wondering if you're still interested in joining our new book club.'

'Yes,' she said. 'Absolutely.'

'Great. We've got our first meeting tomorrow night. It'll just be an informal get-together. We won't actually be reading anything. It'll be more of a discussion as to what everyone wants from the club.'

'Okay,' she said. 'I'm up for that.'

'If you drop by the shop for seven thirty, then?'

'I'll be there,' she said.

'I look forward to seeing you,' he said, and she could tell he was smiling from the tone of his voice.

As she put the phone down, Callie found that she was smiling too.

Callie arrived promptly the next evening and she had to admit to being a little nervous. The trouble with being a writer was that everybody automatically thought that you had read everything that had ever been written and that you were terribly knowledgeable about it all too. Of course, Callie was well read, but she wasn't the most confident when it came to talking about books. Writing books was her thing. Reading them too. But talking about them? It was fine talking about books one to one as she had with Sam in the shop, but what would it be like talking about them to a room full of strangers? And that's what she was here – a stranger. Surely everybody else would know each other. The thought made her slightly apprehensive.

She'd allowed herself plenty of time to get there, driving through the deeply dark countryside that still fascinated her with its lack of street lights, enabling one to appreciate the star-studded heavens. She parked in the market square in the centre of Castle Clare. The little supermarket was still open and the fish and chip shop looked busy. The row of shops in the street just off the square were all in darkness. All except one – Sam's.

Taking a deep breath, Callie opened the green door of the bookshop. The bell tinkled as she walked in and she was quite surprised not to see the room full of people.

'Hello?' she called into the empty shop. There was no answer but she was pretty sure that she could hear voices coming from the back room. She took a moment to savour the magic of being in a bookshop at night. There was something intensely special about being allowed to wander amongst the books after the shop had officially closed for the day. The main lights had been switched off, but Sam had left a single lamp lit on a stool and the little pool of golden light turned the shop into a place of enticement and enchantment.

Callie's hand reached out to touch an old hardback spine whose gold letters gleamed in the dim light, but she resisted actually pulling it out. Instead, she let her fingers briefly linger on it, feeling its cool smoothness. She looked around the room, thinking that this must be the same wondrous feeling one would experience in a museum after hours. There was temptation everywhere and she couldn't help feeling slightly naughty being there.

The sound of a scraping chair from the back room, brought Callie to her senses and she thought it best to let her presence be known.

'Anyone here?' she called.

'Through here,' Sam's voice called back and Callie walked through the book-lined corridor into the back room.

'Hello, Sam,' she said.

Sam got up from the wooden chair he was sitting on. 'Callie!' he said. 'So good to see you.'

'Oh,' she said as she looked around the room, noticing a gentleman who appeared to have fallen asleep on the sofa, 'are we the only ones?' Callie asked.

'I'm afraid so,' Sam said, 'and I think Winston's only here because his boiler's packed in.'

'Oh, dear.'

'I think he was hoping for some of Antonia Jessop's cake too, but she couldn't make it tonight.'

Callie looked at the elderly gentleman who was slumped on the sofa snoring sonorously. He was wearing a felt hat and a little purple scarf. An old chocolate Labrador was sleeping by his feet. The scene made her smile.

'Let's give it a few minutes, eh?' Sam said. 'Cup of tea?'

'Thanks.'

They walked through to the kitchen together.

'I've had several apologies from various people,' Sam said as he switched the kettle on. 'Antonia Jessop, who suggested the club, twisted her ankle in her vegetable patch, and Polly was going to be here, but she couldn't get a babysitter for her son. Several other people showed an interest, but perhaps it was a bit ambitious for Castle Clare.'

'I don't think it is,' Callie said gently. 'I think these things just need a bit of time to get up and running.'

'Maybe you're right,' he said as he made the tea. 'I'd really like to see it take off. I think it could be great not only for the bookshop but for the community too. Winston,' he said, nodding to the sleeping man, 'he's a widower. Lives on his own on the edge of town. I don't think he gets out much, but he loves books and he's always got so much to say about them whenever he comes here.'

Callie nodded. 'Books have a way of opening you up, don't they? That's what I used to enjoy about the book club I was part of for a while.'

'The one with the expensive canapés and butlers?'

Callie smiled. 'That's the one. Well, before it all got so ridiculous with the petty rivalries, we'd have really great conversations – not only about the books themselves, but the subjects and issues that they brought up. We learned so much about each other. It was a real eye-opener.'

'I'd love that to happen here,' Sam said as they sat down with their tea.

The shop bell sounded.

'It might be about to,' Callie said as a lady in her late-sixties came into the room.

'Flo, how lovely to see you,' Sam said, greeting the smiling woman with a kiss on each cheek.'

'Hello, Sam dear,' she said.

'Let me introduce you to Callie. She recently moved to our little corner of the country.'

'My dear!' she said. 'How lovely to meet you.'

'This is Flo Lohman,' Sam told Callie. 'She lives just off the Great Tallington Road.'

'Born and bred there,' she said. 'Never known anywhere else, and let me tell you, you've chosen *exactly* the right place to live!'

'I'm glad to hear it,' Callie said, liking Flo Lohman immediately with her bright green eyes full of light, and her slightly wild white curls that shook around her shoulders when she talked.

'Now, I can't stop I'm afraid, Sam dear. I've got a big pot of jam on the go at home. My fruit trees have been groaning with produce this year. I can't move in my garden without squishing something. I'll pop some jars round to you when they're done.'

'I'll look forward to that,' Sam said.

'I just wanted you to know that I'm all for this book club thing, but I have to say that I'm not a fast reader these days and – if I'm honest – I only really like a nice romance. But I'm open-minded,' she said, 'and willing to give anything a go.'

'Good to know,' Sam said.

'What *do* you think we'll be reading?'

'Well, a few classics, I imagine,' Sam said, stroking his chin.

'Classic *love* stories?' Flo asked.

'I would be very surprised if there wasn't the occasional Austen or Brontë title in there,' Sam said.

'Good good,' Flo said, clapping her hands together. 'And will Winston be joining in or is he just part of the furniture?'

'He'll be joining in,' Sam said with a grin.

'Glad to hear it,' Flo said. 'Well, if he ever wakes up, tell him to expect some jam and a couple of squashes from me later in the week.'

'I will,' Sam said.

'And some eggs too. He doesn't get enough to eat by half,' she said.

'Flo?' Sam said, his head cocked to one side. 'Erm – you've got something in your hair.'

'Have I?' she said. 'What is it?'

Sam squinted. 'Something blue.'

'*Blue* you say?' Flo said in horror. 'Oh, dearie me! It'll be a curler.' Her hands flew to the nape of her neck to find the errant curler, and a perfect snow-white curl bounced up as she removed it. 'I thought there was something odd going on back there when I dozed off in my chair this afternoon. I kept feeling something scratchy.'

Callie bit her lip to stop herself from laughing.

'Well, I must get going. I promised to drop some of my bread rolls round to the vicarage and then I've got to get back to that jam before the cats find it. Filey completely ruined a pan of blackcurrant last year by sticking a mucky paw in it.' She waved a hand in the air as she turned to go. 'Toodle pip!'

'Toodle pip, Flo. Thanks for stopping by.'

'What a sweetheart she is,' Callie said after the shop bell had tinkled on her departure.

'They don't come much sweeter than Flo Lohman,' Sam said.

'It's a shame she couldn't stay. I'd like to have got to know her.'

'Oh, there'll be plenty of time for that,' Sam said.

'And a shame nobody else could make it.'

Sam looked thoughtful. 'Maybe my poster wasn't exciting enough,' he said. 'Maybe I should have made it a book *and beer* club.' His dark eyes sparkled.

'How many do you need for it to run?'

'Half a dozen at least,' he said, 'otherwise the conversation might dry up, don't you think? Something like this needs plenty of input.'

The two of them sat down on a pair of wooden chairs and resumed drinking their tea.

'So, how's the writing going?' Sam asked.

'Very well, actually,' Callie said.

'You sound surprised.'

'I am,' Callie said honestly. 'When I first moved here, everything went rotten in fiction land for a while. I couldn't seem to write anything.'

'Well, a move's a big upheaval,' Sam said. 'Perhaps you needed time to settle.'

She nodded. 'Perhaps,' she said.

'Can I ask what you're working on?'

She bit her lip. 'If I told you, I'd have to shoot you.'

'Ah, I see,' he said. 'Sorry.'

'I'm joking!' she said with a laugh. 'It's – well – the truth is, I'm not sure what it is. It's not my usual sort of thing. You know – series writing for middle-grade girls.'

'No? Maybe that's a good thing.'

'It is,' she said. 'It feels right, somehow. Like I've turned a corner. My agent likes it too which is such a relief.'

Sam frowned. 'I've never understood exactly what an agent does.'

'You're not the only one,' Callie said. 'Let me see. An agent. They read your manuscript and tell you to write exactly the opposite of what you've written, then they make you write it all over again and then take fifteen per cent of any money you make from it.'

'Sounds like a fantastic relationship,' Sam said with a grin.

'Well, I mustn't grumble really. My agent's got me some pretty good deals in the past.'

'I'm sure you worked hard for them and deserved them.'

'Thanks,' she said. 'At least she's letting me get on with this new idea. For a while, she was trying to push me into ghostwriting and I really didn't want to do that.'

'What would that have involved?' Sam asked.

'Oh, there was some celebrity who'd been offered a book deal and her publisher was looking for a writer.'

'You mean the celebrity was offered a book deal without her having written anything?' Sam said.

'It happens all the time,' Callie said.

Sam's face took on a baffled look. 'That's the most bizarre thing I've ever heard. I mean, I know it goes on but it's just crazy, isn't it?'

'Like artists who have teams of people to make the art for them?' Callie said. 'I don't want to be one of those people who make art with somebody else's name on it.'

'I don't blame you.'

'There's no joy in that. Not for me, anyway. Writing is about creating your *own* world and getting every little thought and feeling down. It's a very personal journey, a kind of exploration of your own soul.' She smiled. 'Does that sound pretentious?'

'No, not at all,' Sam said. 'It sounds about right to me. I'm fascinated by the writing process.'

'Have you ever written?'

'Good lord, no! But I'm a great appreciator of the works of others.'

'Oh, writers love their readers,' Callie said. 'When your agent is telling you one thing and your editor another, your readers can be your best friends.'

'Do you get fan mail?' Sam asked.

Callie nodded. 'It's so lovely to think of my young fans taking time out to get in touch with me. It's one of the best things about the job.'

'I don't get fan mail,' Sam said, making Callie laughed. 'Actually, I do get a bit. Usually after the book festival. I've got a few nice letters from visitors who've come to events here – you know, author talks and things. That's always nice.'

'I think my mum still disapproves of me being a writer. She doesn't see it as real somehow.'

'But that's crazy!' Sam said. 'You're about as real as they come with your bestselling books and TV series.'

'But it's all so ephemeral,' Callie said. 'It could all end at any moment.'

'So could anything,' Sam said. 'Nobody's job is safe these days. Gone are the days of joining a firm when you're sixteen and staying the course until you're pensioned off.'

'I know,' Callie said. 'And I've tried to explain how much I'd hate a normal job and how much I *love* writing, but she doesn't understand it.'

'Is she not a big reader?'

Callie shook her head. 'A few magazines and maybe a paperback novel on holiday, but we never had many books in the house growing up.'

'So how did you end up loving books so much?'

Callie looked thoughtful. 'I'm not sure,' she said honestly, 'but I remember one day in the school library. It was one of those quiet lessons where you're meant to be reading in silence, and I was sitting there looking at all the books on the shelves, thinking that it was the greatest gift in the world to be able to walk up to any of them and choose one, open it up and dive into a brand new world. That seemed like the most amazing privilege to me.'

'It is, isn't it?' Sam said. 'And it's a thrill that never dies. Once you've discovered the great joy of books, it's a journey that will last as long as you live.'

Callie watched as Sam spoke about books. She adored his passion for the written word and felt that she could talk to him for hours.

'You know, I've never really been able to talk to anyone about all this before,' Callie said at last. 'Except my ex-husband, that is, and that was always more about the business side of books. He was my publisher.'

'He was in publishing but never talked to you about books?' Sam said, a quizzical expression on his face.

'Only in terms of work,' she said. 'He had this tunnel vision and very little got in between him and that vision.'

'When I read a good book, I need to tell everyone,' he said.

'Me too!' Callie agreed.

'I guess I'm lucky that my family is as crazy about books as I am. We can talk for hours about what we're reading or what we want to read.'

'That must be nice,' Callie said. 'That's why I joined a book club. I didn't have anyone to talk to about my obsession with reading and writing. But that didn't work out either.'

'Well, let's hope this one gets off the ground for you,' Sam said and Callie smiled.

There was something wonderfully warm and cosy about sitting there with Sam in the bookshop. Even Winston and his dog snoring gently beside them seemed to add something to the ambience. At least, they did until...

'What on *earth?*' Sam suddenly said.

Callie's eyes widened as an appalling smell assaulted her nostrils. She looked at Sam and he looked at her, each wondering where the smell had come from. The answer came a moment later when a gentle rippling sound came from the sleeping dog on the floor.

'Blimey,' Sam said. 'That's actually quite bad, isn't it?'

'I think I need some fresh air!' Callie said and the two of them got up abruptly and left the room, charging through the shop and hurrying out on to the pavement, trying desperately to hold themselves together as the laughter began.

'Oh, god!' Sam cried as soon as the door was closed behind him.

'That was – that was – *awful!*' Callie said, tears of laughter streaming down her face.

'Poor Delilah!' Sam said.

'Poor *Winston!*' Callie said. 'He has to live with that.'

'If, indeed, it was Delilah.'

'You think it might have been Winston?' Callie asked, more tears coursing down her face.

Sam shook his head. 'It was definitely the dog. At least I think it was.'

Callie mopped her eyes with a tissue and tried to calm herself down. 'This isn't quite what I was expecting tonight,' she said.

'How does it compare to your old London book club?' Sam said, laughing again.

'Oh, *much* more entertaining!'

'Then at least we've achieved something,' he said. 'I'm sorry you've had a wasted trip into town.'

'Are you kidding?' Callie said. 'I've had a brilliant time! I wouldn't have missed it for the world.'

Sam grinned. 'Maybe they'll be more people next time,' he said.

'Not if word gets around about Winston's dog.'

They stood there in silence for a moment.

'Listen,' Sam said, 'you probably want to get home, but I was wondering—'

'Yes?'

'Well, I'd be happy to make you another cup of tea and we could talk some more.'

'Okay,' she said. 'I'd like that.'

She followed him back into the shop and they saw a dazed-looking Winston getting up from the sofa.

'What time is it?' he asked, rubbing a hand over his line-creased face.

'Just gone eight,' Sam told him.

'Did I miss anything?' he asked, giving Delilah a little nudge with the toe of his boot.

'Not really,' Sam said.

'I hope this here dog didn't disturb you,' Winston said as Delilah got to her feet at last. 'She has a terrible habit,' he continued and Callie didn't dare catch Sam's eye for fear of laughing. 'Yes, she's a real snorer.'

'Indeed,' Sam said. 'We heard.'

Winston shook his head. 'My dear old gal, aren't you?' He bent to pat the dog's head and then waved a hand. 'Well, cheerio,' he said.

'Hope we'll see you next time,' Sam said, as he and Callie followed him to the front door of the shop.

'If you make sure that Antonia Jessop's here with her cakes, I'll be sure to turn up,' he said.

'That's a deal,' Sam said, opening the door to the tinkle of the bell and closing it behind them.

'There are some pretty special people here in Castle Clare,' Callie said as Sam turned back into the room.

'Winston's a bit special,' he told Callie. 'He's lived in Castle Clare all his life. As have most of the people round here. He lives in a tiny terrace and suffered some dreadful pension scandal which left him high and dry.'

'Oh, no,' Callie said.

'He gets by,' Sam said. 'His son and daughter make sure he's okay and his neighbours look after him too. That's one of the great things about living in a place like this – nobody lets you be lonely or go without. We all keep our eyes open for each other. Towns like Castle Clare are like an extended family.'

'That's really nice,' Callie said and Sam nodded.

'I'll make us some more tea,' he said.

Callie followed him into the back room and let her eyes glide over the bookshelves there whilst she waited.

'Oh, you've got a copy of *Country Diary of an Edwardian Lady*,' she said. 'I love this book!'

'You have a copy?' Sam said, his head popping out of the kitchen where the kettle was now boiling.

'I used to but I think I lent it to someone who didn't return it.'

'Ah,' Sam said. 'That's a cardinal sin as far as I'm concerned.'

'With me too,' Callie said.

'I hope you excommunicated them,' he said in all seriousness, returning to the tea things.

'I got a court injunction on her,' Callie said. 'She was prohibited from coming within half a mile of my books.'

Sam laughed and, a moment later, walked back into the room with the tea and they sat down on the sofa together.

'I loved that book,' Callie said. 'Edith Holden's writing was so vivid and real, and her watercolours were so exquisite.'

'I love how she punctuated her own prose with the poetry of others,' Sam said.

'Me too,' Callie said and she got up from the sofa and took the book from the shelf. 'I'd forgotten how much I loved this book. I'm going to have to buy it from you.'

'Then it's yours. It's my gift to you.'

'Oh, but you've already given me a book. You must let me pay.'

'No, no,' he said. 'See it as a welcome to Suffolk gift.'

'Well, that's very kind of you.' She hugged the book to her like a lost friend and then opened it up to a random page, taking in a glorious painting. 'Now, where is it?' she said, flipping through the pages until she reached October. 'There!' She sat down next to Sam again and showed him the painting of the red toadstools.

'Fly agaric,' he said. 'Stunning but horribly poisonous.'

'Yes,' Callie said, remembering Leo's words about them. 'I saw some out on a walk the other day and I thought of this picture.' Her fingers hovered over it now. 'It's over a hundred years since she painted this, but I was carrying it in my mind just the other day. Isn't that wonderful?'

'A good book lives forever,' he said.

'I sometimes think it's easier to love a book more than a person, don't you think?' she said. 'A book doesn't change – it remains constant and perfect no matter how many times you read it.'

Sam looked at her intently. 'Somebody must have hurt you really badly to make you say that.'

Callie closed her eyes. 'I shouldn't have said that.'

'But you obviously needed to,' Sam said gently. 'Who was it?' he asked. 'Who was it that wasn't constant and perfect in your life? Was it your husband?'

Callie took a deep breath. 'Yes,' she whispered.

Sam nodded. 'I'm very sorry to hear that,' he said.

'But it's all over and done with now,' she said. 'Apart from every time I think of him.' She gave a wry smile.

'Ah, yes. Our memories are fickle friends and will betray us at a moment's notice, won't they?' He looked at her. 'I told you I recently got divorced, didn't I?'

'Yes.' she said. 'I'm sorry.'

'Her name was Emma and we'd been married for six years and I thought we were happy. We had our ups and downs like any couple, but we never had any real worries.' He raked a hand through his dark hair. 'I just think she's one of these people who get bored. Perhaps she wanted some excitement, I really don't know.'

'So, what happened?' Callie asked.

'Well, I was doing a house clearance for a fellow called Terence. He's a banker from London and he'd just inherited this amazing old manor house near Long Melford. Stunning place. Timber framed, inglenook fireplaces, walled garden – the works. But, most importantly, quite a good library. I worked with Terence over the next few months, finding buyers for his books and advising him on the conservation of others he wanted to keep. It was a fantastic time. Customers like him don't come along very often and I revelled in every minute I spent at that place. Anyway, there was one day when I was due to meet him, but I'd just caught a horrible cold. I'd taken one of his old atlases into London to one of my collectors there, but he hadn't wanted it. I wanted to return it to Terence straight away and Emma was going to drive by the manor on her way to work so she took the atlas for me. I thought nothing of it and, when I got better, I went over there myself.'

Callie swallowed hard, dreading what he was about to tell her and yet needing to know too.

'I think it must have been about a week later,' Sam continued, 'and I noticed the change in him. He was suddenly very cagey and couldn't look me in the eye and made all sorts of excuses to wrap up the work I was doing. I had this horrible feeling in the pit of my stomach and I just knew.'

'Oh, Sam,' Callie said.

'I cursed that atlas over the next few weeks but, if it hadn't been the atlas, something else would have caused us to part, I'm sure of that now.'

'I'm so sorry.'

'No need to be,' he said. 'Emma and I should never have happened. You know, she married an antiquarian and then complained that I was bookish?'

Callie's eyebrows rose in bewilderment. 'Really?' A giggle escaped her and Sam joined in.

'Isn't that the most ridiculous thing you've ever heard?' Sam said.

'It's up there, I'll give you that.'

Sam laughed. She liked his laugh, but she could see by the look in his eyes that there was still a lot of pain behind it and that he was most certainly putting on a brave face.

When the shop bell sounded, they exchanged looks.

'Did Winston forget something?' Callie asked.

'I don't think so,' Sam said, looking around as he got up from the sofa.

Callie watched as he walked through to the front room of the shop and then she heard a female voice.

'Hello, Sam.'

'What are you doing here?' he asked.

Callie sat forward on the sofa, wondering who the mysterious woman was.

'That's a nice greeting,' the woman said, her voice heavy with sarcasm.

'And how do you expect me to greet you after you sent your maniac brother round here to steal my books?'

Callie gasped. Who on earth would steal Sam's books?

'That's unfair!' the woman cried.

'How the hell is that unfair?' Sam said. 'He punched me in the gut and had Grandpa Joe on the floor. Did he tell you that – your idiot brother?'

'Don't call him that,' the woman said. 'He was doing what he thought was right.'

'Oh, yes. Like that evening he punched that guy in the pub? You can always count on Aidan Jones to do the right thing.'

Callie was beside herself now, desperate to know who it was Sam was speaking to. It couldn't be his ex-wife, could it? Would she get her brother to steal Sam's books? The idea seemed preposterous.

'Well, it was you who stole my book!'

'Emma, for the last time, I didn't steal your book.'

Callie's eyes widened. It *was* Emma, she thought, and how hard it was for Callie to remain in the back room and not sneak through to get a glimpse of the ex-wife Sam had just been telling her about.

'Then where is it?' Emma demanded, her voice rising.

'How should I know where it is?' Sam said. 'Maybe Terence took it.'

'Oh, yes – you'd just love to blame him for everything, wouldn't you? But he's got more important things to think about than your old books.'

Callie tried not to eavesdrop, she really did, but it was impossible not to hear what they were saying because both their voices were raised.

'A distraction,' she whispered to herself. 'I need a distraction.'

Well, what better place to find a distraction for a book lover than a bookshop, she thought, getting up from the sofa and letting her eyes rove across the titles on display. Something, anything, to take her mind off what was happening in the next room because it was none of her business and she really should do her best not to listen.

Her eyes scanned the shelves of the gardening books. Yes, it would be a good idea to lose herself in a few inspirational gardens for a while. She might even pick up a few ideas for her own cottage garden. Now, to choose a book. There was *The English Cottage Garden* which seemed like a pretty sensible one to begin with; *The Victorian Kitchen Garden* which sounded wonderful too but the one that caught Callie's eye was the amusingly titled *Eat Your Own Weight in Veg*. If she could just reach it. The library steps were in the next room and the tempting tome was just above fingertip level even when Callie was standing on tiptoes.

Cursing her lack of height, Callie reached up again, stretching as far as she could until she had the thick spine safely clutched. Or, she *thought* she had it safely clutched until it slipped out of her hand as the heels of her feet came back down to earth. In one of those moments that seemed to both speed up and slow down at the same time, Callie watched in alarm as the book fell to the floor with a sickeningly loud thud.

Her shoulders hunched up and her eyes squeezed themselves shut. The voices in the next room had definitely stopped. Had they heard her?

'What was that?' Emma asked. 'Is somebody back there?'

They *had* heard her.

'I think it's time for you to leave, Emma.'

'Are you hiding something from me?'

'I'm not hiding anything,' Sam said.

The voices were getting closer. *They* were getting closer.

Callie quickly picked the book up from the floor and was just dusting it down when a slender woman with short auburn hair entered the room. Her face was pretty and her features were as dainty as a pixie, but the look she directed at Callie was anything but pretty and her eyes, although beautiful, had a slightly wild light in them.

Sam was now standing behind her.

'You certainly didn't waste any time,' Emma said, turning to him. 'How long's this been going on?'

'There is nothing going on,' Sam said. 'Not that it would be any of your business even if there was.'

'Got somebody else to dust your books already?' she said with a laugh that sounded like a Disney villainess'. She stared at Callie one last time and then turned and left.

'This isn't over, Sam,' Callie heard Emma say as the bell sounded.

'Oh, it's over,' Sam said, his voice full of fury as he followed her out of the room and slammed the shop door shut.

Callie wondered if she should leave there and then or if Sam would want to talk about what had just happened. Indecision flowed through her and, just as she was picking up her satchel, Sam walked into the room. His colouring was higher than normal and he looked utterly exhausted, as if he'd just run to the coast and back.

'Are you okay?' she asked gently.

'I'm sorry you had to witness that,' he said in a low voice and she watched as he gathered up the mugs and took them through to the kitchen where he proceeded to clatter about noisily. Callie stood clueless for a moment, unsure of what she should do or say and, when Sam didn't say anything, she decided that the evening had come to an abrupt end.

'Listen, I'd better get going,' she said.

Sam looked up briefly from the sink and nodded. 'Yes,' he said, and that was it.

Callie hovered, desperate to say or do something to reach out to him, but she could see that the barriers were up and so she said and did nothing.

Leaving the bookshop and crossing the road, she walked through to Market Square where she'd parked her car. She barely registered the dark country roads as she drove home. Usually, she would have revelled in the fact that it was so all-consumingly dark. She might even have pulled up in a lay-by, unwound her window and sat with the engine off, drinking in the silence, the darkness and the brilliance of the stars in the sky. But not now. She was going straight home where she would drink a big round glass of wine, eat the family-sized packet of crisps that she'd hidden from herself under the stairs and then go straight to bed.

But the evening of indulgence was destined not to be because, as her cottage came into sight, she saw a car was parked outside it. A car she instantly recognised.

'Piers,' she said to herself.

What on earth was he doing there?

# CHAPTER 14

Callie parked her car behind her soon-to-be ex-husband's. The evening had been eventful enough without Piers turning up. What was this, she thought – the night of the exes?

'Where the hell have you been?' Piers demanded as soon as she opened her car door, an angry blast of Beethoven coming from his own car.

'What business is it of yours?' she said. 'I don't owe you an explanation.'

'I was worried about you.'

'Oh, really?' Callie said. 'Piers, you barely noticed me when I shared a house with you as your wife, but you expect me to believe you're worrying about me now that we're getting divorced?'

'Well, it's true.'

'What are you doing here?' She opened her satchel and fished inside for her key.

'Still using that god-awful bag?' he said.

'You didn't answer my question,' she said as she walked up the garden path and opened her front door, turning around to block him from entering.

'Aren't you going to invite me in?'

She gave him a quizzical look. 'Are you joking?'

'But I've driven all this way, Callie.'

'And you'll just have to drive all the way back.'

'Come on,' he said with one of his disarming smiles that had, once upon a time, been able to melt her. 'Don't be like that. I just want to see how you are.'

'Couldn't you have rung?'

'Where's the fun in that?' he said. 'I wanted to see you, Callie. I *needed* to see you.'

She stared at him, wondering what on earth she had done in a previous life to deserve this.

'I suppose you could come in, but just for a few minutes, okay?'

she said reluctantly.

Piers walked into the living room and instantly hit his head on a low beam.

'Holy cow!' he exclaimed. 'You could have warned me!'

'What did you expect walking into an old country cottage?'

He rubbed his head, looking sorry for himself and then he turned around, taking in his surroundings.

'God this place is pokey,' he said.

'It suits me just fine,' Callie said.

'Does it? Does it really?' he said in astonishment.

'Yes,' Callie said, watching anxiously as he stalked about the room, poking his head into the kitchen, examining her bookshelves and looking up the chimney.

Callie had taken her coat off and noticed that Piers had too. He was making himself far too much at home for her liking and she had to nip it in the bud.

It was then that she noticed her answer machine was flashing. Her finger hovered over the play button, wondering if she should leave it until she'd managed to get rid of Piers, but curiosity go the better of her and she hit play, instantly regretting it as the sound of Leo's voice filled the tiny room.

'Hi gorgeous,' he said, instantly turning Callie's face red. 'Just wondering how it's going and if you're up for some fun in the great outdoors sometime? Give me a call, okay? I imagine you're spending all your time hunched over that keyboard, aren't you? I'll have to give you one of my famous massages.' He gave a laugh that sent naughty goose bumps across Callie's skin. 'See you!'

'Who the hell was that?' Piers asked as soon as the message was over, his face ashen.

'Just a friend,' she said, turning away from him quickly.

Piers stared at her as if he was seeing her for the first time in his life. 'A friend you have massages with "in the great outdoors"?' he said in a silly voice.

Callie had to will herself not to laugh at Piers's summation of her relationship with Leo Wildman.

'Well, I hear you have a new woman in your life,' Callie said, 'so why shouldn't I have a new man?'

'Who told you that?' Piers said. 'Was it Heidi? Has she been spying on me?'

'Oh, don't be so melodramatic!' Callie said.

Piers looked affronted as he sat down on Callie's sofa.

'What are you doing?' Callie asked.

'I'm waiting for my wife to offer me a cup of tea.'

'Soon to be ex-wife,' Callie said rolling her eyes. She really didn't want him there and couldn't think why he'd driven all the way out of London to see her. They had nothing to say to each other. They hadn't ever really had very much to say to each other especially towards the end of their marriage. But who was she to deny a cup of tea to somebody she'd once been in love with? So, somewhat reluctantly, she headed into the kitchen.

'And a sandwich would be great too,' Piers called.

It didn't take long for Callie to whip up a quick supper for the pair of them. Taking it through to the living room, she saw that Piers had kicked off his shoes. He'd also cranked up the central heating. Alarm bells went off in Callie's head.

'Don't get too comfortable,' she warned him. 'You're not staying.'

'What do you mean?'

'What do you mean, *what do I mean?* I *mean*, you're not staying.'

His face took on a woebegone look. 'But I really don't want to stay in some dreary provincial bed and breakfast.'

Callie looked at him in horror. 'You planned this, didn't you?'

'What do you mean?' he said in all innocence. 'If you'd been here when I'd arrived instead of gallivanting around—'

'I wasn't gallivanting,' she said. 'I was at our local book club.'

'You've joined a little country book club?'

'Why do you always have to sound so snooty about everything?'

'I don't,' he said.

'Yes you do,' she said. 'You're so critical. You were always looking down your nose at my clothes or my satchel or—'

'God almighty – don't bring up that disgusting old bag of yours again.'

'See!' Callie said. 'Plenty of people like satchels.'

'Yeah, like who? Ageing hippies?'

Callie thought of how Sam had taken an instant shine to her beautiful bag and how she'd adored him for it.

'Why did you come here, Piers? I really don't think we've got anything to say to each other.'

She watched in frustration as he finished the food she'd prepared him before he answered her. Looking up from his plate, he ran his hand through his neat brown hair and focused his green stare on her. There had been a time when he'd been able to bowl her over with those eyes of his and his irrepressible grin, but not anymore.

'Piers?' she prompted him.

'Caroline,' he said, sounding her name softly which instantly put her on edge. 'I think I've might have made a huge mistake.'

'Yes, you shouldn't have come here,' she said.

'You know what I mean,' he said.

She wasn't quite sure what to say because she didn't want to hear what else he might have to say.

'Don't,' she said, getting up from the sofa and taking their plates back through to the kitchen. He followed her.

'Listen,' he said, 'I've been trying to work out what went wrong between us and I know it was probably all my fault, but I want to make up for that now.'

'Are you serious?' She turned around to face him. 'Or is there some hidden camera somewhere recording all this for some warped TV show?'

'Callie! I miss you,' he cried.

'But you never even talked to me. All the times I tried to get us to just talk and you ignored me. You *ignored* me, Piers. Have you any idea what that felt like? I've never been lonelier in my life than when I was married to you. A writer's life is lonely enough, but to be married to somebody who doesn't even talk to them...' Her voice petered out as tears rose in her eyes. She didn't want to go back to that time; she didn't want to think about it ever again.

'I'm so sorry, Callie,' he said. 'But you know what my job's like.'

'Yes, I do,' she said. 'It's always been more important than me, hasn't it?'

'No, never,' he said.

'Don't lie to me,' she said. 'I was there. I should know! You locked yourself away from me for hours – not just physically but emotionally too. We never really connected, did we?'

'How can you say that? We were *married*, for God's sake!'

'No we weren't,' she said. 'Not really.'

He stared at her for a long time, his green eyes seemingly full of sorrow.

'I messed up,' he said, looking down at the floor.

'I thought you were seeing somebody else,' she said.

'I don't care about her,' he said. 'I want you back. Can't we try again, Callie? Come back with me – tonight!'

'Piers! No! We're getting divorced. I've left London. I've got my own place,' she said just in case he hadn't noticed. 'And I'm *happy*.'

'You're seeing somebody, aren't you? That massaging guy.'

'That has nothing to do with how I feel about you,' she told him. 'We just didn't work. You've got to accept that.'

'But what if I can't?'

Callie shook her head. 'We should have had this conversation a long, long time ago.'

'But it's *not* too late,' he told her, grabbing hold of her shoulders.

'It's *much* too late,' she said. 'Do you know how many nights I waited up for you, waiting for you to leave that study of yours and come and talk to me? I was *so* lonely, *so* desperate for your company. And then our baby.' Her voice was barely above a whisper now. 'I can't ever forget how quickly you were able to move on from that, but I wasn't and you weren't there for me, Piers! I felt like I was on my own, fighting my way through that grief without you there to help me.'

'I know that now,' he said, 'but I can make it up to you.'

'You're not listening to me,' she said, getting frustrated. 'I don't *want* you to make it up to me now.'

'But you're still wearing your wedding ring,' he said.

'It's stuck,' she said. 'I've been meaning to get it cut off, but I haven't got round to it.'

A horrible silence hung between them.

'Listen, this is just for tonight, you understand. You're not to make a habit of it. I'll get you a pillow and some blankets,' Callie said at last, her innate kindness winning out over reason. 'You can sleep on the sofa.' She made to leave the room and he grabbed her arm.

'Callie,' he said, 'I'm so sorry.'

She nodded before leaving the room.

When Callie awoke the next morning, the first thought to enter her mind was that something was wrong and it didn't take her long to remember what it was.

'Piers,' she said to herself. He was in her house.

It had taken an age for her to fall asleep the night before as her head had filled with so many sad memories of their past together, and of the things he'd said to her and of the things he'd also never said to her.

She'd found it impossible to switch off as she heard her soon-to-be ex moving around her little cottage, sloshing around in her bathroom upstairs and then cursing as he bumped his head on the living room beam downstairs. She was dreading going downstairs and secretly hoped that he'd have had the good sense to leave early, but he hadn't.

She was just making her way to the bathroom when she heard the sound of rustling pages from her study.

'Piers?' she called from the landing. There was no reply. She tiptoed along the bare floorboards in her slippers, tightening the belt around her dressing gown as she peered into her study.

'PIERS!' she cried as she saw him sitting at her desk, washed and dressed, the printed pages of her new manuscript in his hands.

'Jeepers!' he yelled, physically jumping in the air. 'You scared the hell out of me!'

'What are you doing in here?'

'I was just having a look at this,' he said, holding the pages aloft.

'You've got no right to go poking through my things.'

'But I'm your publisher,' he said, looking puzzled by her anger.

'That doesn't mean you can just barge in here,' she said, doing her best to remain calm when what she really wanted to do was to hit him over the head with her pot of pens.

'I didn't know you were writing something new,' he said, resolutely not moving from her desk.

'Well, of course I'm writing something new. What did you think I was doing – vegetating in the country?'

'I think the beginning needs a bit of work, but it really has something,' he continued.

'Please put it down.'

He shook his head. 'I'm taking this straight back to London with me.'

'Oh, no you're not,' Callie said.

'I need to show it to my assistant. I think she's going to love it.'

'Piers – you're not listening to me. I'm not giving you my new novel. We are *never* going to work together again.'

'Are you crazy?'

'No, I'm perfectly sane. Now please put it down and leave.'

'No,' he said.

'I'm warning you,' she said.

He stood up, the manuscript still in his hands. 'Oh, you're warning me, are you?' he said, his left eyebrow raising as if he was mocking her. The expression tipped Callie over the edge and she lunged forward, but he was too quick for her, holding the printed pages high above his head.

'Give them here!' Callie cried, feeling Piers's hands at her waist. 'What are you doing?' But she knew what he was doing: he was tickling her. 'No – don't!'

'Let me take the book, Callie.'

'Stop it!' she yelled, helpless at his tickling onslaught and feeling herself buckling towards the floor.

'Say yes, Callie!' he said.

'No – never!' She was laughing now, as tears of mirth splashed onto her cheeks. 'Let me go!'

He continued to tickle her but, as he reached out to place the manuscript on her desk, she took advantage and made her escape, pushing him away from her. It didn't have quite the effect she wanted, though, and she watched in horror as he dropped the pages which fell to the floor in completely the wrong order.

'Oh, Piers!' she shouted.

'It was an accident,' he said, laughing at the mess of paper.

Callie stood up, straightening her hair and nightgown. Her heart was racing madly and she felt weak with having laughed so much. They hadn't messed around like that since their very early days together when everything was still light and fun between them and they'd actually spent time together.

She looked at him now as he made a mad scramble to collect all her pages together and put them back into order.

'Leave it,' she said.

'No, I made the mess,' he said. 'I'll tidy it up.'

'Piers,' she said softy and something in her voice caught his attention and he put the pages of the manuscript down on her desk and turned to face her.

'I think it's time you left,' she said.

He stared at her without speaking, his eyes full of sadness at her words. 'We were good together once,' he said.

'Once,' Callie said and he nodded.

'I'll get my things,' he said quietly, placing a hand on her shoulder and bending to kiss her cheek before leaving the room.

Callie didn't follow him downstairs. Instead, she watched from the window of her study as he got into his car, her heart breaking all over again as a little piece of her past drove away with him.

# CHAPTER 15

It was Sunday and early morning clouds had parted to reveal a pearly blue sky. The days were getting noticeably shorter now and the country footpaths were slowly being engulfed by mud, but Leo had persuaded Callie that there was still lots to see in the great outdoors and so she'd donned her wellies and the two of them had walked across the green at Newton St Clare and taken a footpath into the wood which was a blaze of coppery colour.

Truffle and Blewit ran ahead along the path, sticking their noses into the piles of leaves that littered the floor of the wood, making a magical carpet of bright colour.

'Aren't you glad you came out?' Leo said.

'I am,' Callie said with a laugh.

'You writers would happily spend all day cooped up indoors,' he said, shaking his head. 'I don't know how you can do it. It would drive me mad.'

'But I like it,' she said.

'And you'll like it even more later for having been outside now.'

'I know,' she said, taking in a deep breath of clear, crisp air and feeling all the better for it.

How quickly she and Leo had got into an easy routine of meeting up and going out. They still hadn't done anything more formal than having a pub lunch together, but Callie enjoyed that and she liked seeing Leo in his natural environment. There was something wonderfully attractive about how well-suited he was to the fields and the woods. Looking at him now as he watched over his beloved spaniels, she couldn't help but wonder what it would be like to be in a long-term relationship with him.

*But that's not what you want*, a little voice inside her said and she nodded to herself because any sort of relationship was the very last thing on her mind. Yet, as she looked at the handsome man with the weather-beaten face and a huge smile, she couldn't help imagining a possible future with him. That was the curse of being a writer, she thought. One's imagination always ran away, and how easy it was to imagine what a life with Leo would be like, with a lifetime of walks to beautiful places to look forward to, of bonfires, foraging and camping out under the stars. She could almost hear the children too. She was sure there would be at least half a dozen little Leos and Leonoras, and how much fun would that be? It would be a wonderfully chaotic, noisy existence with never a dull moment.

Don't go there, the little voice said. Remember what happened when that imagination of yours started after meeting Piers? And look where that got you.

Callie was still feeling pretty shaken by Piers's surprise visit and she was still trying to process her feelings about Sam too, and the strange encounter she'd had with his wife, Emma. It was all much more than she'd bargained for when she'd chosen to escape to Suffolk.

'You okay?' Leo suddenly said, breaking into her thoughts. 'You look all serious.' He cocked his head to one side in that adorable way of his and she thought of how much she could scare him if she confessed to what she'd been thinking about.

'I'm fine,' she said. 'Just thinking too much.'

'That'll *never* do you any good,' he said.

She laughed, knowing he was right and that the best things to ever happen were often spontaneous, light and fun. And that was the reason she was with Leo now, she reminded herself. This wasn't meant to be getting all heavy and serious. It was meant to be a wonderful, carefree fling.

They continued walking, climbing over a stile which the dogs jumped through and following a little brook until they were in the very centre of the wood.

'You've got a beech leaf in your hair,' Leo told Callie.

Callie's hands flew up to her hair. 'Where?' she asked, tipping her head forward.

'Just there,' Leo said as half a dozen leaves cascaded down on her from above.

'What?' Callie cried, looking up.

'You're covered in them,' Leo said.

'Did you just–' she asked, but stopped as she saw him bending down to scoop an armful of bright leaves from the floor of the wood.

'Absolutely covered in them,' he said as he dropped the leaves on top of her.

'LEO!' she shouted.

He laughed.

'Right!' she said. 'This is war!'

If anybody else had been walking in the wood that morning and heard the noise that Callie and Leo were making, they wouldn't have believed that it wasn't a couple of children playing as armfuls of leaves were gathered up and thrown at one another. The spaniels thought it was a brilliant game and did their best to get involved, barking loudly and running around in circles until Callie begged for mercy.

'You are totally crazy, you know that?' Callie said, completely out of breath.

'Only about you,' he said, moving closer to her.

Oh, dear, she thought. Things had gone back to being serious again.

'I think we'd better head back,' she said.

'Callie!' he said, taking hold of her hand. 'I really like you.'

'I know,' she said, 'and I really like you too.'

'So, we're two people who really like each other,' he said. 'That's good, isn't it?' He held her gaze and the intensity of the moment made her breathe all the harder. His hand reached up and stroked her hair. It was a gesture she hadn't expected and she flinched.

'Leo,' she said softly. 'I'm not ready.'

He continued to stroke her hair gently. 'It's okay,' he said.

'Is it?'

He nodded. 'Whatever this is, I'm happy with it.'

'You are?'

He grinned. 'You're such a worrier, aren't you?'

She nodded. 'I have a lot to worry about,' she said.

'Well, there's no need to with me,' he said. 'I like being with you. I'm not thinking about anything more than what we have right now because it's good. It's *really* good. Isn't it?'

She looked into his bright eyes, seeing their joy and warmth. 'Yes,' she said.

'Come on,' he said. 'I don't know about you, but walking always gives me a good appetite.'

She loved how he was always hungry – for food and for life. He simply gobbled it all up, living very much in the present and not ever worrying about the future. Callie knew that she would do well to learn by that.

As they emerged from the woods and headed across the village green back towards Owl Cottage, Leo began to laugh.

'You've still got a leaf in your hair,' he said.

'Have I?' Callie said, stopping as he removed it and handed it to her. She looked at the bright chestnut colour of the leaf and smiled at its beauty before putting it in her pocket. She would place it in a book and keep it as a memory of this day with Leo.

He whistled loudly for Truffle and Blewit as they approached the main road through Newton St Clare and the two dogs came nicely to walk by his heels.

'Looks like somebody's having car problems,' Leo said as they saw an old Volvo that had broken down outside Callie's cottage. A dark-haired man in a tweed jacket was getting out and he didn't look happy.

'Sam?' Callie said.

'You know him?' Leo said.

'It's Sam from the bookshop in Castle Clare,' she said, her speed picking up. 'Hey!'

'Callie?' Sam looked up.

'Are you okay?' she asked.

'I'm fine,' he said, 'but I think my car might have finally died.'

'Oh, dear,' she said. Leo joined her. 'Sam – this is Leo. Leo – Sam.'

Leo held out a hand and Sam shook it, a guarded look in his eyes.

'Can I help? Do you need a lift somewhere?' Callie asked Sam.

'I was just on my way to my parents' house. It's kind of tradition on Sunday. The whole family gets together for lunch.'

'That's nice,' Callie said, never having experienced such a thing herself. 'Can I give you a lift then?'

'Oh, no,' he said. 'I can ring home. Someone will come and pick me up.'

'It's no bother. This is my car right here,' she said, 'and my home.' She pointed to Owl Cottage.

'Well, if you're sure I'm not interrupting anything,' he said.

'You're not,' Callie said. 'Come on.' It was then that Callie remembered something. 'Oh, Leo!'

'It's okay,' he said, raising his hands as if in defeat. 'I'll catch you later, okay?'

Callie nodded, wondering for a brief moment if he was about to lean forward to kiss her goodbye and how she'd feel about that in front of Sam. But he didn't. He merely turned, whistled for his dogs again, and headed off across the green.

Eleanor Nightingale was watching her husband. It was one of her favourite things to do even after thirty-seven years of marriage, and even though he was doing nothing more interesting than raking up leaves in the garden. Even at this dreary time of year, he'd find a dozen little jobs to do out there whether it was washing out terracotta pots in preparation for planting in the new season, pruning the fruit trees in the orchard or aerating the lawn with his trusty old fork. The last week had been filled with cold mists and bitter winds, but a pair of thick socks, a woolly cap and the scarf Nell had knitted for him at least twenty years ago, and he was ready for anything.

She loved watching him out there and could never make her mind up if he looked more at home in his favourite armchair with a good book or out in the garden waist deep in plants. But one thing was for sure – it was time for him to come back inside.

She opened the French windows of the dining room and called across the lawn to him.

'Frank!'

He looked up, leaning on his rake and waving a hand in acknowledgement.

'Time to clean up,' she called, knowing it would take him at least ten minutes to actually make it indoors because he would spot all sorts of little jobs to do as he headed back.

Eleanor returned to the kitchen, a long light room at the back of the house, permanently warm from the heat of the shiny red Aga above which hung an old-fashioned clothes wrack. It was a wonderful treat in winter to come downstairs on a cold frosty morning and retrieve a pair of Aga-warmed socks. Now, there was a family-sized roast cooking for the Sunday lunch that Eleanor looked forward to all week. Frank had pulled up a couple of winter cabbages in honour of the occasion and the potatoes had come from the storeroom, dug up from their vegetable plot earlier in the year.

She looked in the Aga now, a blast of warmth greeting her. Everything looked perfect, she thought, closing the door and busying herself with a heap of linen napkins, folding them and placing them in a neat pile to take through to the dining room.

She then checked the fridge. There were a couple of bottles of nice white wine for her, Frank, Nell and Joe and anybody else who wasn't driving. There was elderflower cordial for Polly and a bottle of something fizzy and disgusting for her grandson, Archie. Well, he did only have fizz once a week, Polly had assured her mother.

At last, Frank made his way to the back door.

'Boots!' Eleanor cried as he entered the kitchen. 'I just wiped the floor down this morning.'

'I know,' he said. 'Boy, it's cold out there today. Wouldn't be surprised if we have a good frost tonight.' He took his thick winter coat and hat off and hung them up in the adjacent cloakroom where he then washed his great gardener's hands in the butler sink. 'You okay?' he asked as he came back into the kitchen.

'I'm worried,' Eleanor confessed.

'Who are you worried about?' Frank asked, knowing that it was usually a *who* and not a *what* that worried his wife. 'Which child's in trouble now?'

'All of them,' she said.

'*All* of them are in trouble?' Frank said, his eyebrows shooting northwards.

'No!' she said, batting him with the back of her hand. 'I'm just *worried* about all of them.'

'Well, there's nothing out of the ordinary in that, is there?' he said as he took a glass from a cupboard. 'Too early to crack open the wine?'

Eleanor nodded. 'Grandpa Joe still seems out of sorts, don't you think?'

'You mean after that business with Aidan?'

'Sam should have called the police.'

'That wouldn't have solved anything,' Frank told her.

'You're so alike, you two,' she said, shaking her head.

'If that means we prefer peace to chaos then – yes – we are alike.'

'Well, I think that man should have been arrested,' Eleanor said. 'When I think what might have happened to your father.'

'But it didn't,' Frank said.

'But it *might* have!' Eleanor said.

'You worry too much,' he said. 'You always have. I don't know how we've managed to raise five children and keep you sane with the way you worry about them all.'

'I'm their mother – it's my job to worry about them.'

'Not when they're grown up with homes and families of their own.'

Eleanor shook her head. 'But I can't help it,' she said. 'I seem to be worrying about them even more these days.'

Frank put his glass down and walked across the room towards her, taking her face in his hands.

'My goodness, you're cold,' she said.

'And you're warm,' he told her. 'Give me a kiss.'

'Frank! The children could come in at any moment.'

'Well?' he said. 'They know we kiss. If we didn't, none of them would exist!'

That made her smile and she allowed herself to be kissed.

'There,' he said. 'All better now?'

'Not really,' she said. 'I've been thinking about Polly. She's so sad and withdrawn these days. I can't remember the last time I heard her laugh.'

'She's all right,' Frank said. 'I've never known anyone who can cope with catastrophe as well as our Polly. She's a born survivor.'

'I'm not so sure,' Eleanor said. 'I keep trying to get her to talk to me, but she always brushes things aside and tells me she's all right.'

'Then she probably *is* all right,' Frank said.

Eleanor sighed, unconvinced. 'And Bryony's been on some awful dating website. You can meet all sorts of loons on those places.'

'Then let her meet them,' he said. 'She knows how to deal with loons. She grew up in a house full of them.'

'And as for Sam and the business with Emma and Aidan–'

'Darling,' Frank said, placing his hands on her shoulders, 'you simply can't worry about everyone. There aren't enough hours in the day.'

'And I don't even want to start worrying about Nell,' Eleanor said.

'What's wrong with her?' Frank asked.

'You must have noticed, Frank,' Eleanor said. 'She's getting more forgetful by the day.'

'Is she?'

As if on cue, Frank's mother walked into the kitchen. 'What's for lunch?' she asked.

'A roast, Mum,' Frank told her. 'It's Sunday.'

'Is it?' she asked, a pretty smile lighting her face as she turned around and shuffled back out.

'See what I mean?' Eleanor said.

'It's easy enough to forget what day of the week it is,' Frank said. 'I do it all the time since retiring from the bookshop.'

'Yes but–'

'We'll keep an eye on her,' he said. 'Now stop worrying for one minute and let's get at least one bottle of wine open.'

Eleanor smiled. It was impossible to stop worrying about everyone, of course, but wine always had a wonderfully calming effect, didn't it?

'I'll just change out of my boots,' Callie told Sam. 'Come on in.' She opened her garden gate, took her key out of her pocket and opened the door.

'Funny you should break down outside my cottage,' she said. 'I mean, not *funny* funny – obviously.'

'It was very lucky that I did,' he said, walking into her home behind her. 'I was just collecting some books from a woman over in Monk's Green.'

'Oh, that's where Leo lives,' Callie said, noticing that Sam frowned at this titbit of information.

'Anyway,' he said, 'it's very kind of you to help me out.'

'It's no bother. I'm happy to help,' she told him as she climbed out of her wellies. 'Welcome to Owl Cottage by the way.'

'Thank you. It's lovely,' he said. 'Just the sort of place I imagined you in.'

'Really?'

He nodded. 'Full of character.'

'And books.'

'Of course,' he said. 'I would expect no less.' He cast his eyes over the many cases and shelves.

'I've got heaps more upstairs,' she said. 'I really must have a sort out some time.'

'You mean, throw some away?'

Callie winced. 'When you say it like that, I know I'll just back down and keep absolutely everything.'

'I had to have a bit of a clear out after Emma and I separated and

I moved into the flat above the shop.'

'That must have been hard,' Callie said.

'Not really. The books became part of my stock.'

'A definite advantage to owning a bookshop,' Callie said.

'But the really wonderful thing about parting with books is that it makes room in your life for new books.'

Callie nodded as she put on a pair of shoes. 'The collecting of books never really stops, does it? Your collection might change over the years when you swap a few titles here and there, but a real book lover – a person who can't ever walk by a bookshop without popping in and browsing – can never stop adding new titles to that collection.'

Sam nodded and their eyes met. 'I agree.'

'It's one of the great pleasures in life, isn't it?'

'Indeed.'

'Perhaps the greatest,' she said.

He frowned very slightly and looked as if he was about to say something but she beat him to it.

'Right,' she said. 'Ready to go?'

# CHAPTER 16

'Listen,' Sam said as they left the cottage. 'I hope I wasn't interrupting anything. I hate to bother anyone, especially at Sunday lunchtime.'

'You weren't interrupting anything,' she said.

Sam cleared his throat and Callie could tell what was coming. 'Is he your–'

'Friend,' Callie interrupted. 'Leo's a good friend.'

Sam nodded. 'Not that it's any of my business but I'm glad you're making friends.'

They got into her car.

'Right, you'd better tell me where we're going'

'As if you're heading into Castle Clare only take a left by the junction at Castle Park.'

Callie nodded and they started the short journey.

'So, you always have lunch with your family every Sunday?' Callie asked.

'Oh, yes,' Sam said. 'It's a family tradition that Mum insists upon although my youngest sister, Lara, is away at university and she can't always make it home for Sunday lunch. There have been times in all our lives when we've been travelling or had commitments which meant we couldn't get home but, for the most part, there are ten members of the Nightingale family around that table every Sunday.'

'*Ten* members?'

'I'm one of five,' Sam explained. 'You've met Josh and Polly. Then there's Mum and Dad, Grandpa Joe whom you met in the shop, and his wife, Grandma Nell, and young Archie, Polly's son. Then Bryony and Lara.'

'That's a big family,' Callie said. 'It must be nice to belong to a big family.'

'It's noisy,' Sam said with a grin. 'Noisy and meddlesome. Everybody knows your business *all* the time.'

Callie laughed.

'But there's a comfort in that too because you know that, no matter what happens to you, no matter what life throws at you, there'll be a circle of people who care about you around that table every single week.'

'Wow,' Callie said. 'That's really special.' For a moment, she tried hard to imagine what it must be like. She'd often written about large families in her stories and it was probably a sort of wish fulfilment because, growing up as an only child with parents who seemed constantly baffled by her presence, she'd often longed for siblings or cousins to talk to and play with. And what would it be like now, she wondered, having brothers and sisters she could turn to? Would it have made a huge difference when she was struggling to cope with her miscarriage – when she knew for sure that her marriage to Piers was over? Would picking up the phone to a brother or talking things through with a sister have made the pain ebb away that little bit faster?

'Left here,' Sam said, breaking into Callie's thoughts as she realised they'd arrived at the turn off for Castle Clare.

She took the unfamiliar road out of the town which soon became a country lane as the neat Victorian terraces were replaced by detached cottages and large country houses.

'Listen,' Sam said as they took a bend in the road near a pretty flint and brick church. 'I wanted to apologise for the other evening.'

'There's nothing to apologise for,' she assured him.

'But there is,' he said. 'I was rude. I think I was a bit shaken after seeing Emma.'

'You don't have to explain,' she told him.

'Well, that's kind of you, but I feel really bad about it. I shouldn't have let her spoil that evening. I was having a great time.'

'Me too,' Callie said.

'I hope you'll give it another go sometime,' he said.

'Of course I will!' she said. 'You can't get rid of me that easily. In fact, the only thing that would really put me off would be a room full of Delilahs. I'm not sure my system could cope with that.'

Sam laughed. 'Oh, man! Someone will have to tell Winston about that.'

'I think that someone might be *you*,' she told him.

'Oh, no!' he said with a groan.

'Well, you don't expect *me* to do it, do you?'

'You were a valuable witness,' Sam pointed out.

'I'm having nothing to do with it!' she said with a laugh.

Sam shook his head. 'I think it may be something we have to endure. 'Oh, turn right here.'

The country lane they turned into was surrounded by the sort of lushly green, undulating fields which made England the envy of the world. Tall hedgerows gave way to panoramic vistas that made Callie want to park the car and just drink it all in.

'Left after the post box,' Sam said, nodding to a little red post box that was almost completely screened from view by ivy.

'The driveway here?'

'Yes.'

Callie slowed the car down, turning into a neat driveway whose long wooden gate had been left open. There were already several cars parked there.

'Here we are,' Sam said. 'Campion House.'

Callie gasped as she got her first view of the grand Georgian facade of Campion House.

'You grew up here?' she asked.

'This is the family home.'

Again, Callie experienced a pang of envy as she thought about her own childhood and how many different homes she'd known. Her mother liked to move house and Callie must have lived in at least five growing up, so the idea of having a family home that one could come back to was a completely alien concept to her.

'It's beautiful,' she said, looking at the great sash windows which were at once imposing and yet friendly with their chintzy curtains and pots of geraniums on the windowsills.

'You'll have to come in for lunch,' Sam said, turning to her.

'Oh, I couldn't possibly.'

'There's always plenty,' Sam said. 'Mum makes masses of food and then sends us all home with doggy bags.'

'I don't want to impose,' she said.

'But I imposed on you,' Sam said, giving her a little grin.

'No you didn't,' she said.

'Please – come on in.'

Callie was just about to say no again when the front door was opened and a beautiful woman with long dark hair worn loose approached the car.

'You've been spotted,' Sam warned her as he got out of the car. 'There'll be no getting away now.'

'There you are!' the woman said, walking across the driveway with a couple of dogs in tow. 'We were getting worried about you.'

'Hi, Mum,' Sam said, giving her pale cheek a kiss. 'I had a spot of trouble with the car.'

'And this kind lady gave you a lift?'

'Mum, this is Callie.'

Callie got out of the car. 'Hello, Mrs Nightingale.'

'Eleanor,' she said. 'Call me Eleanor. And it's lovely to meet you, Callie. I take it you're joining us for lunch?'

'Oh, well, I–'

'I've already asked her to,' Sam said.

'I should hope so,' Eleanor said.

'That's very kind,' Callie said, 'but I wouldn't want to–'

'There's always plenty to eat,' Eleanor said, ushering her into the house.

Callie's eyes widened as she took in the homely splendour of Campion House. It was a house full of books, lamps and comfortable chairs in which to read, and Callie instantly fell in love with it even though she felt a little nervous about joining them for lunch unannounced.

'A real family home,' she whispered to herself.

'What's that, my dear?' Eleanor asked.

'It's a beautiful home,' she said.

'We've been very happy here,' Eleanor said. 'Although it's been a lot of work over the years. It was a bit of a shell when we first moved in. Took years to make it truly ours.'

'Well, it's lovely.'

'Thank you,' Eleanor said, taking Callie's coat as she took it off. 'So you're the writer?'

'Yes,' Callie said.

'And you've just moved to Suffolk?'

Callie cleared her throat, wondering just how much Eleanor Nightingale knew about her already.

'That's right,' she said.

'And you're happy here, I hope?'

'Oh, I love it,' Callie said. 'I can't imagine living anywhere else now.'

'Suffolk has that effect on you,' Eleanor said. 'Once you've discovered how lovely it is, it's impossible to leave. Now, let me introduce you to everyone. You've already met Hardy and Brontë.'

'Have I?' Callie said.

'She means the dogs,' Sam said. 'Hardy's the black and white pointer and Brontë's the liver and white spaniel.'

'Oh, I see,' Callie said, wondering where the dogs had disappeared to.

'So, the rest of the family,' Eleanor said.

'Get ready for the onslaught,' Sam whispered from behind her and Callie felt her body spike with nerves as she was led through to the living room. It was an elegant room at the front of the house, the large sash window letting in plenty of autumn light. The far wall was lined with a floor to ceiling bookcase and there were beautiful oil paintings of local landscapes on the other walls. There were two huge sofas covered in heaps of cushions and a richly-coloured rug gave the room a warm feel.

Callie immediately recognised Polly from having met her in Sam's shop.

'Hello,' Polly said with a warm smile. Her dark hair was scraped back away from her face and she was sitting on one of the sofas next to a young boy. 'This is Archie. Say hello to Callie, Archie.'

The big-eyed boy looked up from the book he was reading. 'Hello,' he said with a goofy grin.

'What are you reading?' Callie asked.

'Perry's Planet,' he said.

'It's good, isn't it?'

'Have you read it?' he asked.

'I have,' she said, 'and I know the writer.'

'Really?' Archie said, his mouth dropping open as he looked to his mother to either confirm or debunk Callie's statement.

'Callie's a writer too,' Polly said.

'Cool!' Archie said in awe.

'Although my books are mainly aimed at girls,' she confessed.

'Why?' he asked her with the unnerving directness of the young.

'Erm–' Callie went blank for a moment. 'Perhaps because I was a little girl once.'

'Oh,' Archie said. 'Well, boys are better.'

Callie laughed. 'I'll bear that in mind when I'm writing my next book.'

Next to Polly and Archie on the sofa was Josh whom Callie had met in the shop next door to Sam's.

'Hi Callie,' he said, getting up and shaking her hand. 'How are you getting on with that Roger Deakin book?'

'Very well,' she said. 'Beautiful prose. Puts my own to shame,' she said. 'That's the curse of a good book, I'm afraid. It either inspires you with its greatness or intimidates you into believing that you'll never write decent word yourself again.'

'Well, let's hope for more inspiration than intimidation,' Josh said.

'Callie,' Sam said, 'let me introduce you to our grandmother, Nell.'

Callie turned to see an elderly lady with a pretty round face and masses of curly white hair.

'Grandma, this is my friend Callie.'

'Pleased to meet you,' Callie said, bending to shake the old lady's hand.

'Have we met before?' Nell asked, looking confused.

'No, Grandma,' Sam said. 'Callie's just moved to Suffolk.'

Nell nodded, but she still looked confused.

'And this is my dad,' Sam said, as a large man strode into the room, clapping his great hands together.

'Your mother tells me we have a guest!' he said. 'Very pleased to meet you, young lady. I'm Frank.'

'Good to meet you too,' Callie said, shaking hands.

It was then that Grandpa Joe entered the room, clocking Callie immediately.

'You made it!' he said.

'But I wasn't expected,' Callie said in confusion.

'You'd have found your way here eventually,' he said.

'Take no notice of him,' Sam said. 'I've only to mention a woman's name once and he's got my whole future mapped out.' He shook his head. 'Callie gave me a lift, Grandpa. My car broke down in her village.'

'Oh, yes,' he said, stroking his chin. 'I think that happened to my car once when I was trying to date your grandma.'

Sam rolled his eyes. 'I apologise on behalf of my grandfather,' he said.

Callie just laughed.

'Where's Bry?' Sam asked.

'On her way,' Frank said.

'Isn't that her now?' Josh asked from the sofa as a screech of tyres was heard on the gravel driveway outside.

'Auntie Bryony!' Archie shouted, dropping his book and leaping up from the sofa to run to the front door.

'Be careful with your book!' Eleanor cried as she came into the room. 'Honestly, you'd think he'd know better growing up in family of booksellers.'

'I'll do that,' Polly said, getting up from the sofa to retrieve the discarded book just as Eleanor bent to pick it up. 'Archie always turns completely wild whenever Bryony's around. She's a very bad influence on him.' This was said with a fond smile and Callie began to look forward to the aunt who could inspire such rebellion.

'I'm here everyone!' a singing voice called from the hallway a moment later as the front door was opened. 'Hello Archie!'

'Auntie Bryony – Uncle Sam's brought a writer with him.'

'Really?'

'Come and meet her. She's nice even though she only writes books for girls,' Callie heard Archie say.

A moment later, Archie appeared back in the room having dragged his aunt by the hand so that she wouldn't hold things up.

'CALLIE LOGAN!' Bryony cried as soon as she laid eyes on her.

Josh roared with laughter.

'Have we met?' Callie said, quite sure that they hadn't.

'No, but I've just been having a look at your website,' Bryony said, her big brown eyes wide with excitement. 'Sam mentioned you'd been into his shop and I was so jealous. He's been keeping you all to himself!'

'Don't be so melodramatic, Bry,' Sam said.

'I thought I was destined *never* to meet you!' Bryony said. 'Sam met you, then Josh and Polly.'

'*I* met her before you too,' Archie said with a grin.

'That's right!' Bryony said, coming forward to shake Callie's hand. 'I think everybody in the whole world has met you before me and that really isn't fair at all.'

'It's great to meet you,' Callie said, smiling at the wall of enthusiasm she was greeted by.

'Why haven't you come to my shop yet?' Bryony continued without, it seemed, drawing a single breath.

'Don't hassle her,' Sam said.

'I'm not,' Bryony said. 'Am I hassling you?'

'No, of course not,' Callie said.

'See, Sam?'

'Well, she's not likely to admit that you are, is she?' Sam said.

'Oh, he's such a bore. Let's go somewhere nice and quiet – just the two of us – so we can talk all about setting up a book signing for you.'

'Leave her alone,' Sam told his sister, his voice sterner this time.

'But she must!' Bryony said to her brother before turning back to Callie. 'You simply *must*! You can't be a writer living near Castle Clare and not do a book signing. You know about our festival, don't you?'

'I've heard of it, yes,' Callie said, wondering how on earth she was going to get out this pickle. 'But I–'

'We'll arrange everything for you,' Bryony went on in her bulldozing manner. 'All you need to do is to turn up and be your brilliant self. We'll have children and parents queuing right around Market Square to meet you, I'm sure of it. It'll be the best event ever!'

Callie swallowed hard. Avoiding public events such as this had been one of the reasons why she'd chosen in Suffolk as her new home.

'Bryony,' her mother said in a warning tone. 'Now, if everyone's here, let's eat.'

'At last,' Josh said, getting up from the sofa and clapping his hands together.

'At last!' Archie echoed, receiving a ruffle of his already tousled hair from his uncle.

'This way,' Sam said, escorting Callie into the dining room.

Callie gasped. 'A real dining room!' she said.

'Of course,' he said, smiling at her bemusement.

'I mean – a real dining room that's used as a dining room.'

He gave her an enquiring look.

'My mother never used her dining room. At least not for family meals. It was always *for best*, she used to say.'

'Like Christmas and birthdays?' Sam asked.

'No,' Callie said. 'For visitors. Only we never really had any.'

'Sit next to me!' Bryony said, interrupting her.

'Callie is Sam's guest,' Eleanor said. 'She wouldn't get a chance to eat a single mouthful if she sat next to you.'

155

Bryony looked much put out by this and Callie was ushered to a chair in between Sam and Eleanor.

Sitting down, she admired the beauty of the table with its pretty plates, silver cutlery and glassware. Three small glass vases filled with colourful dahlias graced the middle of the table and beautiful linen napkins lay beside each place setting. It was all wonderfully elegant, but there was an informality about it too because of the happy faces around the table. This was not the sort of stuffy family gathering which would make a stranger feel ill at ease; it was just a regular Sunday lunch and Callie was looking forward to it immensely.

'This is a lovely surprise,' she told Eleanor who was sitting to her right.

'And for us too,' Eleanor said as Frank made a start carving the roast and everyone else passed dishes of potatoes, parsnips, carrots, cabbage and peas up and down the length of the table. 'Do you have family close by?' Eleanor asked.

'No,' Callie said. 'They live in Oxfordshire.'

'What do they think of your new home?' Frank asked her.

'They've not seen it yet,' Callie confessed.

'How long have you been there?' Polly asked.

'Since September.'

There was a stunned silence around the table.

'Don't worry,' Callie said, 'that's normal. They never saw either of my homes in London either.'

'Why not?' Bryony asked.

'Bryony – that's none of our business,' Eleanor said.

'No, it's okay,' Callie said. 'It's just–' she paused. What exactly was she going to say? How could she explain to this large, happy family that her own was so small and antisocial? She'd been faced with that situation many times in the past whenever people asked her what she was doing for Christmas and she'd have to try and explain that she didn't really have a home to go to because she was never invited. 'They – erm – they're not really–'

'Callie,' Sam interrupted, laying a hand on hers, 'don't be bullied by my family. They're horribly nosy.'

'Yes, everyone,' Frank said from the head of the table. 'Respect the fact that we have a guest today and pipe down a bit.' He said this with an indulgent smile at his tribe.

'It's okay,' Callie said. 'I don't mind – really – but there's not much to tell, that's all. My family is small. There's just me, in fact. And my parents...' she faltered again, 'they – they don't see me much.'

Bryony frowned and exchanged a puzzled look with Polly, whilst Josh's eyebrows rose and Grandpa Joe looked deeply concerned.

'They don't see you much?' Grandpa Joe barked from the far end of the table.

'That's right,' Callie said.

'What did she say?' Grandma Nell asked her husband.

'She said she doesn't see her family much,' Grandpa Joe said.

'That's nice, dear,' Nell said, and there was a chorus of light chuckles from around the table. Even Callie managed a little smile.

'I envy you all,' she said. 'I really do. I can't think of any families that get along together let alone see each other every week. You're really lucky.'

'That's sweet of you,' Eleanor said.

'I can't imagine us all not seeing each other,' Bryony said from across the table. 'It's weird enough when Lara's away. But there's always a good group of us here each week.'

Callie nodded, secretly wondering if Sam's ex-wife, Emma, had been a part of the Sunday gatherings and what they thought of her absence now. Did they talk about such things? They seemed a fairly open bunch. Then something else occurred to her: Polly had a son but no partner. What was the story there, she wondered? And had Bryony and Josh ever been involved with anyone? It was all so fascinating and something she'd missed out on being an only child. What would it be like to have brothers and sisters, she thought? And to be an auntie too?

'Have you heard from Lara?' Polly asked her mother.

Eleanor took a sip of wine and nodded. 'She's struggling with an essay on *Hamlet*.'

'Ah, the Dane!' Grandpa Joe said dramatically. "O, that this too too sullied flesh would melt, thaw and resolve itself into a dew."'

'That's disgusting!' Bryony said.

Archie giggled.

'That's the Bard,' Grandpa Joe said, and then he began again, holding his knife aloft, "*Frailty, thy name is woman!*"'

'Grandpa, *really!*' Polly cried as Archie dropped a forkful of peas into his lap as he giggled again.

Grandpa Joe sighed. 'Ah, I should have treaded the boards!'

'What boards, Grandpa?' Archie asked.

'The theatre, my boy!'

'You really wanted to be an actor?' Josh asked.

Grandpa Joe chewed thoughtfully on a roast parsnip. 'At one time, acting was my whole life. I lived and breathed it, playing all the great roles.'

'Really?' Josh said.

'So what happened?' Bryony asked.

'I left school and got a proper job.'

'Oh, Grandpa!' Bryony said with a laugh. 'You only acted in school?'

He gave a little chuckle.

'I don't know about that,' Frank said from the other side of the table. 'He's certainly been acting up ever since.'

Grandpa Joe shook his head. 'Underappreciated,' he said. 'There is nothing worse than being underappreciated by one's own family.'

'I still appreciate you,' Grandma Nell said, giving his hand a little squeeze, 'even after all these years.'

'Good grief!' Josh complained. 'Not whilst we're eating!'

Everybody laughed.

The lunch continued with much banter. Callie was so enjoying it all, hearing all the stories from each of the Nightingales – stories about the books that had come into stock that week, the customers they'd met as well as everyday things like why Bryony's radiators were still making really rude noises.

When Eleanor was absolutely sure that nobody could manage yet another roast potato, Polly and Josh got up from the table to clear the plates away.

'I'll get the dessert,' she said.

'Polly's made two apple tarts,' Sam told Callie. 'They're to die for.'

'Can I help with anything?' Callie asked.

'Absolutely not,' Frank said. 'You're our guest.'

'You can help the next time you come,' Bryony said. 'You'll be given a great big list of chores then!'

Callie didn't know if she was joking or not, but she smiled politely, knowing that it would be unlikely for her to be invited again.

Sam was right about Polly's apple tart. It was delicious, especially as it was served with rich local cream. Callie particularly loved the fact that Polly had made two large tarts so that everybody could have seconds.

'It's expected,' Sam told her with a grin.

Tea and coffee followed in the living room where Grandma Nell promptly fell asleep with a crocheted blanket over her knee, and where Josh was trying to teach young Archie the finer points of chess.

'You'll wow the girls at school if you can master this game,' Josh told him.

Bryony frowned. 'Wow the girls with *chess?*' she said in undisguised horror.

'I don't like girls,' Archie said.

'You will,' Grandpa Joe said.

'And girls love a man who can use his skill on the chess board,' Josh said, moving his knight into an intimidating position.

'Are you sure about that?' Bryony said.

'Always worked for me,' Josh said.

'Really? I'm learning something new about my brother today.'

'I used to teach all the cute girls how to play,' Josh said.

'Are we still talking about chess?' Sam asked, winking at his sisters.

'Now, I'm not saying that they were all one hundred per cent interested in how to play the game,' Josh said,' but it yielded me one or two kisses.'

'Yeah,' Bryony said, 'they were all so bored, they knew the only way they could get you to stop wittering on was to kiss you!'

Everyone laughed.

'Can I read my book now, Uncle Josh?' Archie said.

Josh rolled his eyes. 'If you must,' he said.

'Never discourage a bookworm,' Grandpa Joe said.

'Anyone want to finish this game?' Josh asked.

'No,' everyone chorused.

'More tea, Callie?' Eleanor asked.

As much as Callie would have liked to have stayed and enjoyed the warm hospitality at Campion House, she felt it was time to go.

'I should probably be getting back,' she said, getting to her feet.

'Really?' Bryony said. 'Already?'

'I've got some work I shouldn't put off any longer,' Callie explained.

'Let me get your coat,' Eleanor said and Callie followed her through to the cloakroom at the back of the house where Hardy and

Brontë were sleeping.

'I hope you haven't found us all too much,' she said. 'I know we can be a little intimidating *en masse*.'

'Not at all,' Callie said. 'I really enjoyed it. I don't often get to be a part of a big family. I mean, I don't *ever* get to be a part of one.'

'I can't imagine not having this house full every week,' Eleanor said.

Callie smiled as Eleanor handed her coat to her.

'You're welcome here any time,' she said.

'Thank you,' Callie said.

They walked into the hallway together and Callie popped her head round the living room door.

'I'm off!' she said. 'It was lovely meeting you all.'

'Bye, Callie! Drop by the shop sometime soon,' Josh said.

'Drop by *my* shop sometime soon!' Bryony said.

'Goodbye,' Grandpa Joe waved from his chair. 'Nell – *Nell!*'

'What is it?' Grandma Nell asked, waking up with a startled look on her face. 'What time is it?'

'Callie's leaving.'

'Who's Callie?'

'The nice young woman Sam brought with him.'

'Are they getting married?' Nell asked.

'Not today,' Grandpa Joe told her to the sound of much laughter.

Sam got up and joined Callie in the hallway. 'Sorry about all that,' he said.

'Everyone's so funny,' she said.

'Yes – funny *strange*. They should all be locked up!' he said, but he was smiling as he said it. 'Well, thanks again for getting me here on time.'

'You're welcome,' she said.

'You okay finding your way home?'

'I think I can manage,' she said. 'What's happening with your car?' she asked.

'Oh, Josh is going to tow it for me tomorrow.'

'I'll keep an eye on it tonight,' she said.

'I think it'll be safe in Newton St Clare.'

'I think you're right,' she said.

There was an awkward pause.

'I'm glad you came,' he said.

'Me too. I had a really great time,' she said. 'You've got an amazing family.'

'That's a very kind thing to say.'

'It's just the truth,' she said. 'You're lucky.'

'I know,' he said. 'They wind me up and drive me insane, but I couldn't imagine life without them.'

He opened the front door and Callie stepped outside.

'Bye,' she said, waving a hand.

He waved back and watched as she got into her car and drove off.

When Callie arrived back at Owl Cottage and shut her front door behind her, the silence wrapped itself around her and, for the first time, it wasn't completely welcome. She realised how much she'd loved the noise and chaos of the Nightingale family, and how warm and inviting it had all been. Even when she'd been embarrassed by their questions, she'd thought that it was rather wonderful to be a part of such a happy clan.

Suddenly, she had an impulse to reach out to her own small family and she picked up the phone before she could change her mind. She was always a tad nervous when ringing her mother because she never knew if her call would be well received or not.

'Hello, Mum!' she said a moment later.

'Oh, Caroline? Is that you?'

'Yes,' she said, only slightly annoyed that her mother should ask her that question as Callie was the only person in the world to call her *Mum*.

'I'm just heading out. It wasn't important was it?'

'No, Mum, it wasn't important.'

Callie had long since realised that she was not a priority in her parents' life.

'Is everything all right?'

'Yes of course it is.'

'Then why are you ringing?' her mother asked.

'I just wanted to talk to you.'

'That's rather strange, don't you think?'

Callie sighed. How she longed to have a normal conversation with her mother – to swap silly stories like the Nightingales did, to be able to casually chat about anything and everything. But it wasn't to be, was it?

'Your father and I were in Suffolk last week,' her mother said.

'Really? Where?'

'Bury St Edmunds.'

'But that's only twenty minutes from me,' Callie said, astonished that her mother hadn't got in touch about the trip.

'It was a last minute thing. Your father was visiting an old work colleague. We thought you'd be busy.'

Callie didn't know what to say. Her parents had been only twenty minutes from her new home and they hadn't bothered to call in to see her.

'Look, I've got to go,' her mother said, sounding flustered. 'Bye.' And she rang off.

Callie stood holding the receiver, feeling quite numb. Had that really just happened?

She sighed in defeat. 'Why do I do this to myself over and over again?'

# CHAPTER 17

Sam had stood at the front door of Campion House until Callie's car had left, delaying the moment when he returned to face his family because he knew what he was in for.

Sure enough, as soon as he entered the living room, he was set upon with everybody talking at once.

'SAM!' Bryony yelled. 'Why didn't you tell me she was coming?'

'You've kept this all very quiet, Bro,' Josh said.

'Is she your new girlfriend, Uncle Sam?' Archie asked.

'She's a very nice young woman,' his father said. 'I hope we'll be seeing her again soon.'

'Who are they talking about?' Grandma Nell said now that she was wide awake.

Sam shook his head and left the room.

His mum, who'd been straightening things in the dining room, motioned him into the kitchen and Sam knew there was no escaping.

'That lot been giving you earache?' she asked.

'Something like that,' he said, knowing full well that she would be doing just the same thing only in her quieter but well-meaning way.

'I'm so pleased your car broke down in front of Callie's house,' she told him, wading in gently. 'Although you didn't need that excuse to invite her here, you know?'

'I know that, Mum,' he said.

'Then why haven't we met her before today? She's been in Suffolk since September.'

'We're just friends, that's why,' he said. 'I don't invite all my friends to Sunday lunch with my family.'

'I know,' she said, 'but she seemed rather special.'

'I suppose she is,' he said.

'There's no supposing about it,' she said. 'That young woman has special written all over her and, what's more, she looked like she needed a friend.'

'She has one,' Sam said.

'Good,' she said.

'No,' Sam said. 'I don't mean me. I meant,' he paused, 'a *special* friend.'

'Who?'

'Leo Wildman,' Sam said, sounding the name with some distaste. 'She was with him when my car broke down in her village.'

'With him as in *with him*?' Eleanor asked, eyebrows raised.

'I think so,' Sam said.

'Oh,' she said. 'That's not good news.'

'You've heard of him?'

'Sure I have,' she said. 'I met their mother at that sewing group I used to go to. Her husband died a few years ago. There were two boys – Leo and,' she paused, 'Rick, I think. I met them both a few years ago. Very handsome.'

'Yes,' Sam said with a scowl.

'And very – what's the word?'

Sam looked at his mother with anxious eyes. 'What? He's very what?'

'Well, *popular*,' she said at last. 'Those Wildman boys are very popular with the women. At least, that's what I've heard.'

'Well, it's none of our business whom Callie is seeing,' he said.

'No, not if you don't care about her,' Eleanor said, 'but I think you *do* care about her, don't you?'

Sam walked across the kitchen and looked out of the window onto the back garden. A blustery wind was sending spirals of leaves dancing down from the trees and great grey clouds were hanging heavy in the sky.

'Sam?'

'What?' he said, turning back to look at her.

'You do care about her, don't you? I don't mean to pry, but I couldn't help but notice how things were between you.'

'What do you mean?'

She shrugged. 'Oh, just the little looks that passed between you.'

'You have a *very* vivid imagination, Mum,' he said with a grin.

'No,' she said, 'I have a very astute sense of what's going on with my children, that's all.'

He made to leave the room. 'I'll take my chances in the living room.'

'Sam?'

'Yes?'

'I know you've had a really rough time of things recently – rougher than anyone should ever have to experience – but I hope you don't think you'll never fall in love again. It will happen, you know that, don't you?'

Her face was tender with emotion and, even though Sam wanted to run about a million miles away from that particular conversation, he knew that she had nothing but his interest at heart and so he nodded.

'I know, Mum,' he said.

'Do you?' she asked, her eyes fixed on him and seeming to see into his very soul.

He stood there for a moment, suffering under the relentless gaze of his mother. 'I've got to go,' he said at last.

Since moving to Owl Cottage, Callie had managed to avoid going into London, but she could put it off no longer. Her agent had been hollering at her non-stop.

'We need to talk,' she kept saying. 'I hope you're not expecting me to come out to the wilds of Suffolk. Not in these shoes.'

Callie had finally taken pity on her city-bound agent and had bought herself a ticket, catching the train into London and taking the tube to Covent Garden. It was a strange experience to be in London again, pushing her way through the crowded underground and having her ears blasted by traffic and tourists. She'd forgotten how exhausting it was just to walk and breathe in London and, even after only half an hour in the capital, she longed to get back to her little place in the country where she could stride across the woods and fields without knocking into people.

Her agent had booked them a table at a small restaurant in a side street off the piazza in Covent Garden, but wasn't there when Callie arrived which didn't surprise her because her agent was always running late. She was one of those people who always tried to squeeze twenty appointments into ten slots and was known to juggle phone calls and text messages whilst simultaneously holding a meeting with a person in the same room with her.

It was ten minutes after Callie had sat down that her agent arrived, catching her eye from the door whilst flinging her heavy winter coat at a waitress.

Margot Marsden was a terrifying woman. At five foot eleven in heels, with the breadth and carriage of a headmistress from the strictest of schools, she still made Callie feel slightly ill at ease even though they'd been working together for years. But she was one of the best literary agents in the business and worked around the clock making sure that her clients got the very best deals and author care from their publishers.

'Hello, darling!' she said, air kissing Callie before sitting down opposite her with a weary sigh. She didn't apologise for being late because, as far as Margot was concerned, she never was.

'So, Piers wants your new book,' Margot said, launching straight into business without bothering with any niceties first, as she usually did. 'He's been emailing and texting and filling up the office answer machine.'

'I'm so sorry, Margot – I did tell him, quite firmly, that I wasn't interested.'

'You did *what?*' she asked, her voice booming across the restaurant, causing several heads to turn.

'I told him I wasn't going to work with him again – ever!'

'You *never* tell an editor that,' she said, leaning in closer. 'You simply tell them to put their best offer forward and you play them off against all the other publishers.'

'But what's the point if we're going to turn him down?'

'Because he might encourage the other players to up their offer,' Margot said. 'Honestly, have you learned nothing in your time with me?'

'Obviously not,' Callie said.

'All writers should be sent to business school in my opinion,' Margot said, ordering lunch for the two of them together with a bottle of very expensive wine. 'Business school followed by a course in fashion.'

Callie looked down at the outfit she'd cobbled together from items in her wardrobe. She'd thought she'd passed muster before Margot's jibe, but she could see how her simple, rather bohemian dress might be viewed with suspicion by a lady who lunched slightly more often than Callie did.

'So, you're okay with me sending Piers the first draft of your opening chapters?' Margot said, and Callie could tell it was a statement rather than a question.

'I'd really rather you didn't,' she said.

'But he's practically drooling over this novel.'

Callie winced. The image of her ex-husband drooling just as she was about to have lunch was too much.

'I've said no,' Callie said, standing her ground which was never easy with Margot.

'Fine!' Margot said. 'Have it your own way, only let me do my job here and find out what his offer actually is before we turn him down. He might surprise us. I'll send it out to a few other editors too and see what sort of offers they come up with too.'

Callie shook her head in despair. No matter how many times she'd say no, and no matter how many times Margot appeared to listen to her, Callie knew that her beloved manuscript would appear in her ex-husband's inbox before the day was out.

It was after lunch with her agent and en route to meet up with her friend, Heidi, that Callie spotted the bookshop. It was a small independent with a window crowded with new editions of classics as well as the latest chart-topping titles.

Hesitating, Callie wondered if she dared go in. It had been months since she'd walked into a London bookshop and even longer since she'd last looked for her own books on a shelf. Taking a deep breath, she walked inside, making her way to the children's department which was warm and inviting with its bright, cheerful colours.

It was always a loaded moment for an author to walk into a bookshop and Callie realised that she'd almost stopped breathing as she approached the shelves, looking along the great length of book spines in the 'L' section, her eyes resting as they came to the place where anything by Callie Logan would live.

There was nothing there.

Callie swallowed hard and looked again. Maybe her titles had been put in the wrong place, but a quick glance to the left and the right revealed nothing. She simply wasn't there.

All at once, all the old insecurities came flooding back. What if she was never published again? What if her time as a writer was up and nobody ever bought her work again or stocked her books or read them?

*Calm down*, she told herself. *If Piers loves your new book, other publishers will too.* But what if they didn't? What if it was only Piers's offer on the table? What would she do then?

She turned to leave the shop and that's when a little table caught her eye on which was a large cardboard sign which read, "Staff recommendations". And there in the middle of the display were three of Callie's very own books from her *Perdita* series, including a reprint of *Perdita's Key* – the book which Sam was trying to find her a first edition of.

She breathed a sigh of relief and beamed a smile at one of the shop assistants as she left.

Heidi had grabbed a seat in a quiet corner of the small cafe and was there waiting for Callie.

'I've ordered two huge hot chocolates to fend off the cold,' she told Callie who nodded in approval. 'So, tell me *everything* that's been going on with your wild man of the woods!' Heidi insisted after giving her friend a warm hug.

'Oh, you know,' Callie said evasively.

'No, I don't know,' Heidi said, 'because my so-called *friend* doesn't keep me updated with all the gossip! Honestly, Callie – normal girlfriends text each other all the juice every five minutes.'

'But there isn't any juice,' she said, wrinkling her nose at Heidi's use of that particular word.

The hot chocolates arrived and Callie hoped that Heidi would change the subject, but quickly realised that that wasn't going to happen.

'So, you're telling me that *nothing* is going on with the gorgeous Leo Wildman? You're not *totally* immune to his tremendous masculinity, are you? I mean, a blind nun would be tempted by him!'

'Heidi!' Callie cried, but she couldn't help but laugh at her friend's outrageous comments.

'Don't tell me you're still not over Piers because I won't believe you.'

Callie stirred her hot chocolate. 'He visited me.'

'Nooooo! When?'

'Last week,' she said. 'He wants us to try again.'

'You're kidding!' Heidi said. 'What did you do? What did you say?'

'What do you think I said?'

'I don't know,' Heidi said. 'I can never quite tell with you.'

'I told him it was too late,' Callie said.

'Thank goodness for that,' Heidi said. 'For a minute there, I thought the reason things were on hold with Mr Wild Man of the

Woods was because you were rekindling things with your ex.'

'Please! Give me *some* credit.'

'I can't believe the nerve of him. He ignores you when you're living in the same house as him, but suddenly drives to the middle of Suffolk once you're gone.'

'I know,' Callie said. 'I pointed out that we were getting divorced and that I'd bought my own house. He genuinely seemed to have forgotten those details. But—'

'What?' Heidi asked.

Callie took a deep breath. 'He did say sorry.'

Heidi swallowed hard and reached out across the table to take Callie's hand. 'I should think so too,' she said. 'But that's way too little way too late, isn't it?'

'We can never be together again,' she whispered. 'I feel like the part of me that loved Piers died along with our baby.' Tears swam in her eyes.

'Now, don't you go getting all upset about it all again!' Heidi said, her voice firm. 'You have made yourself a brilliant new life and virtually have the whole of the male population of Suffolk after you.'

Callie smiled.

'Anything happening with that bookshop guy, by the way?'

Callie dabbed at her eyes with a tissue, glad that her friend had moved the conversation away from Piers. She'd had her fill of him that day.

'I had lunch with him,' she said.

'You had lunch with the book guy and didn't *tell* me?' Heidi's eyes widened and she shook her head in exasperation.

'Lunch with him and his whole family. Well, most of them. One of them was away, I think.'

'You went to his house?' she said. 'I'd say that was pretty serious.'

'Not really – it was quite by accident,' Callie explained. 'And it wasn't his house; it was his parents' house. His car broke down in my village, I gave him a lift and his mum insisted I stay for lunch.'

'Well, I'd say that is far more serious than him inviting you round to his own home,' Heidi said.

'It was just a casual thing.'

'A friend thing?' Heidi said, suspicion in her voice.

'Exactly,' Callie said.

Heidi nodded. 'So, let's get back to Mr Wildman,' she said with a naughty twinkle in her eye. 'How do you feel about him? I mean, *really?*'

Callie looked thoughtful. 'Leo's so carefree,' she said at last. 'He's so much fun to be with and I feel so light and breezy around him.'

'Light and breezy is good,' Heidi said, 'especially as you said you didn't want anything serious.'

'But—' Callie paused. What was she trying to say? That she knew she wasn't the light and breezy sort of girl? That she could never just have a fling because she wasn't made like that.

'Don't tell me you've suddenly changed your mind about that?' Heidi said. 'Have you?'

Callie sat staring at her empty cup. 'I don't know,' she said.

'What do you mean?' Heidi's eyes narrowed as she scrutinised her friend. 'Have you gone and fallen in love?'

'*What?*' Callie cried.

'Because that would be *exactly* like you, Caroline Logan! You're a hopeless romantic and you would sooner fall head over heels in love than have a nice light-hearted fling, wouldn't you?'

'I don't know what you're talking about,' she said defensively.

'Yes you do,' Heidi said, 'and you're blushing. I'm right, aren't I? You've fallen in love, haven't you?'

Callie didn't say anything; it was probably best not to because, until Heidi had mentioned the word *love*, the truth of the matter hadn't really registered with Callie, but it was true, wasn't it? Slowly, almost imperceptibly, she'd been falling in love, even though she'd done her very best to shut those feelings down inside herself.

'I think it's wonderful,' Heidi went on, squeezing her hand again. 'Really wonderful. Good for you.'

But whereas Heidi was talking about Leo Wildman, Callie was thinking very much of Sam Nightingale.

# CHAPTER 18

Once Bryony Nightingale had an idea in her head, there was no stopping her and there was definitely no shutting her up.

'Come on, Sam – it's a brilliant idea!' she said, pacing the carpeted area of her children's bookshop, her long patchwork skirt swishing madly in a medley of colour.

'I don't know,' Sam said, scratching his chin and generally looking uncomfortable.

'I don't see what's *not* to love about this,' she said. 'I run a children's bookshop, and a children's writer – one of the most famous of the last five years – has just moved to Suffolk and is already best friends with my brother.' She gave him a cheeky little grin.

'But you saw how awkward she felt about the whole thing when you were pressurising her on Sunday.'

'I wasn't pressurising her!' Bryony said.

'No? Are you sure about that?'

'I was just being enthusiastic.'

'Oh, is that what it was?' he said.

'You know what I'm like,' she said, unclipping her wild curly hair and stuffing the pin in her mouth as she twisted her ponytail and retied it.

'I do know what you're like, but Callie looked absolutely petrified by that enthusiasm and I really don't think you should push things with her. I want to *keep* her as my friend, all right?'

'Do you?' Bryony said.

'Of course I do.'

'Just as a friend?' Bryony asked.

'Don't start that again,' Sam said.

'I can't help it,' she said. 'I worry about you.'

'Yeah, well don't.'

'*Everyone's* worried about you after that awful business with Emma and her mad brother.'

'That's all in the past,' he told her. 'I want to forget about it.'

'Yes, but it's only the very recent past and you're still letting it affect your present,' she said, sinking down onto a beanbag.

Sam groaned. 'You sound exactly like Mum,' he said, flopping down on a beanbag opposite his sister, his long legs bent like a grasshopper's.

'Which proves my case exactly,' Bryony said. 'Everyone wants to see you happy again, Sam, and that can't happen when you refuse to let love into your life.'

'Good grief, Bry – have you been reading some self-help manual?'

'No I haven't. I got that phrase from an online dating agency. "Let love into your life" is their slogan,' she said with a giggle.

Before Bryony could continue the examination of her brother's love life, the little bell above the door tinkled and a young man with neat, sandy-coloured hair entered the shop.

'Hi Colin,' Bryony said. Tellingly, she didn't get up from her home on the beanbag.

'Just taken a batch of fruit scones out of the oven,' he said with a grin. 'Thought you might want first refusal.'

'Oh, you do know how to spoil a girl,' Bryony said. 'Bring half a dozen round. What I don't eat will go straight in my freezer for evenings in front of the TV.'

'Sure thing,' he said with a nod before leaving.

'Are you two seeing each other?' Sam asked as soon as the door was closed.

'Not yet,' Bryony said. 'Not officially.'

'What does that mean?'

'It means– ' Bryony paused and puffed out her cheeks.

'It means you're hoping somebody better will come along and sweep you off your feet in the way that poor old Colin the baker never could?'

'Sam Nightingale! What a thing to say,' she said in outrage.

'So I'm right, then?'

She sighed. 'Colin's just – well – Colin, isn't he?'

'You could do a lot worse than Colin,' Sam said. 'He's a good guy.'

'I know,' Bryony said, flapping her hands in the air, 'but he's not terribly exciting, is he? I can't imagine ever getting *really* excited about being with him and that's not right, is it? Love should be mad and thrilling, shouldn't it?' She looked at him with wide brown eyes dancing with light.

'You've never really got over Ben, have you?' Sam said.

Her mouth dropped open. 'I thought I told you *never* to say his name again,' she snapped, getting up from her beanbag.

'So it's okay for you to put *my* love life under the spotlight, but it's not okay for me to talk about yours?'

'That's right,' she said.

He shook his head and got up from the beanbag. 'Right,' he said. 'I'm off.'

'Oh, don't go, Sam!'

'Bry – we just seem to be goading each other.'

'But I didn't mean to goad you,' she said, crossing the shop and putting her arms around him, and how could he be angry with her when she did that?

'You're such a girl,' he told her.

'And you love it,' she said, kissing him on the cheek.

When he returned to his own shop a moment later, Grandpa Joe was waiting for him at the till.

'You missed a huge rush of sales,' he told his grandson.

'Did I?'

'Nope,' he said with a wink before shuffling off in his slippers to his favourite sofa in the back room where he was reading a book about the history of cinema. He would occasionally read little bits and pieces from it in an attempt to convince Sam that he *was* actually reading it and not just looking at photographs of Brigitte Bardot.

Standing in the silence of the shop, surrounded by millions of words, Sam wished he could formulate at least a few of his own to describe how he was feeling. But the truth of the matter was, he'd been trying *not* to think about how he was feeling over the last few days. Or months. It had all been much too painful. But his whole family seemed determined to make him think about it all.

So, what was going on with him? He'd been telling everyone he was fine. He was getting over Emma, or at least he had been until that nasty business with her brother. He'd made himself a great little home in the flat above the shop. It was a tad smaller than the marital home and there wasn't a lot of furniture, but he was happy enough there and the commute to work was, of course, unbeatable. Work was good. In the secondhand book trade, one could always happily use a few more sales here and there, but business was generally good.

He had nothing to complain about and no real worries, so why were his family so concerned about him?

But he knew why. Sam had always been happiest when he was in love, from the early teenage girlfriends he'd bring home to lunch, to the serious relationships throughout his twenties, to his marriage with Emma. There hadn't been much time in his life when he hadn't been involved with someone. Maybe that's where he'd been going wrong, he thought. Maybe he wasn't meant to be with anyone. That was the message he'd taken from the disastrous marriage, and his brief flirtation with the idea of dating again when he'd met Callie Logan had been well and truly trounced by her rejection. If only his family would let him get on with the business of being a born again bachelor.

'Like that's going to happen,' he said, picking up a rather battered copy of love poems by the Romantics and putting it back in its rightful home.

Callie had done her best to throw herself back into her novel as soon as she'd got home from London, and she'd done her very best to stop thinking about Sam Nightingale too, only that wasn't so easy. When she'd made up her mind to leave Piers, she'd told herself that she was never going to let herself fall in love again. She just couldn't put herself through that sort of pain a second time. But the human head and the human heart were two very different things and Callie hadn't been able to stop the feelings that seemed to be surfacing whenever she thought about Sam.

She thought about the easy way they talked to each other, sharing their passion for books and the written word, she thought about his gentle humour and his warm smile, and she thought about that desperate look on his face when he'd asked her out and she'd said no. Had he truly forgiven her for that, she wondered? She'd probably lost him forever because of her abruptness and she was regretting it because, although they had a lovely friendship, she had a feeling that it would never be anything else now because of the night she'd told him no.

Sitting at her desk, she felt so unutterably sad about the whole thing and couldn't help wondering what would have happened if she'd said yes to Sam. That was one of the curses of being a writer: one spent far too long thinking about the *ifs* and *maybes* of life.

'If I'd said yes, where would we be now?' she whispered into the empty room, allowing herself a brief moment of daydreaming about finding a soulmate in Sam Nightingale who would help erase all the heartache of the past. But then she silently cursed herself for even going there with her silly *ifs* and *maybes*. She would just have to forget about him and the whole Nightingale family. Maybe it was best if she never even went into Castle Clare at all. She'd probably be better off shopping in Bury St Edmunds or driving into Cambridge.

She was just printing out her latest chapter so that she could edit it the old-fashioned way – with a red pen – when the phone rang.

'Callie?'

'Hello?' Callie said, not recognising the woman's voice.

'It's Bryony. Bryony Nightingale.'

'Hello,' Callie said, instantly on her guard.

'I was wondering if you've given any thought to doing an event in my children's bookshop.' Her voice was warm and light-hearted, and Callie immediately felt guilty because she knew she was going to say no.

'I haven't, I'm afraid,' she said.

'It would be an honour – a *real* honour – to have you in our little shop. We have great links with the local primary school and the reading club at the library. It would be so much fun. The kids would love it. They're a really brilliant bunch in Castle Clare too. I'm sure you'd love them. So what do you think?'

'I – erm – well–'

'Now, I know we can't promise tube posters like your big London events, but we can run to a few simple A4 posters and flyers.

Callie didn't know what to say so she said nothing which meant there was an awful pause.

'Oh, I'm sorry,' Bryony said at last. 'Sam told me not to push things with you and I've gone and pushed anyway.'

'What did he say?' Callie asked.

'He told me not to be a bully and to leave you alone, but I can't. I just can't! I found your business card in that big old book Sam keeps in the shop and, well, you're a children's author and I'm a children's bookseller. That's a match made in heaven, isn't it?'

Callie couldn't help but smile at that.

'I just had to push this a little bit more,' Bryony went on. 'I hope I haven't offended you.'

'You haven't offended me,' Callie assured her.

'Oh, good!' Bryony said. 'Because I'd never forgive myself if I had and Sam would absolutely kill me if he found out I was ringing you. He's very fond of you, you know?'

'Oh?'

'And he'd absolutely kill me if he knew I'd told you that as well.'

Callie caught her breath. Sam Nightingale was fond of her and he'd told his sister not to bother her. Did that mean he cared about her?

'Bryony?'

'Yes?'

Callie was on the verge of saying no, very politely but very firmly, but then she remembered all the fears and insecurities that had surfaced when she hadn't been able to find her titles in the little bookshop in London and, although she'd finally spotted some of her *Perdita* books, they might easily have been overlooked or not even in stock. There were so many variables in the publishing business and she would be considered truly mad by her fellow writers at turning down such a wonderful opportunity as doing an event with Bryony. It was publicity on a plate and, what was more, it might actually be good fun.

'Callie?' Bryony said, and Callie realised that she must have gone horribly quiet.

'I'll do it!' Callie told her.

'You will?' Bryony said, giving a scream of joy that almost shattered Callie's right eardrum. 'You won't regret it. It's going to be brilliant! Just leave it all to me and I'll arrange it all, okay?'

'Okay,' Callie said, and they said their goodbyes, promising to keep in touch.

So much for keeping my distance from the Nightingales, Callie thought as she returned to her desk.

Archie Prior was sitting on the top of one of the library steps in the front room of Sam's shop.

'What are you reading, Arch?' Sam asked his young nephew as he looked up from the book club advert he was drafting to put up in the local library and the rest of the Nightingale bookshops.

'I'm not sure,' Archie said.

'Hold it up,' Sam said and Archie revealed the cover. 'Ah, that's

*King Lear.* I'd come back to that in a few years if I was you.'

'It wasn't very good anyway,' Archie said, stretching up to replace the book before climbing down from the library steps. Sam grinned. Archie had been in the bookshop for just over an hour after a friend of Polly's had picked him up from school and dropped him off. In that time, he'd worked his way through most of the shelves, declaring that the books were boring.

'Come on,' Sam said to him now, 'time to get you home.'

'Is your car fixed?' Archie asked.

'Yep,' Sam said. 'Cost an absolute fortune but it's up and running again.'

'Does that mean we won't break down?'

'I hope so.'

'Oh.'

'You *want* to break down?' Sam asked.

Archie nodded as they shut up the shop early and walked round to the back where Sam's car was parked. 'Tiger's car broke down the other day and this massive yellow truck came to pick it up.'

'I see,' Sam said.

'He sent me the photos – look!'

Sam looked down at Archie's phone. Everything was photographed and shared these days, he'd noticed. 'What's that?' he asked, as Archie scrolled to another photo.

'My dentist's nose,' Archie said.

'You took a photo whilst you were in the dentist's chair?' Sam asked.

Archie nodded.

They got in the car and left Castle Clare. A moment later, they pulled over at a small cottage on the left.

'Have we broken down?' Archie asked, glee filling his face.

'No. Just stopping to get some eggs,' Sam said, nipping out of the car and returning with a box that had been left on a small table of produce outside a cottage. 'Flo Lohman's free-range hens lay the best eggs in the county.' He handed the box to Archie who immediately opened it.

'Oh, gross!' he said.

Sam laughed. 'Just a bit of mud.'

'There's feathers in here too.'

'You can have a feather omelette for tea.' Archie didn't look impressed. 'Hold onto them tightly.'

They drove the short distance to the village of Great Tallington which had a large green surrounded by cottages in the traditional Suffolk pink, and a fine flint church guarding the inhabitants.

Polly lived in a lane overlooking Church Green, in a neat terraced row of brick and flint cottages.

'Be nice and quiet for your mum, Arch,' Sam said, as they got out of the car and walked up the garden path to the front door.

'I will,' he said.

'We're here, Poll!' Sam called as they entered the kitchen, bending to pet Dickens, the liver and white spaniel who greeted him. Archie placed the eggs on the pine table and then shot off into the living room where he switched the TV on. Sam followed him through. 'Not too loud.'

Archie nodded, turning the volume down.

Sam looked around the room, noticing that, despite his sister suffering from a debilitating migraine, she'd still managed to keep the house in order. There wasn't so much as a cushion out of place.

As with every member of the Nightingale family, there were books galore, and Sam's eyes roved over the shelves in the living room now, knowing – instantly – that there were no new editions. Polly had really had to cut down on her spending since Sean's disappearance.

He looked at the little table by the sofa on which sat a wedding photo of his sister and brother-in-law.

Where the hell are you, Sean? he said to himself. What in the world happened to you?

Leaving Archie to watch TV, and letting Dickens out into the back garden, Sam walked through to the kitchen to start preparing something for tea. It was then that Polly appeared.

'You okay?' Sam asked as she walked into the room. Her hair was loose and her face was pale. She nodded but looked weak and shaky. 'Sit down. I'll make you something to eat.'

'Bloody migraines,' she said, going to the fridge and pouring herself a glass of orange juice. 'Is Archie okay?'

'He's fine,' Sam said. 'Was it a bad one?'

'No such thing as a good one,' Polly said. 'But it's ebbing away now.' She sat down at the kitchen table and Sam got on with tea.

'I've brought some eggs,' he said.

'There's a bit of cheese in the fridge if you want to make an omelette. Some tomatoes too.'

Sam nodded. 'So, any more ideas about drumming up business for the book club?' he asked her.

'I'm sorry, Sam, I haven't had a chance to give it any thought yet. But I will.'

'That's all right,' he said. 'Plenty of time. It's probably just a case of letting it grow organically.'

'The people of Castle Clare don't like surprises,' she said. 'They like things that have been established for at least ten years.'

Sam laughed. 'I don't know if I've got the patience to give it that long!'

'It'll happen,' she said.

Breaking three eggs into a bowl and whisking them, Sam continued. 'Bryony came in today. She's set up an author event with Callie.'

'I thought Callie didn't want to do one,' Polly said.

'I thought that too, and I told Bry not to push it, but you know what she's like.'

'Yes I do,' Polly said. 'But maybe Callie just changed her mind. Have you spoken to her?'

'Not since I rang to thank her for the lift on Sunday,' Sam said. 'Maybe I should give her a call.'

There was a knock on the door.

Sam turned around from the cooker. 'Are you expecting anyone?'

Polly shook her head and then winced, the movement obviously hurting her.

'I'll get it,' he said, leaving the eggs and going into the hallway. When he opened the door, he was met by a tall young man who had to bend himself into the doorway. He had messy fair hair that looked too long to Sam and he was holding a guitar.

'Is Archie there?' he asked.

'Erm, yes. Who's calling?'

'Jago,' he said. 'Come for Archie's guitar lesson.'

'Oh?' Sam said in surprise. 'I wasn't aware he had one.'

The young man looked puzzled. 'I spoke to him this morning.'

'Jago?' Archie cried as he came running through from the living room.

'Hi, mate!' Jago said.

'I'm sorry,' Sam said, 'but Archie's mum's not feeling well. I think you'd better come back another time.'

'Archie? Who is it?' Polly asked, appearing in the hallway.

'Hi, Mrs Prior. I'm Jago. Archie's friend.'

Sam watched as his sister tightened the belt on her housecoat and frowned at the intruder.

'Jago's going to teach me to play the guitar!' Archie said.

'Oh, is he?' Polly said. 'Well, I don't know anything about that.'

'I was going to square it with you, of course,' the young man said.

'We can't afford guitar lessons,' Polly said. 'Archie's already learning the piano.'

'Oh, Mum!' Archie groaned. 'I *hate* the piano!'

'Archie – go through to the living room,' Polly said, giving him a warning glare. 'I'm afraid you've wasted your time,' she said, turning back to the young man who was still bent at an odd angle in her doorway.

'I wasn't going to charge,' he said.

'Then what's in it for you?' Polly asked, her voice full of suspicion.

'Just the pleasure of passing music on to a young 'un,' he said with a lopsided grin.

Sam watched the exchange.

'I don't think so,' Polly said, turning around and heading into the living room.

'Sorry,' Sam said. 'She's had a rough day.'

'No problem,' the young man said, waving a hand in the air before heading off with his guitar.

As he closed the front door, Sam could hear Polly talking to Archie and joined them in the living room.

'You can't just go around asking strangers into our home!' Polly cried.

'But he's not a stranger, Mum.'

'You said you only met him this morning when you got your lift to school. We don't know anything about him.'

'But he lives over the road.'

'Where over the road?'

'With Mrs Solomon.'

'He's Mrs Solomon's son?' Polly asked.

Archie shrugged. 'Don't know.'

Polly sighed and sank into an armchair. 'You can't just invite people round when you have a whim to.'

'But he said—'

'I don't care what he said,' Polly said, clutching her head as she closed her eyes.

'That's enough, Arch,' Sam said.

'But he was going to teach me the guitar,' Archie said, stomping out of the room leaving the TV on.

Sam switched it off before walking towards Polly and giving her shoulder a squeeze. 'You okay?'

'I could have done without this today,' she said.

'He seemed like a nice enough chap,' Sam said.

Polly looked up. 'Did he?'

'You didn't notice?'

'I think I'm going to go back to bed,' she said, walking slowly out of the room. 'You okay with Archie for a bit?'

'Sure,' Sam said.

'Archie – come down and have some tea,' Polly said as she climbed the stairs to her bedroom.

'I'm not hungry,' Archie said.

Sam, who was standing at the foot of the stairs, shook his head and took himself back into the kitchen where he finished making the three-egg omelette for himself.

# CHAPTER 19

Bryony's bookshop was everything that a children's bookshop ought to be: bright, warm and inviting, and Callie instantly fell in love with it.

When she'd arrived in Castle Clare for her signing, she hadn't been sure what to expect but, walking to the shop from the local car park by the antiques centre, she'd been surprised to see a long queue of people on the pavement outside ready for the three o'clock event.

'It's her!' a young girl cried as she spotted Callie.

'Callie!' another girl shouted. 'Sign my book! Sign my book!'

Callie smiled politely, her cheeks flushing red, as she rushed into the shop.

'I told you there'd be a good crowd,' Bryony said, a huge smile on her face as she ushered Callie in.

'I can't believe it,' Callie said, feeling amazed that Bryony had managed to organise such an event in such a short space of time.

'Everybody is so excited,' she said. 'When I popped into the primary school, all the girls were jumping up and down in their seats.'

Callie laughed. 'Well, I hope I don't disappoint them.'

'Disappoint them? Are you kidding? They're going to *love* you,' Bryony said. 'Now, let's get you seated. Will you be okay here?' She motioned to a chair and table she'd set up by the window.

'I think so,' Callie said, smiling again as a group of young girls waved at her through the window.

'You okay?'

Callie nodded. 'I always get so nervous at these things. Silly, isn't it? I mean, everyone's always so nice and kind, but I can't help it. I guess I'm so used to spending hours on my own that suddenly being out in public can be a bit daunting.'

'You've got absolutely nothing to worry about,' Bryony said. 'Polly's helping out on the till.'

'Hi,' Polly said, emerging from the stock room with an armful of books which she placed by the till.

'And I'll be right by you the whole time to open all the books at the right page for signing.'

Callie nodded. 'It's a really lovely display,' she said. 'Thanks so much for all the trouble you've gone to.'

Bryony stepped forward. 'Your hands are shaking,' she whispered.

'I know,' Callie whispered back.

'Let me get you a cup of tea before you begin.'

'I don't want to keep everyone waiting.'

'They won't mind,' Bryony said. 'Come in the back and have a cup of tea, okay?'

'I feel so silly,' Callie said. 'I don't know why I get so nervous about these things.'

'It's not silly at all,' Bryony said. 'I can only begin to imagine what it must be like to face a ravenous crowd of mad fans.'

Callie's face drained of all colour.

'Sorry,' Bryony said. 'Wrong phrase to use.'

Bryony quickly made two cups of tea and they perched on a pair of stools in the stock room.

'I'll be all right in a minute,' Callie said. 'I'm sure I will.' She gave a little smile.

'I read the *Perdita* books again this week,' Bryony announced.

'Really?'

'Of course,' she said. 'I wouldn't have an author here if I hadn't read their books. They're really wonderful, Callie. You should be so proud of them.'

'They made me very happy writing them,' she said.

'So why did you stop? Or am I overstepping the mark by asking that? You must tell me if I am because I do that all the time.'

'She does,' Polly said, popping her head into the stock room.

'Well, I think it was coming to a natural end in terms of storytelling and the market was changing. Children's books have been getting a lot darker, haven't they?'

Bryony nodded. 'Yes. It's all dystopian settings now, isn't it? I don't like it.'

'I was also going through a separation and then I was sorting out moving here and I found I couldn't write at all for months. It was really scary. So I came into Castle Clare and visited Sam's bookshop.'

'And you were inspired to write again?' Bryony asked.

'Very soon afterwards.'

'That's great. So what's the new book about?'

'Now you're overstepping the mark,' Callie said with a grin as she finished her tea.

Bryony laughed. 'Fair enough,' she said, standing up and taking Callie's mug. 'Shall we get this show on the road?'

'I think we'd better,' Callie said, taking a deep breath before heading out into the shop.

Sam had a pretty good view of the proceedings from his shop on the opposite side of the road. He'd been watching as the queue slowly got shorter and then the final mother and daughter had ventured inside and the door of the shop had been closed behind them.

'You want to go over there and show your support?' Grandpa Joe asked. He didn't normally come into the bookshop on a Saturday, but he'd found out about Callie's signing and had obviously wanted to keep an eye on things.

'I'm not sure it's my place to,' he said.

'Nonsense,' Grandpa Joe said. 'I'm sure she'd appreciate it.'

'Yeah?'

He nodded. 'Of course,' he said.

'Well, maybe I could just pop my head in for a minute.'

'I'll hold the fort here,' Grandpa Joe said.

Sam looked around the shop as though he'd lost something.

'Go *on*, then!' Grandpa Joe told him.

'Right,' Sam said, leaving the shop.

The final mother and daughter were just leaving as Sam entered Bryony's and Callie was stretching her arms out in front of her.

'Oh, my goodness!' Bryony said. 'That was so amazing! Wasn't that the *best* signing ever?'

'It's definitely up there,' Polly said. 'I'm exhausted!'

'Yes, thanks so much for manning the till,' Bryony said. 'Sam – you should have seen how wonderful Callie was. The kids loved her!'

'I'm sure she was fantastic,' he said, exchanging smiles with Callie as she stood up.

'I thought I'd rooted there,' she said.

'Do you want another cup of tea?' Polly asked.

'Oh, she'll want something stronger than that!' Bryony said. 'Sam – why don't you take Callie to The Happy Hare for a celebratory drink? We'll be along after closing up.'

Sam hadn't been expecting Bryony to suggest that and couldn't help feeling surprised, but pleasantly so. 'Would you like to?' he asked Callie.

'Erm, sure,' she said. 'I'll just get my bag. Oh, thanks,' she added as her satchel was thrust at her by Bryony who'd already retrieved it from the stock room.

'We'll see you there,' Bryony said, giving Sam a sly wink. 'Later.'

He rolled his eyes and left the shop. Subtlety was *not* his sister's strong point.

Once outside the shop, they crossed the road.

'Oh, there's your grandpa,' Callie said, waving back to the old man who was flapping an enthusiastic hand in the air.

Sam cleared his throat. 'I'd better check he's okay shutting up.' He opened the shop door and poked his head in. 'You all right if I–'

'I'll shut up shop,' Grandpa Joe interrupted, giving him a saucy wink which Sam hoped Callie didn't see.

'Right,' Sam said as he closed the door, 'ready for that drink?'

'Am I ever?' Callie said and they walked the short distance to the pub together.

The Happy Hare was the sort of pub where you instantly felt at home. With its dark beams and cosy corners, it was just the sort of place to warm up on a cold winter's afternoon.

'Grab that seat by the fire,' Sam said, 'I'll get the drinks. What would you like?'

'Just an apple juice,' she said.

'You sure?'

'I'm driving home.'

'Of course,' Sam said. 'An apple juice it is, then.' He turned to the bar and ordered the juice and a glass of wine for himself and then joined her by the fire.

'I am *so* glad that's over!' she said.

'You tired?'

'Funnily enough, not as tired as I thought I would be. I'm still kind of numbed by it all. It went by in such a blur of busyness that I feel a bit like it didn't happen at all.'

He laughed. 'Bryony's events often make people feel like that,' he said. 'Her author signings are some of the most popular I've ever seen.'

'She works hard, doesn't she?'

'She does,' he said, 'but it was you signing all those books.'

'Yes and I probably won't be able to write for weeks now. I've got a very sore arm!'

Sam's phone beeped and he took it out of his pocket. It was a text from Bryony.

We'll leave you two love birds to it! x

He put his phone back immediately.

'Everything okay?' Callie asked.

Sam cleared his throat. 'Bryony's asked me to say a huge thank you for today.'

'Isn't she coming?'

'She's – erm – no, she's not,' Sam said. 'Something came up.'

'Oh,' Callie said. 'What a shame.'

Sam took a sip of his wine, suddenly feeling awkward which was ridiculous really because he loved being in Callie's company. It was just the constant pushing from his family to turn his relationship with her into something else – something it could never be – that made him feel uneasy around her.

'Are you okay?' she asked him.

'I'm fine,' he said, doing his best to pull himself together. 'Do you think it's too early to eat?'

She smiled. 'I'm absolutely starving,' she confessed.

'Yeah?'

She nodded. 'Let's order something, shall we?'

Two large plates of lasagne, chips and salad were soon served up and they both got stuck in.

'Pub food's the best in the world, isn't it?' Callie said.

'I think so,' Sam said.

'I saw my fair share of London restaurants when I was living there and they were fun, but they always used to make me a bit nervous with their and fussy little portions. Give me a good plate full of simple home-cooked food any day,' she said.

'So, tell me about the signing,' Sam said. 'Any awkward customers?'

'Not at all,' she said. 'Everyone was really lovely.'

'Good.'

Callie looked thoughtful, her fork resting on her plate. 'Sam?'

'Yes?'

'Bryony told me about Aidan.'

He frowned. 'Did she?'

She nodded. 'Just at the end of my signing before you came into the shop. She didn't go into any detail or anything. Did you get all your books back?'

'Yes,' he said, making a mental note to personally strangle his sister at a later date.

'That must have been really scary,' she said. 'I can't imagine why somebody would do that.'

'Greed,' Sam said simply. 'My ex thought I had something expensive that belonged to her and she wanted it back. She didn't want it because it was a beautiful item. Nor did she want it because it had been given out of love. She wanted it because it was worth a little bit of money.'

'I'm sorry,' Callie said gently. 'That's really awful.'

'I'm trying to forget about it,' he said, 'but that isn't always easy in a small town and with a big family who keep reminding you about it every five minutes.'

'And then I go and raise the subject too,' Callie said. 'I'm sorry. I shouldn't have mentioned it.'

'I wasn't blaming you,' Sam said. 'Please don't think I was.'

They smiled at each other.

'Another drink?' he suggested.

'I'd love a glass of wine,' she said.

'What about driving home?'

She chewed her lower lip. 'How about I get a taxi and collect my car tomorrow?'

'You sure?'

'A big glass of white!' she said with a laugh.

Sam laughed too. 'Coming right up.'

Callie watched as Sam ordered drinks at the bar and willed herself to remain calm. She was feeling strangely energised after her book signing. She was floating on a euphoric little cloud somewhere beyond herself and she didn't want to go home just yet. She spent too much time on her own, she knew that, and – for tonight at least – she wanted to talk and be a part of things for a little while longer.

She remembered the strange pattern of emotions from her public events in London. There'd be the initial swell of pride at being asked to do an event but, as the time of the actual event approached, fear would take over until her nerves were so jangled that she could barely think straight. Then, once the event had begun, and she had met a few readers and heard their sweet messages, she would begin to relax although it wasn't total relaxation, of course – it was more of a coma-like state which carried her through. Then, once it was all over and she was back home, a rush of loneliness would engulf her. Piers had rarely been around for those moments, but Sam was now with food and wine and his wonderfully warming smile.

'Two white wines,' he said as he returned to their table. 'Cheers!'

'Cheers,' she said, clinking glasses.

'And well done on a really successful event.'

'Thank you,' she said. 'Let's hope that keeps Bryony happy for a while.'

'Until the literary festival in the summer at least,' Sam said.

'I'll make sure I'm on holiday that week.'

Sam laughed. She did like his laugh and, thinking of it now, sitting so close to him, made her blush. She really did like this man, didn't she?

'You okay?' he asked. 'You're a bit red.'

'It must be the wine,' she said. 'Or the fire.'

'But you've hardly drunk any,' he said.

Callie took a hearty swig. 'But I will,' she said.

They were quiet for a moment.

'I hope I'm not keeping you from anything,' Callie said.

'Not at all,' Sam said. 'Now, let me see. What would I normally be doing on a Saturday night?' He cast his eyes to the ceiling and frowned. 'Hmmmm. Absolutely nothing.'

Callie laughed. 'Me too. Although I'm totally fine with that. Always have been actually. Is that really boring?'

He shook his head. 'If it is then I'm the world's biggest bore. I think Emma used to get a bit fed up of me preferring a night in with a good book than wanting to go out.'

'Did she?'

'She liked to get dressed up, you know?'

'No,' Callie said. 'I'm not one of those women. Well, not very often anyway. I like a nice dress, but I'm not one of these women with miles of wardrobe space. I'd much rather have shelves of books than shelves of shoes.' She took another sip of wine. She was getting through it at an alarming rate and was beginning to mellow which was a wonderful feeling.

'When Emma and I got married, she didn't own any books.'

'What – none at all?'

'Not one,' he said. 'Not even a holiday paperback.'

'That's worse than–' Callie paused, 'worse than not having any food in the house.'

'It is, isn't it?'

'It really is!' Callie said. 'I'd much rather go without food than without books. Well, for up to a couple of days at least.'

'Even if you're not a big reader, isn't it a comfort just to have a few books around you?'

Callie nodded enthusiastically. 'I love how books instantly furnish a room,' she said. 'When I moved into Owl Cottage, unpacking my books was a top priority. I just love the look of them and having them all around me.'

'I think my collection drove Emma mad,' Sam said. 'She once asked why I needed so many.'

Callie laughed. 'What did you say?'

'I said they were part of what keeps me alive just like the air I breathe. I have no more than I absolutely need.'

They talked for a while longer and Callie acknowledged the fact that, once again, they'd slipped into their easy way of rambling from subject to subject, but always coming back to books.

Callie bought the next round of drinks: two more white wines.

'Sam?' she said when she sat back down.

'Cheers,' he said, lifting his glass to chink hers.

'Oh, cheers.'

'What is it?' he asked.

Their eyes met, but Callie quickly turned hers away, looking down into her wine glass. She thought about the man sitting in front of her and how she'd come to realise that she had feelings for him. But did she have the courage to tell him? And did she want to take the risk of giving her heart to somebody else after having had it broken so recently?

'Callie?' Sam asked gently.

'I was just thinking,' she began hesitantly, 'we've had dinner together.' She looked up. Sam was staring right at her.

'Yes we have,' he said with a bemused grin.

'And I was so sure that I didn't want to have dinner with you. You know – when you asked me?'

'I remember,' he said.

'I was really sure that I didn't want this to happen.' She held his gaze.

'What are you trying to say, Callie?' he said, leaning forward slightly.

'I'm trying to say—'

'*Callie?*' a voice interrupted.

She started, looking across the pub.

'Leo?' she said.

'Hey,' he said, crossing the room quickly. 'What are you doing here?'

Callie felt temporarily stunned at the intrusion, but she quickly pulled herself together. 'I've just done a signing at Nightingale's. I sent you a text about it yesterday,' she said, watching as Leo pulled a chair from the adjacent table and sat down.

'Oh, that's right,' he said.

'You remember Sam?' Callie said, thinking of the confession she'd been about to make to Sam before Leo had turned up so unexpectedly.

'Hey,' Leo said with a nod. Sam nodded back. 'I'm sorry I forgot about your event. I'd have loved to have seen it.'

'No you wouldn't,' Callie said with a laugh. 'Anyway, I thought you were out looking for pignuts today.'

Callie couldn't help noticing that Sam gave a little grin at that.

Leo shook his head. 'Wrong season,' he said. 'So, who wants another drink?'

Callie looked at Sam, feeling awkward both for him and for herself.

'I've still got this one on the go,' she said, nodding to her glass of wine, 'and I was just about to call for a taxi.'

'Really?' Leo said. 'But it's so early.'

'I know, but I'm exhausted after the signing,' she said, hoping her face didn't colour up at her lie. Well, it was only a half-lie.

'Let me give you a lift, then,' he said.

'Okay,' Callie said. 'I've got to get something out of my car first.'

'Your car's in town?'

She nodded.

'I can tow it home if you like,' he said. 'My old Landy's used to rescuing damsels in distress.'

'I'm not in distress,' Callie told him.

'How's your car?' Leo asked Sam, clapping a hand down onto his right shoulder. 'Do you need me to tow yours anywhere?'

'No, thank you,' Sam said tightly, getting up from the table.

'You're going?' Callie said, also rising to her feet.

He nodded. 'It's been a great evening,' he said. 'I'll see you.'

He started walking towards the door.

'Sam!' Callie called, crossing the room to catch up with him. He turned to look at her. 'I'm sorry.'

'For what?'

'For this,' she said. 'I mean for not doing this sooner.'

Sam gave her a quizzical look.

'I should have said yes to you that day – when you asked me to dinner.' There, she thought. She'd said it. But she didn't get a chance to say any more because Leo had joined them by the door.

'Ready to go?' he asked, placing a hand on Callie's shoulder and she nodded.

# CHAPTER 20

Callie was sitting at her computer, but her eyes weren't focussed on the screen in front of her and she wasn't playing out the next scene of her story in her mind. Instead, she was replaying the scene from the night before in The Happy Hare, over and over again until she felt she was going quite mad.

And then the questions began ricocheting around her frazzled brain. What would have happened if Leo hadn't turned up? What exactly would Callie have told Sam and, more importantly, how would he have responded? She'd half-expected to hear from him this morning; hoped with all her heart that he would have called, but he hadn't and she hadn't had the courage to ring him either.

Getting up from her desk, she went downstairs to boil the kettle for a cup of tea. She wasn't getting any writing done. Perhaps she should just give up and go out for a walk, but the sky was lead-grey and uninviting and Callie really didn't fancy it.

She thought about what had happened after she'd left the pub. Leo had towed her car home from Castle Clare and she'd felt obliged to invite him in to Owl Cottage and he'd sat on the sofa in the living room, telling her something about his cocker spaniels that she couldn't remember.

'Callie?' he'd said a minute later. 'We're all right, aren't we?'

She'd been standing awkwardly in front of a bookcase, sliding titles out and sliding them in again without really paying attention. When she looked up at his kind, handsome face, she honestly didn't know what to tell him.

'We're all right,' she'd said at last, taking the coward's way out.

'Good,' he said, getting up and giving her a kiss. 'I'm going to leave you to it. You really do look exhausted. I'll call you tomorrow, okay?' And he'd gone.

Now, a part of her wished that she'd had the courage to break things off with him. It was unfair to keep stringing him along when she knew that she didn't have feelings for him.

'And when you have feelings for someone else,' she said to herself.

She thought about ringing Heidi, but she really wasn't in the mood to talk to anyone so, taking her cup of tea upstairs, she sat back down at her desk for some more staring at the blank screen in front of her.

'So, what happened with you and Callie at the pub?' Bryony asked Sam the second she managed to corner him in the kitchen of Campion House after Sunday lunch. 'I didn't want to ring you last night in case you'd taken her home.'

'As subtle as usual, aren't you?' Sam said, throwing the tea towel he'd been holding at her.

'No point in pussyfooting around, I always say.'

'And can I just ask what business was it of yours to tell her about Aidan's little visit?' Sam said.

'I thought she should know,' Bryony said. 'She cares about you.'

'That is my personal business,' Sam told her. 'It's grubby and it's embarrassing, and the fewer people who know about it, the better.'

'I'm sorry,' she said. 'I didn't mean to upset you.'

'I know,' Sam said, 'but you really should think before you speak sometimes, Bry. You're going to get yourself into trouble some day.'

'So, how did it go?' she asked. 'You're not getting away without telling me.'

Sam tutted and was about to make his excuses when Polly entered the kitchen.

'I'm just asking Sam how his date went with Callie,' Bryony said.

'It wasn't a date,' Sam said.

'No? What would you call it, then?' Bryony said.

'A set-up,' Sam said.

'Oh, so you'd rather not have spent the evening with her?' Bryony asked with a grin.

'I didn't say that.'

'So you got on okay?' Polly asked.

'Of course we did. We always do,' he said, feeling hounded in the two-against-one situation he now found himself in. 'We had dinner.'

'Ooooh, dinner!' Bryony said.

'With wine?' Polly asked.

Sam tutted, but he couldn't help smiling at the line of questioning. 'Yes, with wine.'

'I thought she'd driven into town?' Polly said.

'She was going to get a taxi back,' Sam said.

'*Was* going to?' Bryony said. 'What happened?'

'Leo bloody Wildman turned up and gave her a lift home, towing her car with his bloody Land Rover.'

'Uncle Sam swore!' Archie said as he entered the kitchen with an empty glass.

'Yes,' Polly said. 'He's a very bad uncle. What have you come in here for, Arch?'

'Some more fizz.'

'No more fizz today.'

'Awww, Mum!'

'You'll have a glass of water if you're still thirsty.'

'I'm not *that* thirsty,' he said, handing his mum the glass and leaving the kitchen.

'I keep telling him that all his teeth will fall out if he drinks too many fizzy things, but he doesn't seem worried.'

'Kids don't worry about teeth,' Sam said. 'It's one of the great joys of being young – you believe everything is going to last forever.'

'Anyway – back to last night,' Bryony said. 'What happened next?'

'Nothing happened next,' Sam said. 'She went home with Leo.'

'And you let her?' Bryony said.

'What was I meant to do?' Sam said.

Bryony shook her head. 'You were meant to *fight* for her. Make a big play for her.'

'In The Happy Hare?'

'Absolutely!'

'Bry, you are a crazy romantic with unrealistic notions about how the world works.'

'I am not!' she protested. 'Polly – back me up here, why don't you?'

'I'm with Sam here,' she said. 'If something's meant to be then it'll work itself out. I wouldn't be tempted to push things.'

Bryony rolled her eyes.

'Look,' Sam said, 'Callie and I are friends. Good friends. That's all, okay?' He watched as Bryony puffed out her cheeks in frustration and left the room. Polly took Archie's glass to the sink and then started fiddling around with the dishes. Sam joined her and stared out of the window into the wintery garden. He was tempted, just for a moment, to tell Polly what Callie had said to him as she'd left the pub. Heaven only knew he'd been thinking about it ever since.

'I should have said yes to you that day – when you asked me to dinner.'

She'd looked at him with such tenderness in those beautiful hazel eyes of hers, but what had she meant? Did she just mean that she enjoyed his company and that they should spend more time together talking about books or was it more than that? Was she beginning to have feelings for him as he was towards her?

He sighed. He was, wasn't he? He was beginning to feel something much stronger than friendship towards Callie. It had been creeping up on him so quietly that he couldn't really pinpoint when it had first begun. But it was there. Of that he was quite sure.

'Sam?' Polly said, breaking into his thoughts by placing a hand on his arm. 'You okay?'

'Just thinking.'

'I'd love to know what about. Or whom,' she said, 'but I am not Bryony and so I won't ask.'

'Thank you,' he said, giving her a little smile.

'But don't wait too long to tell me, will you?' she said, going up on tiptoes to give his cheek a kiss.

It was just beginning to get dark and it had started to rain when Polly noticed something wasn't quite right. The family were all sitting in the living room, in that comfortable, casual sprawl that always seemed to follow Sunday lunch.

'Where's Grandma?' Polly asked, closing the paperback book she'd been reading and looking around the room.

A few heads looked up from their own books, newspapers and cups of tea.

'Did she go for a lie down?' Eleanor asked.

'I don't think so,' Grandpa Joe said.

'I'll go and check,' Polly said, on her feet in an instant and making her way to her grandparents' rooms on the ground floor.

'I'll check the kitchen,' Frank said. But she wasn't in the kitchen. Nor was she upstairs.

'I've looked everywhere,' Polly said when she came through from her grandparents' wing a moment later.

'Is she in the TV room?' Eleanor asked.

'No,' Bryony said, coming out of that very room.

'Mum,' Josh said, running through from the dining room. 'The patio door was open.'

Eleanor looked at her husband.

'I'll get some torches,' Frank said.

'Her coat's still hanging up,' Sam said from the hallway. He grabbed it and then put his own on.

'I'll get some blankets,' Bryony said. 'It's freezing outside.'

'Do you really think she's out there?' Polly asked.

'She's not in the house, is she?' Sam said. 'Where's she likely to have gone, Grandpa?'

Grandpa Joe scratched his head, his face was deathly pale. 'I don't know,' he said. 'I really don't know.'

'Think, Dad,' Frank said. 'Is there anywhere she likes to walk to these days?'

He shook his head, looking vague. 'She likes the old wooden bridge over the ford, I guess,' he said, 'but I don't think she'd go there on her own.'

'There's a first time for everything,' Frank said.

'Would she really have gone there in the dark and the rain?' Josh asked.

'It might not have been dark or raining when she left,' Eleanor pointed out, 'and you know how she loses track of time these days.'

'Come on,' Frank said, once everyone had their coats and hats on. 'We've got no time to lose.'

'Should we take the dogs?' Josh asked.

'Good idea,' Frank said. 'You take Hardy and I'll take Brontë.'

Polly grabbed hold of Archie's hand. 'Now, stay with me, okay? We don't want you getting lost as well.'

The little boy nodded as everyone headed outside.

The late afternoon air was bitterly cold. The wind had picked up and the rain chilled everyone's face and fingers in an instant.

'Okay,' Frank began, holding the spaniel's lead tight in his hand, 'Polly, Archie, Bryony and Eleanor – search the garden. Check the greenhouse in the walled garden and the potting sheds. Everybody got a working torch?'

'Yes,' everyone echoed. If there was one thing country living taught you, it was to have plenty of torches.

'Josh – could you head out across the field with Hardy?'

'The footpath to the woods? Sure, Dad,' he said, the pointer at his side waiting anxiously to get moving.

Frank nodded and everyone instantly looked nervous at the thought of Grandma Nell wandering into the woods in the dark.

'Sam–'

'I'll go down to the ford,' he said.

'And Grandpa and I will head the other way along the road. Have we all got our phones?'

Everyone nodded.

'Okay, let's get going.'

The night air filled with cries as the Nightingale family spread out.

'Nell?'

'Grandma!'

'Mum? Where are you?'

Polly, Archie, Bryony and Eleanor fanned out around the garden, the lights from Campion House as well as their torches helping to guide them. Sam watched as Josh headed for the footpath to the wood and then he walked out of the driveway, turning right along the lane which led to the ford and the little wooden bridge.

His bent his head low as he faced into the wind. He hated the thought of his grandmother out there in the dark somewhere.

'Grandma?' he shouted, but the wind carried his voice across a hawthorn hedge and off over a field.

The country lane from Campion House was narrow and twisted through the countryside. The road was slick with rain tonight and Sam found himself sloshing through several deep puddles. Was his beloved grandma really out on such a night? The thought terrified him.

He scanned the gaps in the hedges with his torch as he went, stopping at each and every field opening in case she'd walked into one, but there was no sign of her. He could only imagine how his grandpa must be feeling. He'd looked completely winded when he'd been told that Nell wasn't in the house.

Sam thought of the special love his grandparents had for each other and how much they'd been through in almost sixty years of marriage. Sam loved hearing the stories from their past and Grandpa Joe loved telling them whilst he kept his grandson company in the shop. Sam had heard all about the early years of their marriage and how hard they'd struggled to open and expand the bookshops in

Castle Clare. There were funny tales about Sam's dad and uncle, the young Frank and Ralph, and countless reminiscences about Sam and his siblings, some of which he'd sooner forget like the time they'd had a picnic in a nearby field by the river and Sam had trod in a cow pat, seeming to sink right up to his four-year-old knees. Grandpa had dangled him over the river to wash the mess away and Grandma had given him an extra lollypop. Her pockets had been filled with lollypops and jelly babies in those days, Sam remembered with affection.

'Grandma?' he shouted into the dark now as he headed towards the ford. It was coming up around the next bend. He sent the beam from his torch as far ahead of him as he could and caught a glimpse of water. The downpour had swelled the ford and, as he approached it, it sounded like a small river.

He flashed his beam to the left of the lane where the wooden bridge was, but there was no sign of anyone on it.

'Grandma!' he called again, crossing the bridge. Would she really have come this far?

Sam had his answer as soon as he stepped off the little bridge when the thin beam from his torch picked out a pair of slippers and the fallen body of his grandmother.

# CHAPTER 21

Callie was just drawing her curtains against the night when a pair of headlights lit up the lane. It was Leo's Land Rover. He hadn't called and she wasn't expecting him, but she was beginning to learn that that was one of the ways of country living: people did have a habit of just dropping by unannounced.

'Leo?' she said in surprise as she opened the door to him a moment later.

'I got caught in that downpour. Did you hear it?' he asked, entering the cottage before actually being invited in. 'I've been out all day,' he said.

'I can tell,' Callie said, looking down at his trousers which were more mud that material.

'Ah, sorry. I should have gone home first, but I was so close to yours and I wanted to see you.' He bent forward to kiss her, his stubble scraping the soft skin of her face.

'Where are the dogs?' she asked.

'Asleep in the car.'

'Won't they be cold?'

'They're snuggled up together on their blankets.'

'Well come and get warm yourself,' she said. 'I've got the wood burner going.'

'Brilliant,' he said, taking off his great big boots, his wax jacket and his cap. His dark hair was wet at the edges and his face had a rainy sheen. If Callie had been a writer of romance novels then Leo Wildman would be prime material for a hero, she couldn't help thinking.

'What have you been doing today?' he asked her as he sat himself on the rug in front of the stove, his long legs crossed yoga-style.

'Oh, not much,' she said, 'mostly staring at a blank screen and wondering where all my words have gone.'

'Oh, no,' he said. 'A computer malfunction?'

'No, an *author* malfunction.'

'Perhaps you need somebody to turn you off then turn you on again,' he said with a wink.

She grinned but chose to ignore his suggestion. 'Would you like something to eat?' she asked him.

'I would *love* something to eat.'

'Well, it won't be anything spectacular from the local hedgerows; it'll just be a simple pasta.'

'That sounds great,' he said, getting up from the rug. 'Anything I can do to help?' He winced.

'You okay?'

'A bit wet around the legs,' he said. 'I don't suppose I could have a bath?'

'Oh,' Callie said in surprise. 'I – well, of course.'

'Great,' he said. 'So, where is it?'

'Right, well, it's upstairs, on the left. Towels are in the airing cupboard on the landing. Help yourself.'

Callie watched as he walked up the stairs and then she went in to the kitchen to make a start on dinner. She heard the bathroom door shut and then came the sound of running water.

There's a naked man in your bathroom, she thought as she boiled the kettle.

'I'm not going to think about that,' she said to herself, and she really tried not to because the thoughts that had been tumbling around in her mind lately all pointed to one thing.

'You've got to tell him,' she said as she walked to the fridge to see if there might be something worthy of Leo's palette in there. 'This has got to be the first and the last time he's naked in your home.'

She nodded to herself. It was unfair of her to keep stringing Leo along when she knew that she was having feelings for another man. Leo was a lovely guy – one of the loveliest she had ever met – and she'd had so much fun with him, but he wasn't quite right for her.

'And Sam is?' she said to herself, remembering how she'd come to Suffolk with one very clear vision in mind: to avoid men and anything approaching a romantic relationship. So what had happened to that idea?

'Sam happened,' she whispered, pouring the water from the kettle into a big copper pan. Gentle, smart, sweet Sam, and she couldn't stop thinking about him.

'Oh, this is ridiculous,' she said. 'You're meant to be happily single again and putting all your time and energy into your work, not mooning around like a lovesick schoolgirl.'

But it was too late for that. Much, much too late.


In a dark country lane just a few miles away from Owl Cottage, Sam Nightingale was dealing with a crisis all of his own.

'Grandma?' he cried, rushing forward. 'Are you okay? Are you hurt?'

'No, no,' she said in a faint voice. 'Who is it?'

'It's me – Sam,' he said. 'Can you get up?'

'I'm not sure,' she said. 'I can't feel my legs.'

'You're frozen,' Sam said, 'and wet through. We need to get this coat on you and get you indoors. Can you move? We've got to get you off the road.'

Gently, Sam scooped his arms around her, lifting her slowly until she was sitting up, then placing her coat around her and removing his winter hat and placing that on her head.

'How do you feel? Do you remember what happened?'

'I was walking across the bridge and slipped.'

'You know where you are, then?'

'Yes,' she said, 'but I'm not quite sure how I got here.'

'I'm going to call Dad, okay?' He got his phone out of his pocket. 'Dad?' he said a moment later. 'It's Sam. I've found her. She's here by the ford, but she's had a fall. Okay. We'll see you in a minute.' He hung up. 'Grandpa and Dad are bringing the car. We'll get you home in no time, all right? Get you nice and warm.' He gave her a hug, rubbing his hands up and down her back. 'Do you hurt anywhere?'

'I can't tell,' she said. 'I think I hurt everywhere, but maybe it's just the cold.'

'Very likely,' Sam said. 'The cold and damp. Do you think you can move to sit on my lap.'

'But then you'll get all wet and cold,' she said.

'Doesn't matter,' Sam said, sitting down on the road and easing her onto him before wrapping his arms around her.'

'I could murder a cup of tea,' she said.

Sam laughed and kissed her cheek which was terrifyingly cold. 'We'll get you a cup of tea.'

It was then that they were lit up in a sweep of headlights and the sound of car doors opening greeted them.

'Mum!' Frank cried. He was by her side in an instant. 'Sam – help me get her into the car. Is it safe to move her?'

'I think so,' Sam said.

'Nell?' Grandpa Joe said, taking her hand. 'My old darling. Can you hear me?'

'Of course I can hear you,' Nell said. 'I'm not dead yet!'

Grandpa Joe gave her a big kiss and then they all helped to lift her into the car and drove her home as fast as was safely possible along the wet country lane.

'Oh, thank God!' Eleanor said as they arrived home. Nell was now on her feet although being supported by Sam and Frank, and was surrounded by the entire family.

'Don't crowd her,' Eleanor said.

'We should ring an ambulance,' Josh said.

Eleanor shook her head. 'We need to get her straight into bed. A nice warm bed with a hot drink. That's what she needs.'

'But something might be broken,' Josh said.

'I don't think it is,' Frank said, 'but I think we should call Dr Ward. He's just down the road. He can be here faster than any ambulance.

Eleanor nodded. 'I'll boil a kettle.'

'I'll do that, Mum,' Bryony said.

'Thanks, darling,' Eleanor said, following Grandpa Joe, Sam, Frank and Nell along the hallway towards Joe and Nell's rooms on the ground floor.

There was then a flurry of activity as everyone did something to help. Bryony brought in a hot water bottle and a mug of sweet tea, Eleanor helped Nell get ready for bed, Frank got in touch with Dr Ward, Polly and Archie dried the dogs off and fed them, and Sam comforted his grandfather who had turned quite ashen.

'She's never done this before,' he whispered to his grandson. 'What did she say to you?'

Sam sighed. 'She seemed quite lucid when I arrived on the scene. She knew where she was, but she didn't seem to know how she'd got there.'

Grandpa Joe shook his head. 'What are we going to do?'

'We're going to make her comfortable and let Dr Ward see what's what,' Sam said in a calm voice although a tumult of emotions was churning inside him.

Grandpa Joe nodded and then walked towards the bed where he sat on the edge, taking Nell's right hand in his.

'All right, my Nell?' he asked, bending forward and giving her a kiss.

'Did I scare you?' she whispered, looking up at him.

'You certainly did,' he said, 'but you're safe now.'

Sam watched the scene, his grandmother's frail hand in his grandfather's great strong one, and something touched him deeply inside. They had shared so much life together and the thought of one of them being without the other was too much to bear.

He left the room, blinking back the tears that had caught him by surprise.

'How is she?' Josh asked as he entered the living room. Polly, Archie and Bryony were also in there waiting for news.

'She's resting.'

There was a knock at the door. Sam went to answer it, letting Dr Ward in. 'She's through here,' he told the older man, leading him through to his grandparents' bedroom.

Sam told Dr Ward where he'd found his grandmother and he examined her and there passed an anxious few moments with the whole family hovering by the bedroom door. Grandpa Joe, who'd refused to leave Nell's side, was sitting in a chair by the bed, only relinquishing her hand when the doctor absolutely insisted.

'Well,' he said once he'd finished his examination, 'bed's definitely the best place for her.' He motioned for the family to leave the room and they all went into the living room at the front of the house.

'How is she, doctor?'

'I wouldn't want to move her tonight and I don't see that there's any need now that you've all done such a splendid job in getting her comfortable. She's obviously had a shock and will need monitoring, but it's the memory lapse that concerns me most.'

'It's been worrying me for some time now,' Eleanor said. Frank put his arm around his wife and hugged her to him.

'We'll need to run some tests,' the doctor said.

'Of course,' Frank said.

'As soon as you feel she's ready,' Dr Ward said. 'Give me a call in the morning, okay? Or sooner if you're worried about anything.'

'Thanks for coming so quickly,' Frank said, seeing him out. When he returned to the living room, Sam couldn't help noticing that his father looked completely drained.

'I'll get everyone some tea, okay?' Polly said. 'Grandpa?'

'I'm going to sit with your grandmother,' he said, shuffling out of the room.

Sam watched as his parents sat down on the sofa together, arms around each other.

'I've never been so scared in my life,' Frank said. 'Well, other than every time you went into labour with each of our children.'

Eleanor kissed his cheek. 'She's safe now,' she said.

'I should have listened to you. You've been worried about her for a while, haven't you?'

She nodded. 'Her memory isn't what it was,' Eleanor said softly.

'I know,' Frank said. 'I've been stupidly believing that it's just part of the ageing process, but maybe there's more to it than that.'

'Well find out,' she said, patting his hand.

'I'll go and give Polly a hand,' Sam said, leaving the room.

His sister was arranging mugs on a tray in the kitchen when he entered.

'Hey,' he said. 'You holding up?'

She turned and nodded. 'That was pretty scary, wasn't it?'

'I don't think I've ever been more scared in my life,' Sam admitted. 'What if we hadn't found her? What if she'd got herself lost in a wood or fallen into a quarry or banged her head on the road or–'

'Shush!' Polly said, approaching him and resting a hand on his arm. 'She's safe. Safe in bed and surrounded by her family.'

'But what if it happens again?'

'We've got to make sure it doesn't,' Polly said pragmatically, as if it was simply a case of her making up her mind that the incident would never be repeated. She moved to the kettle and began fussing over the tea things.

'I'll take Grandpa his.'

'I haven't made one for Grandma. She's had some and I imagine she's sleeping now.'

Sam left with two mugs of tea.

'Grandpa?' he said quietly as he entered the bedroom.

'Sammy,' he said, looking up.

'Is she sleeping?'

'Yes,' he said from the chair beside the bed.

Sam handed him his tea and then took an appreciative sip of his own.

'To think of my Nell out there alone in the dark,' he said, shaking his head. 'How could I have let that happen?'

'It wasn't your fault.'

'It feels as if it's my fault,' he said.

Sam pulled up a chair from his grandma's dressing table and sat down next to his grandpa.

'Did I ever tell you about the time we got lost in Venice?' Grandpa Joe said.

Sam frowned. 'No,' he said. 'I didn't even know you'd been to Venice.'

'Ah, well, you don't know everything about us, you know,' he said, a little of his familiar humour coming back to him now. 'We'd been shopping along the Rialto Bridge. Window shopping, you understand. Venice is horribly expensive.'

Sam smiled. His grandpa was a notorious skinflint.

'Well, your grandma turned one way and I turned another and, before you knew it, we were parted. It was before the days of mobile phones, you know. Took us over two hours before we found one another.'

'Couldn't you have met at the hotel or something?' Sam asked.

'Nell didn't know where that was. You know she's the world's worst map reader.' He gave a little chuckle. 'I'll never forget the fear of those two long hours. I thought I'd entered the set of that film where the little kid in the red coat is running around the backstreets of Venice.'

'Don't Look Now?'

'Why?' Grandpa said, looking around the room.

'That's the name of the film, Grandpa.'

'Oh,' he said. 'Well, anyway, we found each other and your grandma had managed to buy three Venetian masks and presents for everyone. See what happens when she's not under my watchful eye?'

Sam grinned.

'Hold on to the ones you love,' Grandpa Joe told him now. 'Hold on to them tightly and tell them that you love them at every opportunity because you just don't know when you'll be parted from them.'

Sam looked at the great tenderness with which his grandfather watched over the sleeping figure of his wife. There were decades full of love in his eyes and Sam swallowed hard as he observed it. He felt as if he was a witness to a very private moment although there was little of privacy in the Nightingale family. Somehow, though, this seemed like an extraordinarily intimate moment.

Not wanting to intrude anymore, he gave his grandpa a hug and left the room. His family was gathered in the living room, drinking their tea in numbed silence. His parents still had their arms around each other and Sam couldn't help thinking about how very fragile life was, and how quickly things could spiral out of control in the space of a moment.

'I've got to go,' he said from the door.

'Already?' Eleanor said.

He nodded, walking into the room and bending to kiss his mother's cheek.

'You okay?' she asked him.

He took a deep breath. 'It's been quite a day.'

'Never to be repeated,' his father said. 'We've all got to make sure of that.'

'We will,' Sam said. 'Call me if there's any change, okay?'

'We will,' his father said.

Sam said his goodbyes and left Campion House.

As he drove back along the country lanes, he couldn't shake the emotions that had been welling up inside of him at the events of the day. Nor could he forget the great love and tenderness he'd seen shared between his grandparents and his parents too. After so many years together, each couple still had such strong feelings for each other.

And that's when it happened. That's the moment when Sam realised something with such clarity that it stunned him: he had to tell Callie how he felt about her.

Sam knew that he couldn't go on locking his feelings away from her or denying them. Grandpa Joe had been right; Sam was only fooling himself if he thought he couldn't ever fall in love again, and he had been totally in denial believing that romantic love no longer had a place in his life. It was in his very genes and he knew that, even if he experienced a tiny fraction of what his parents and his grandparents felt for each other, then his life would be all the richer for it.

Sam slowed the car to a stop as he came to the junction. The road straight ahead would lead him into Castle Clare and home; the road to the right would take him to Newton St Clare and Callie.

He paused, hesitating, and then he turned right.

# CHAPTER 22

When Leo entered the living room, he was wearing a towel around his waist.

'Is this okay?' he said. 'I couldn't bear to put those wet trousers on again. Mind if I dry them by the wood burner?'

Callie, who'd been laying the table, looked at him in silent surprise as she took in the long bare legs in the middle of her cottage, but what could she say.

'Oh, right – sure,' she said, feeling horribly certain that she was blushing.

'They won't take long to dry,' he said, coming over to the little table and pulling out a chair to sit down. With his bare legs.

Callie turned away. 'I'll just warm up the legs.' She paused. '*Plates!* I mean plates!'

She hid herself in the kitchen as she tried desperately to die from her mortification.

'You need a hand?' Leo called through.

'No thanks,' she called back. She didn't want his hands as well as his legs getting in on the action.

You've got to tell him, a little voice inside her said. You've got to tell him to put his trousers on and leave. This has to stop. It isn't fair on him.

Callie nodded to herself. She'd do that. As soon as they'd eaten, she'd tell him.

The lane leading to Newton St Clare was puddle-strewn and Sam had to slow down and drive in the middle of the road at one point because the sides had turned into little rivers. He parked across the road from Owl Cottage, switched off his headlights and sat in the darkness, gathering his thoughts. There was a Land Rover parked outside Callie's cottage, but he didn't give it a second thought. He had other things on his mind.

'You can do this,' he told himself. 'You *should* do this.' And he knew in his heart that it was absolutely the right thing to do.

Getting out of the car, he crossed the road, opening the gate into Callie's garden and pausing, just briefly, before knocking on the front door.

Time seemed to stand strangely still and Sam was acutely aware of the world around him from the coldness of the evening air on his face to the sound of the wind in the trees on the village green. He thought that the door would never be opened and so he knocked again.

And there she was.

'Sam?' her bright eyes widened and he swallowed hard at the vision of her. 'What a surprise.'

'I wanted to see you,' he blurted without preamble.

'Is everything okay?'

'It's been quite a night,' he said.

'What's happened?'

'We had a bit of a scare with Grandma Nell.'

'Oh, no! Is she okay?'

'She is now,' he said. 'But it made me realise something. Something I should have told you before.'

'What?' Callie asked, her eyes wide and expectant.

Sam cleared his throat. 'Can I can come in?'

'Well, I–' she began.

'What is it?'

'Leo's here.'

Sam frowned.

Leo must have heard his name because, all of a sudden, he was standing there in the doorway wearing a bath towel and a big fat grin.

'Oh, it's Sam, right? How are you?' he said.

'I'm fine,' Sam said, doing his best not to look at him which wasn't easy with the amount of bare flesh on display.

'Want to join us? Callie's just made some pasta,' Leo said.

'No – I – erm,' he stumbled, noticing that Leo's hair was wet and that he'd obviously had a bath or shower. In Callie's Cottage. 'I'd better be going.'

He glanced at Callie whose face had turned quite red and then he turned to go.

'Sam!' she called after him, but he was through the gate and across the road. 'It's not what you think!'

She was behind him as he opened the car door.

'You don't have to explain to me, Callie,' he told her.

'But I want to,' she said, 'and you wanted to say something to me too, didn't you? *Didn't* you?'

He paused, glancing at her briefly. 'It doesn't matter,' he said quietly, getting into the car.

'Sam!' she cried. 'Don't leave like this. *Please!*'

But he had to and he did, with thousands of words tumbling around in his head which he knew would never be spoken now.

Callie watched Sam's car disappear into the darkness and then turned back to her cottage. Leo was still standing in the doorway and she couldn't help wanting to shout at him, but it really wasn't Leo's fault and she knew it would be wrong to blame him.

As she entered her garden, Leo left the door and, by the time she entered the living room, he was getting dressed – putting on his not-quite-dry trousers.

'I think we'd better talk,' he said, turning to face her as he did up his belt and she nodded.

He sat down on the sofa and Callie sat next to him.

'What's going on?' he asked. Callie had never seen him looking so serious and it upset her.

'Leo, I'm so sorry,' she began hesitantly.

He gave a deep, sad sigh that nearly broke her heart. 'Were you ever going to tell me how you feel about Sam?'

'Of course I was,' she said, 'I just didn't get the chance. It's all been so confusing.'

'How? How's it been confusing? I thought we had something special going on here.'

'We did,' she said. 'You're such a brilliant guy, Leo, you really are, and I've had the best time ever with you, but–'

'You don't love me,' he said. 'Is that it?'

Callie didn't know what to say. The intense look in his eyes was so painful to behold and no words seemed sufficient to try and explain herself to him.

'When I left London,' she began, trying desperately to make sense of the situation she now found herself in, 'I didn't want to get involved with anyone. I really didn't. I needed some space, some time. I needed to be alone. But then I met you.'

'And Sam.'

'Yes, and Sam,' she said.

'So, what's going on now? He saw you first so he's the winner?'

'Leo – please!'

'I'm just trying to understand what's happening,' he cried in frustration.

'I know,' she said, 'and I'm trying to work it out too.' She took a deep breath as if that might help to sort out the mess in her head. 'Things sometimes happen that you're not entirely in control of.'

'Like what?'

'Like going out with you,' she said.

'But you were in control of that,' he said, obviously perplexed.

'Yes, but–'

'But what?'

Callie chewed her lip. How could she explain this to him?

*As truthfully as possible*, a little voice inside her said.

'Remember my friend Heidi?' she said slowly.

'Of course,' he said.

'I think she was more ready for me to go out with you than I was,' Callie said. 'I think she was worried that I was going to lock myself away in this cottage and never see the light of day again let alone go out with a man.'

'You didn't want to go out with me?' Leo said, rubbing a hand over his stubbly jaw line.

'If I'm really honest – no, I didn't. But Heidi made a very good case for you.' Callie smiled gently at him and picked up one of his hands in both of hers. 'I had the best time ever with you,' she told him. 'I really have.'

'So you always knew it wasn't going to last?'

She shook her head. 'None of this was planned, Leo. I didn't plan to meet you or go out with you or have feelings for you. And I didn't plan to meet Sam or have feelings for him either. I really didn't think I had a right to all this – not after the way my marriage ended. It's all been so–' she paused, 'so *overwhelming*.'

'And where does this leave us?' Leo said.

Callie looked down at her lap. 'I should have told you what was happening. I was going to this evening.'

'You were going to tell me about Sam?'

Callie nodded. 'I feel awful about this. I never ever meant to hurt you.' She looked up at him again and the wounded look in his eyes nearly destroyed her.

'It's the books, isn't it?' he said.

'What do you mean?'

'This Sam's really into books like you, isn't he? And I don't read much.'

'It's not because you don't read much,' she said.

'No?'

'*No!*'

'Then what is it?' he asked. 'Because I really want to know.'

Callie frowned. 'I don't know if I can explain it to you. It's just somehow different with Sam. *I'm* different. Does that make sense?' She paused, searching desperately for the right words. 'He takes me out of myself. And right into myself too.'

'*That* doesn't make sense!' Leo said, giving the tiniest of smiles.

Callie dared to smile back.

'I think he has feelings for you too,' Leo said. 'He was going to tell you tonight, wasn't he? That's why he came over.'

'I don't know,' Callie said.

'I saw the way he was looking at you,' he said. 'It was the same that night in the pub. I interrupted you then too. I could see he hated me for it.'

'He didn't hate you.'

'Well, he hates me tonight,' Leo said, getting up off the sofa.

'Are you going?' she asked him as she stood up too.

'I think I'd better,' he said.

Suddenly, there were tears in Callie's eyes and he moved forward, wrapping his arms around her and kissing her forehead.

'You're one of the sweetest girls I've ever met,' he said, 'and I'm never going to forgive you for breaking up with me before I got to show you the bluebell wood.'

'Oh, Leo!' she cried.

He shook his head. 'Don't cry,' he said, but she was quite sure she could see tears in his own eyes. 'You're right – we've had a really great time together.'

'We have, haven't we?'

'And if you ever get fed up of that book guy, you know where I am.'

'I'm not sure that book guy will want to see me after tonight,' Callie said.

'Don't kid yourself,' he said.

'I really hope we can still be fr–'

'Don't say that,' Leo interrupted. 'It could never work out, could it? I mean, what do you think Sam would say if I turned up to take you foraging in the woods one day?' He gave her a wink and then, without another word, he left Owl Cottage.

# CHAPTER 23

Monday mornings. What was it about them that made one want to crawl under the duvet, especially when it followed a particularly gruelling Sunday evening in which Callie had upset not just one man but two.

She wasn't sure how long it had taken her to fall asleep the night before, but she'd seen one o'clock, two o'clock and three o'clock glowing malevolently on her alarm clock.

She was just hauling herself out of bed when her phone rang. Realising that it was now ten o'clock and the rest of the world must have been awake for hours, she rushed to answer it.

It was her agent.

'I hope you're sitting down,' Margot began

'I'm almost lying down,' Callie said.

'Pardon?'

'Nothing.'

'Well, I've got some rather good news for you.'

'Go on,' Callie said, automatically crossing her fingers as she wondered which publisher might have made an offer for her book.

But Margot didn't give Callie the name of the publisher. She just gave her a figure. A very large figure.

'Wow,' Callie said. 'That's quite impressive.'

'Quite impressive? It's the *best* offer I've had in all year!'

'And you're sure that's just for the one book?'

'That's the offer although they want to have an option on your next book.' It was then that Margot revealed the name of the publisher.

'Right,' Callie said. It was the news she'd been dreading.

'So? What should I say?' Margot pressed.

'Can I think about it?'

'What's there to think about other than how quickly you can get the contract signed? I could courier it over to you today.'

'I'd really rather think about it,' Callie said and she heard Margot groan.

'Don't make this deal about things it isn't about,' Margot said. 'This is business, Callie. Remember that.'

'It's easy for you to say. You won't be the one working with Piers.' She took a deep breath. As much as she would welcome the money, this wasn't the outcome she'd hoped for. 'Did anyone else offer?' she asked, keeping her fingers crossed.

'Oh, yes,' Margot said, and she told her the three other offers that had been made by publishers – all were considerably lower than the one that had come in from Piers.

'But you told me his offer would encourage the others to up their game,' Callie said.

'It did,' Margot said. 'You should have seen them before.'

'This puts me in a very awkward position.'

'I don't see why,' Margot said. 'It's not like he'll actually be editing your work.'

'Are you kidding? If we sign this deal, Piers will make it his sole mission in life to make sure he's my editor.'

'Well, take it or leave it,' Margot said, 'although, as your agent, I'd advise you to take it.'

As her agent hung up, Callie thought about what the money would do for her – how she would have plenty to live off for the next year whilst she wrote more. Wasn't that what she'd been hoping for with her new book? Wasn't that what every writer dreamed of?

When the phone rang a moment later, she nearly didn't pick it up because she thought it might be Piers, but it wasn't. It was Joe Nightingale – Sam's grandfather.

'Callie?' he said.

'Hello, Mr Nightingale. How are you?'

'Can't complain. Can't complain.'

'How's Nell?'

'You heard about Nell?'

'Sam called round last night – briefly.'

'I thought he might have,' Grandpa Joe said. 'I take it all didn't go well between you two?'

'You could say that.'

'Ah. Well, that explains his mood today,' Grandpa Joe whispered.

'Oh, dear,' Callie said, feeling absolutely awful. 'Is he okay?'

'I wish he'd talk to me so I could find out. But Nell is stronger this morning, thanks for asking.'

'I'm glad to hear it.'

'I wanted to stay with her today, but she threw her pillow at me and told me I had to go to work.'

Callie laughed.

'Listen,' Grandpa Joe continued, 'I had a feeling Sam wouldn't ring you with this today, but I thought you'd want to know that your book's in.'

'*Perdita's Key*? The first edition?'

'The very one.'

'That's great!' she said. 'I didn't think Sam would be able to track it down.'

'He's very tenacious when it comes to such things,' Grandpa Joe said.

'Is he around today?' Callie asked.

'Kind of,' he said. 'Why? Did you want to see him?'

'I did,' she said. 'I do.'

'Then I'll make sure you do,' Grandpa Joe said. 'I'm sure he'll want to see you.'

'Thanks,' she said. 'I'll pop by soon.'

When Callie put the phone down, she found she was shaking which was ridiculous. What did she have to be nervous about? Apart from everything, that was. But the thought of seeing Sam again after what had happened the night before made her uneasy. Would he even want to see her again, she wondered? She wouldn't be surprised if he refused and yet she knew he wasn't the kind of person who would be awkward and never speak to her again, and she took comfort from Grandpa Joe's kind words.

'I'm sure he'll want to see you.'

'But does he?' Callie said to herself, wishing she felt as certain as Grandpa Joe. Well, even if he didn't want to see her and even if he didn't want to speak to her ever again, Callie was jolly well going to speak to him and tell him how she felt.

With a crazy kind of determination, Callie grabbed her satchel and left for Castle Clare immediately. There was no point putting these things off, she thought, washing and dressing quickly before leaving Owl Cottage and getting in her car.

The country lanes were slick with rain from the night before, forcing Callie to take things slowly which made the short journey a kind of torture and, when she turned the corner by the wood, she was forced to stop completely as a gaggle of geese made their slow stately way across the road. Callie loved the country lanes, she really did, but they could be absolutely infuriating if you were in a hurry.

Finally, she made it into town, the wheels and sides of her car splattered with mud and her nerves in tatters. She gave herself a few minutes to calm down, watching the people of Castle Clare going about their Monday morning business. It wouldn't be long before the shops were stuffed full of glittering displays for Christmas, she thought. Callie had heard from her neighbours that lights would be strung up all across Market Square and an enormous tree would be erected at its centre. She couldn't wait to see that.

Getting out of the car, a leaf-littered wind blowing around her, Callie didn't immediately make her way to Nightingale's. Instead, she walked straight into a little shop on the other side of the square. There was something she had been putting off for far too long; something she needed to do before she saw Sam.

Ten minutes later, her business complete, she crossed Market Square again and made her way to Sam's bookshop, stopping to look at the beautiful shopfront before opening the door and hearing the familiar ring of the bell.

'Callie!' Grandpa Joe said, looking up from the newspaper he was reading as he stood on till duty.

'Hello,' she said with a bright smile which belied her nerves.

'I have your book ready and waiting,' he said, turning around and reaching down to a shelf behind the counter. 'Here we are.'

Callie smiled as he handed her the little paperback of *Perdita's Key*. It was a modest volume, one which most people wouldn't have looked twice at, but it had been part of a small print run at the very beginning of Callie's career and she'd been so desperate to see it again having given away what had turned out to be her last copy.

'Thank you so much,' she said, getting out her money to pay as Grandpa Joe took the book from her to pop into a brown paper bag.

'Don't thank me,' Grandpa Joe said, handing her the bag. 'You want to thank Sam, don't you?' he said, a bushy white eyebrow rising.

'I do,' she said.

Grandpa Joe nodded. 'He's upstairs,' he said. 'Hiding out with a box of new acquisitions. He's asked not to be disturbed, but I think we can make an exception, eh?'

'Are you sure?' Callie asked.

'Get yourself up there,' Grandpa Joe said with an encouraging smile.

Callie took a deep breath, her nerves rising again as she walked through the shop to the back room and up the stairs which led up to Sam's flat. She'd never been up there and she didn't know what sort of welcome she was going to receive when she got to the top of the stairs, but she went up anyway, her tread slow and her feet managing to find every single squeak in the old floorboards.

The door to Sam's flat was ajar and she caught sight of him sitting in the middle of the floor completely surrounded by books.

'Grandpa – there' some really interesting volumes here. Come and see.' He looked up. 'Callie!'

'Hi,' she said.

'I thought you were Grandpa.'

'He said it was all right if I came up,' she said. 'Is it?'

Sam got up from the floor and brushed himself down. 'Of course,' he said.

Callie entered the room and looked around, noticing the numerous book cases and shelves stuffed to overflowing with hardbacks and paperbacks. It was the sort of room she could instantly feel at home in, but then, she wasn't there to feel at home and so she cleared her throat.

'I wanted to thank you for the book,' she said.

'I'm glad we finally tracked down a copy for you,' he said, running a hand through his dark hair and straightening his glasses. 'It's really nice condition too. I don't think it's been read.'

'I know. Although that's a mixed blessing for an author, isn't it?' she said with a stab at humour.

'I guess so,' he said.

'Anyway, I can't thank you enough. I thought I'd never see it again.'

'All part of the service,' he said, and there was one of those dreadful, silence-drenched pauses when neither knew what to say.

Callie swallowed hard, knowing that it should be her who spoke first.

'Sam,' she said, 'I wanted to explain about last night.'

He shook his head. 'You don't owe me an explanation.'

'But will you let me explain anyway?' she asked.

'Callie, what goes on between you and Leo Wildman is none of my business.'

'But there *is* no me and Leo,' she all but cried.

'But I thought—'

She shook her head. 'I like Leo. I really do. But he's just a friend and – well, he's probably not even that after what happened when you left.'

'What happened?' Sam asked and then shook his head. 'Sorry. Not my business.'

'It is your business,' she said, 'because it very much involved you.' She held his gaze. 'Do you think I could sit down?' she asked.

'Of course,' he said, motioning to the small sofa and quickly moving a couple of large hardbacks to make room for them both.

'I told him,' she began, 'I told Leo that I never planned to get involved with anyone again, that I wouldn't allow myself to have feelings for anyone. Not after what I went through with Piers. Not ever.' She twisted her hands into knots in her lap. 'That's what I thought, anyway. I came to Suffolk to start again. To be *just me*. I needed to get back to that most basic of things – learning to live by myself. But then...'

'What?' Sam asked after a moment's silence.

'But then I met you,' she said in a half-whisper, looking anxiously up at him. His gentle brown eyes looked straight back at her. 'I wish you'd say something,' she said.

'Callie,' he said, 'I've been *trying* to say something to you for ages.' He gave a tiny smile. 'I was trying last night and that night in the pub, and the time I wanted to take you out to dinner and you said no. Remember?'

'*Please* don't remind me,' she said. 'I wanted to say yes and I really should have, but I was scared.'

'But I'm scared too,' he confessed with a little laugh. 'You're not the only one to have just come out of a bad relationship and you're certainly not the only one to have sworn off falling in love again because I did that too.'

'You did?'

He nodded. 'I'm terrified, absolutely terrified, of history repeating itself and I'm sure you are too, but here's the thing: I'm not Piers and you're certainly not Emma.'

He held her gaze and she nodded. 'No,' she said. 'You're right.'

'So,' he asked with a grin, 'what do you think about us being scared... *together*? About giving things a go even though we're both absolutely terrified and have promised ourselves that we'd never get involved again. What do you think, Callie? Do you want to give it a go?'

She smiled. 'You *really* want to be with me?'

'I really do,' he said.

'But I feel I have absolutely nothing to give you,' she said.

'And I feel I've absolutely nothing to give you too!' he said.

She laughed and he joined in.

'But maybe we have,' he said, taking her hands in his. 'Maybe this second chance is the one that's meant to be – the one we were both working towards.' He paused.

'What is it?' she asked

'You're not wearing your wedding ring anymore.'

'I've just had it cut off at the jewellers in Market Square,' she said. 'It wouldn't shift and I've been desperate to get rid of it.'

Sam's fingers gently stroked hers and she watched as he closed the space between the two of them and kissed her lips so gently and so sweetly that Callie knew she was lost forever and that this second chance Sam had spoken of could be the very best thing to have ever happened to her.

'Sammy?' Grandpa Joe's voice came from the top of the stairs.

Callie and Sam leapt up from the sofa as if they'd been ejected from it.

'Grandpa – have you been eavesdropping?' Sam said, walking towards the landing. Callie followed and saw Grandpa Joe standing there with a great big smile on his face.

'Eavesdropping? Wherever do you get these notions from?' Grandpa Joe asked. 'I was just wondering if I should ring your mum and tell her to set an extra place for Sunday lunch from now on.'

Sam sighed and shook his head. 'I'm sorry, Callie,' he said. 'I should have warned you. If you have *anything* to do with me, you're going to have to get used to this sort of thing.'

She smiled and laughed. 'I'd *love* to get used to this sort of thing!' she said and she wasn't a bit surprised when Grandpa Joe walked towards her and wrapped her up in a big warm hug.

# Rules for a Successful Book Club

# VICTORIA CONNELLY

Book two in The Book Lovers series will be out in 2016.

# ABOUT THE AUTHOR

Victoria Connelly was brought up in Norfolk and studied English literature at Worcester University before becoming a teacher. After getting married in a medieval castle in the Yorkshire Dales and living in London for eleven years, she moved to rural Suffolk where she lives with her artist husband and a Springer spaniel and ex-battery hens.

Her first novel, *Flights of Angels*, was published in Germany and made into a film. Victoria and her husband flew out to Berlin to see it being filmed and got to be extras in it. Several of her novels have been Kindle bestsellers.

To hear about future releases sign up for Victoria's newsletter at: www.victoriaconnelly.com

She's also on Facebook and Twitter @VictoriaDarcy

# ALSO BY VICTORIA CONNELLY

**Austen Addicts Series**
A Weekend with Mr Darcy
The Perfect Hero
published in the US as Dreaming of Mr Darcy
Mr Darcy Forever
Christmas with Mr Darcy
Happy Birthday, Mr Darcy
At Home with Mr Darcy

**Other Fiction**
The Rose Girls
The Secret of You
A Summer to Remember
Wish You Were Here
The Runaway Actress
Molly's Millions
Flights of Angels
Irresistible You
Three Graces
It's Magic (A compilation volume: Flights of Angels,
Irresistible You and Three Graces)
Christmas at the Cove
A Dog Called Hope

**Short Story Collections**
One Perfect Week and other stories
The Retreat and other stories
Postcard from Venice and other stories

**Non-fiction**
Escape to Mulberry Cottage
A Year at Mulberry Cottage
Summer at Mulberry Cottage

**Children's Adventure**
Secret Pyramid
The Audacious Auditions of Jimmy Catesby

Printed in Great Britain
by Amazon.co.uk, Ltd.,
Marston Gate.